"What begins as a misguided pr[...]
ful journey of second chances an[...]
ciate this diverse cast of characte[...]
faith, family, and future dreams."
　　　　　—NICOLE DEESE, Christy Award–winning author

"Angela Ruth Strong shines in this witty and endearing romance that will have the reader grinning from ear to ear. Striking the perfect balance of lightheartedness and depth, Strong has created a masterpiece of escapism and reflection that few authors can pull off. Highly recommend!"
　　　　　—SARAH MONZON, author of *All's Fair in Love and Christmas*

"Angela Ruth Strong is a master at weaving God's truth into the rom-com genre. From the beginning of *Fiancé Finale*, I was captivated and didn't want to stop reading. Angela made the characters come alive for me as I laughed, pondered over truth, and swooned with all the feels. This book is definitely my favorite of the series and one I will revisit."
　　　　　—TONI SHILOH, Christy Award–winning author

"Once again Angela Ruth Strong delivers spiritual truths in a story brimming with humor, swoon, and wit. Grab some popcorn. *Fiancé Finale* is the perfect happily-ever-after to this must-read series!"
　　　　　—BECCA KINZER, author of *Dear Henry, Love Edith* and *Love in Tandem*

"Angela Ruth Strong knows how to not only write rom-com but weave Christian details into her comedy with finesse and fun! That takes real skill. Her snappy writing voice brings her characters to life through their internal monologues and their fantastic (and funny) dialogue. And Charlie? Sigh . . . If you're looking for a fun, deliciously romantic rom-com that incorporates a solid faith throughout, this book is for you!"

—PEPPER BASHAM, ECPA best-selling author of
Authentically, Izzy

"*Fiancé Finale* flips readers from tears to laughter with the skill of a martial artist. Strong has crafted an endearing romance between a smart, savvy heroine and an out-of-the-box, clueless hero. The story breathes unique and meaningful moments, and the last few chapters sneak up on the reader in a delightful way."

—SHANNON SUE DUNLAP, author of *Love Overboard*

"Angela's done it again! Likable characters, funny moments, and a path to romance I wasn't expecting. The ending to this series left me with a happy sigh."

—HEATHER WOODHAVEN, author of *The Secret Life of Book Club*

"Angela Ruth Strong weaves a second-chance romance with a strong thread of faith and all the familiar faces you love from her earlier books. If you love to read about ex-fiancés, challenging family and church situations, and workplace romance, then this is the book for you!"

—JESSICA KATE, author of *A Girl's Guide to the Outback*
and *Drive You Crazy*

Fiancé Finale

A Novel

LOVE OFF SCRIPT SERIES
Husband Auditions
Hero Debut
Fiancé Finale

We Three Kings: A Romance Christmas Collection

Fiancé Finale

A Novel

Angela Ruth Strong

KREGEL

PUBLICATIONS

Fiancé Finale: A Novel
© 2024 by Angela Ruth Strong

Published by Kregel Publications, a division of Kregel Inc., 2450 Oak Industrial Dr. NE, Grand Rapids, MI 49505. www.kregel.com.

Published in association with the Books & Such Literary Management, 52 Mission Circle, Suite 122, PMB 170, Santa Rosa, CA 95409-5370, www.booksandsuch.com.

The persons and events portrayed in this work are the creations of the author, and any resemblance to persons living or dead is purely coincidental.

Scripture quotations taken from the Holy Bible, New International Version®, NIV®. Copyright © 1973, 1978, 1984, 2011 by Biblica, Inc.™ Used by permission of Zondervan. All rights reserved worldwide. www.zondervan.com. The "NIV" and "New International Version" are trademarks registered in the United States Patent and Trademark Office by Biblica, Inc.™

Library of Congress Cataloging-in-Publication Data
Names: Strong, Angela Ruth, author.
Title: Fiancé finale : a novel / Angela Ruth Strong.
Description: First edition. | Grand Rapids, MI : Kregel Publications, 2024.
 | Series: Love Off Script ; book 3
Identifiers: LCCN 2024013888 (print) | LCCN 2024013889 (ebook)
Subjects: LCGFT: Romance fiction. | Christian fiction. | Novels.
Classification: LCC PS3619.T7756 F53 2024 (print) | LCC PS3619.T7756
 (ebook) | DDC 813/.6—dc23/eng/20240329
LC record available at https://lccn.loc.gov/2024013888
LC ebook record available at https://lccn.loc.gov/2024013889

ISBN 978-0-8254-4795-2, print
ISBN 978-0-8254-7070-7, epub
ISBN 978-0-8254-6973-2, Kindle

Printed in the United States of America
24 25 26 27 28 29 30 31 32 33 / 5 4 3 2 1

Dedicated to Pepper Basham,
for her inspiration.

Chapter One

NICOLE

It is better to be hated for what you are than to be loved for what you are not.
—André Gide, *Autumn Leaves*

It's rare for me to wake up to a text message because hardly anyone gets out of bed before I do. So when my phone vibrates on my nightstand, I'm lost in the dark for a moment. Then I see a glow of blue light and hear the buzz. A rush of warm fuzzies reminds me what day it is, and I don't mean a Thursday in August.

It's the day my campaign launches. And by "my campaign," I mean the one that's going to skyrocket my career in marketing.

It took some finagling, but I finally persuaded a big-time Christian athlete to represent a big-time Christian pizza company. All the ads have been placed, all the billboards designed, all the radio spots recorded, and all the commercials filmed. Hence, I was able to get a good night's sleep for a change. Now I'm just waiting for the audience response, and by the sound of my cell buzzing, I don't have to wait any longer.

I reach for my phone with a smile in my heart.

> **Morgan:** Dante is trending
> on social media.

Already?
I sit up straight, the text more energizing than a shot of espresso.

I'd known my campaign was good, but I hadn't expected such instant results.

I fumble for the switch on my reading lamp while rubbing the sleep out of my eyes with the other hand. If this is as big as I think it's turning out to be, I'm taking myself to Jamaica for vacation. Better yet, Costa Rica. No, wait. Peru.

My pulse stills in a moment of silence over the man who left me for a film gig in South America. I could have gone with him, but that would have required giving up my own dreams. Now look at me. I'm going to have both the job and the journey. Who needs the man?

Anyway, there's another man in my life, and he's a pro golf star. I bite my lip and click on the search engine that might as well be a magic wand, as it's going to make all my wishes come true.

Dante Sullivan. My latest client's name pops up first on the list of popular subjects.

I jump to my feet and do a little dance right there on top of my mattress. "Thank you, Jesus."

I need to pause my celebration long enough to find out exactly what I'm celebrating. Freezing all but my finger, I click on Dante's name. But then I bounce again while waiting for the app to load. I can't help it.

The first trending post reads like a campaign against religion. *Dante Sullivan's golf slice is no slice of heaven.*

I should have expected as much. Christianity can be considered offensive these days. And with the dumb stuff some churches do, I get it. As for Dante, he has a huge platform, so not everybody who sees him is going to be a fan.

I scroll to the next post and cringe at a sexual innuendo left in the comment section. Where is that coming from? Because pizza slices are hot?

I shake my head. Moving on.

The following post is a link to a news article about—

I gasp and smash a hand over my mouth.

Either my phone vibrates with another text, or I'm trembling in shock. Probably both.

Morgan: Dante apparently sent some inappropriate texts to a single mom at the junior golf camp where he's an instructor. Slice of Heaven is dropping him.

"No . . ." My legs give out. I sink into a nest of sheets and pillows, not that I feel any of their comfort. I'm numb. I'm horrified. I'm mad.

My college psychology teacher taught us to use the word *angry* rather than *mad*, because *mad* means crazy. But I think *mad* fits this scenario.

Tingles shoot through my body and my breath comes out in gasps. This is the stuff of mental breakdowns. Or at least panic attacks.

I'm mad at Dante. I'm mad for his wife and kids. I'm mad for the mom he propositioned. I'm mad about his followers who are going to blame his poor choice on God. I'm mad that a company just spent their whole advertising budget on a "pillar in the community" who is turning out to be more like one of the pillars Samson knocked over. I'm mad this is going to affect me.

There's no trip to Machu Picchu in my future. There might not even be a job in my future.

But you know who I'm most mad at? Me.

I should have known this would happen. Everybody falls off his or her platform eventually. It's simply more devastating to a community who prides itself on being wholesome.

This is my dad's fall from Grace Chapel all over again.

I can practically feel a cold sore forming on the outside of my mouth from the onslaught of stress. I rub my lips together. Yep. There's the tender bump. Because public humiliation wouldn't be complete without an open lesion on my face.

My phone rings, startling me back to the present. It's Morgan, of course. Soon it'll be the owner of the pizza chain, my boss, and the press. I don't know whether to laugh or cry.

I'm not one to hide under my covers, but I'm also not sure what I can possibly do about this. I feel the devastation that's coming for all involved. There's no spinning it, and I wouldn't want to.

"Why, God?" I'm not blaming Him. I'm trying to understand.

My phone rings a second time. I take a deep breath of the soothing lavender essential oil in my diffuser, which is not currently cutting it. I must come across as poised. It's my brand.

I look at Morgan's contact picture, her pin curls, chipmunk cheeks, perfectly lined lips, and salty expression staring back at me from behind cat-eye glasses, then I slide my thumb over my screen's slick surface to answer. "I saw the news," I state calmly. "Have you spoken with Dante?"

"I've left messages with his agent and his mom." Her voice dips with displeasure, and mine would too if I'd spoken with Mrs. Sullivan. The matriarch wears an apron with all the charm of June Cleaver, but she also brandishes her rolling pin like a weapon. "There's an apology forthcoming."

I can't hold back my huff. Dante's apology is only going to split the justice and mercy arms of the church even wider, not to mention the impact of his actions on those who don't go to church. What should be used as proof of how badly we all need a Savior will be used as evidence of hypocrisy. Though, honestly, I don't feel like anything can save me right now.

Chapter Two

CHARLIE

Have you ever been in love? Horrible, isn't it? It
makes you so vulnerable. It opens your chest and it
opens up your heart and it means that someone can
get inside you and mess you up.
—NEIL GAIMAN, THE SANDMAN, VOL. 9:
THE KINDLY ONES

I get tired of first-world problems. There are much bigger issues on earth than another supposed superstar putting the "player" in playing golf. I'm not here to judge him.

In fact, I'm only here until I get a contract with a ministry in the Philippines to film its need of training for midwives and to highlight how many mothers and children are dying for lack of health care. My goal is to make the world a better place by educating those who *can* help about those who *need* help. I click my mouse, ignoring Google News, and simply try to search.

My itch to produce another documentary overseas is spreading like chicken pox. I've stayed in Portland, Oregon, since I got back from filming my last foreign documentary because of Nicole. But a guy can only pursue a girl for so long before he starts considering other options. Even if he thinks God told him to marry said girl.

If it's God's will, then the responsibility for our relationship is on the Boss Man, right? Right.

I pull the brim of my ball cap down lower, as if it will help me focus.

I'm finally ready to accept that making a movie in an island country of Southeast Asia is going to be easier than winning back my former fiancée. Though work has always been easier than relationships for me.

My phone rings, and I glance at it from my computer. It's going to take something pretty important to tear me away from my next project.

Momentum Marketing. It's Nicole's firm.

Okay, I'm probably jumping ahead of myself again. Simply because Nicole works for Momentum doesn't mean she's on the other end of this phone call. I've been trying to hire them to promote my latest documentary for a while, but the company has been booked solid. This could be an answer to a different prayer.

I connect the call. "Charlie Newberg."

"Hi, Charlie." The male voice sounds radio-DJ smooth, and I recognize it as Nicole's boss. "This is William Barlow."

If William's calling, then this is a business deal, which should make me ecstatic. I knew better than to expect Nicole. "Hey, William. Did you finally realize what a great opportunity you were passing up when you turned me down?"

He chuckles. "I do like your confidence."

I shrug, then use my shoulder to pin the phone to my ear so I can get back to typing on my computer. "And?"

"I'm assigning Nicole Lemaire to promote your documentary."

I hit Enter on my keyboard, but my eyes don't register the list of sites found by my search engine. The list doesn't matter anymore. Because now I'm going to be working with Nicole.

This is what I've always wanted. Even from back when I interviewed her for a piece on our college's honor society all the way to when she refused to go to Peru with me because she'd been offered the job with Momentum.

"Shouldn't she be the one calling, then?"

"Well . . ." William's pause is a little too long to be positive. "Her schedule opened up unexpectedly, so she's tying up some loose ends. We have a meeting at three, and I thought I'd invite you to join us. We can give her the good news together."

Marketing execs try to spin things, but I call it how I see it. "You're planning to ambush her."

He clicks his tongue. "I like how honest you are, Charlie."

And he likes my confidence. Blah, blah, blah . . . Cut to the chase, man.

"So, I'll tell you the truth. In this business, we're only as good as our last deal, and her last deal was making Dante Sullivan the spokesman for Slice of Heaven Pizza."

I tap the back button on my computer. Moments ago it had splashed Dante's indiscretions as front-page news. Now I'm interested in reading the article. The headline pops up.

Spokesman and Pro Golfer Dante Sullivan Dropped from Advertising Campaign After Questionable Texts Surface.

"Ouch."

"It's not an ambush, Charlie. It's an intervention."

I drop my forehead to my palm. Nicole is going to work with me because I'm her only option. I'm going to save the job she once chose over marrying me.

I lean back, staring up at my bedroom ceiling and, thus, toward heaven. I open my free arm wide. "Why?"

"Why am I telling you?" William misinterprets my question. "I didn't have to. But I know you care more about doing the right thing than observing the court of public opinion."

I snort. Because I'm pretty sure William refers to "the right thing" as whatever most benefits him. Though what is the right thing? Even if one believes it to be God's will, that can still get confusing.

"I'll meet you at three," I say.

Nicole's not going to like working with me. She's been avoiding my calls for years. But maybe it will help if I go early and clarify that I think God wants us to get married.

I clap my hands together. Problem solved.

Chapter Three

NICOLE

*Love doesn't just sit there, like a stone, it has to be
made, like bread; remade all the time, made new.*
—URSULA K. LE GUIN, *THE LATHE OF HEAVEN*

I never miss work. It's my favorite part of life. But for the very first
time, I don't want to be in the office.

My unread email folder remains empty, as if my coworkers think
losing clients is contagious. This is more isolating than the plague. At
least if I were home, I could be cleaning out my refrigerator or beating
up my punching bag. Plus, I wouldn't be running the risk of anyone
seeing this cold sore on my face.

I pull out my compact mirror for the fiftieth time to dab full-
coverage concealer over the little gathering of blisters below the corner
of my mouth. All my attention just seems to make it worse.

William wants to meet with me, and I'm trying not to panic. He
wouldn't really let me go, would he? I haven't done anything wrong.

I narrow my eyes at their reflection. They're dark, serious, and out-
lined flawlessly. My shiny almost-black bob is just as chic. I'm wearing
my powder-blue suit and my favorite Tahitian black pearls. If I turn
my head to the left, I look as though I could grace the poster for a rom-
com. But if I turn my head the other way, I'm the bad guy in a Batman
movie.

In a world where appearances are everything, I have committed
the most grievous of offenses. I'm imperfect.

I need to go home sick. Then maybe William will take pity on me. I'm definitely not going to do myself any favors meeting him like this.

I dab once more at my lip, accidentally popping the fragile top of one of the blisters.

Clear puss oozes out.

I wince and grab a tissue. "Morgan," I call, then look up to find she's already sticking her pudgy face in the doorway to my office.

"Do you want the bad news or the worse news?"

Great. William's going to fire me without even talking with me. Nothing could be worse than that. But at least I don't have to face him now. "Ease me in."

"There are more women coming out with stories about Dante Sullivan. Starting with his nanny."

That's pretty bad, but more so for him than me. This morning's news knocked me down so hard that this second punch misses its mark by flying right over my head.

How did Dante think he was going to get away with cheating? How does anyone? At least I'm just a marketing director and not a member of his family.

"Noted. What's worse than that?"

"Your ex-fiancé is here to see you."

Oh, the poor guy. He probably believes this is his chance to win me back. Now that my career is being flushed down the toilet, he hopes I'll be desperate for his money and attention. Really, his interest isn't too bad either. He's sweet, and he means well. His kind words will be a balm to my aching ego. "Send Tim in."

Morgan starts to pull away, then pauses. Her gaze collides with mine. "It's not Tim."

"Wait . . ." I stand, but she's gone. Clutching my pearls as if I'm one of those little old ladies in the church where I grew up, I have a moment of panic before snapping into action. Though it feels like I'm moving in slow motion.

Kill me now.

I grapple with the clasp of my necklace, my pulse throbbing underneath like a ticking time bomb. Charlie might not even remember when I got the necklace, but on the off chance he does, I don't want him to get the mistaken idea it's a collar he can attach his leash to once again.

Finally, the strand of smooth, round beads slides into my palm. Shoving them inside my desk with time to spare, I exhale in relief. But the movement stretches the tender skin by my cold sore, and I'm reminded of another embarrassing issue.

Ugh. I grab my tissue and dab the blisters furiously. Unfortunately, the tissue rips, and with the day I'm having, I must assume part of it is stuck to my face. I grab my mirror.

Sure enough.

I pick at the little white pieces of Kleenex glued to my lip. I pick too hard, and a pink spot turns bright red before blood trickles out.

Enter Charlie. Or at least I think it's Charlie. He's still rocking his outdoorsy vibe and in need of a haircut, but he's also got a bushy brown beard hiding his cleft chin and exquisite bone structure. His intense dark eyes take in my bloody lip from underneath brooding eyebrows. "What happened to your face?"

The pastor's daughter in me used to appreciate that she never had to guess what Charlie was thinking. I found it a refreshing change from living in a glass house and having everyone in the community judge me while being fake nice. But at this moment, I don't appreciate his reminder of my failure.

I was supposed to have the job and the journey without him. Now all I have is a bloody tissue.

"What happened to yours?" I counter.

He strokes his facial hair. "You like it? I'm entering a contest at the state fair."

"I'm sure you'll win." I shrug to let him know his new look has absolutely no effect on my life. "You always win."

He grins, and he's still cute in a disheveled way. Which isn't fair, since I try really hard and I'm the one left with a smear of blood on my face.

He motions to a corner of his mouth. "You missed a spot."

I knew it. I dab again. "I need to get ready for a meeting with my boss. So, if you don't mind . . ."

"Oh, yeah, I'm going with you."

Bloody lip forgotten, I ball the tissue in my fist to plant against a hip. "What do you mean you're going with me to my meeting?"

In all the possible scenarios that had played through my head, I'd never imagined this one. If I'd fit these pieces into place earlier, I wouldn't have come to work today.

Charlie tried to hire me to promote his films, and I, of course, turned him down. He then went to William, who also turned him down. Our firm is big enough to represent major motion pictures, not his indie documentaries.

Or it was. I was. Until now.

"You've been assigned to the promotion of my latest documentary."

"Oh no, no, no." I sink into my seat, face in my palms, bloody tissue and all. "I am not going to help you succeed in the career you left me for."

"I did what?"

He sounds so confused that I peek through my fingers to find wrinkles lining his forehead.

"I didn't leave you," he contends.

I drop my hands to stare at him. Does he really believe that? "You got on a plane to Peru. That's the definition of leaving."

He shakes his head. "I wanted you to join me."

"On the day before our wedding?" I knew he could be obtuse, but this is a new level of insensitivity. I reach for my pearls, remembering too late that my neck is naked. I end up clutching my throat.

"Was it that close to our wedding day?" He strokes his beard, more contemplative than repentant. "It was the only day my informant could get me into the illegal mine in the Amazon."

I stare at him, daring him to mention the Emmy he'd won for it.

His eyes don't flinch in apology. They don't shine with compassion. Instead, they study me as if I'm a specimen under a microscope. "If you still want to marry me, it's your lucky day."

A guffaw rips from my lips. He can't be serious.

He circles the desk toward my side.

I'm out of my seat again, fists raised in what my kickboxing instructor calls guard position. Though with the tissue sticking out of one hand, I can't look too intimidating.

He drops to his knee and pulls a familiar black-velvet box from his pocket. It's the same ring I used to wear. It's pretty, though I'd secretly been disappointed with a lab-grown diamond. Naturally Charlie hadn't wanted to buy a real gemstone in case it came from illegal mines.

This is a flashback from another life.

"Are you insane?" I ask before he can pop any questions.

He frowns, looking curious. "Actually, I've been waiting for this moment ever since you told my sister you broke it off with that other guy."

I knew he would think the ending of my second engagement had something to do with him. It didn't. "I only told Meri because she seemed really sad that I'd been engaged twice while she'd never been proposed to at all."

"Oh, she's engaged now." Charlie's furry face breaks into a huge grin. The one that's so cute it used to make me forgive him for not understanding matters of the heart. This time it tells me he cares more about his sister's love life than mine. "I get to walk her down the aisle."

I really am happy for Meri, and it's sweet that her little brother is filling in for their father, who passed when they were young, but talking about her engagement with a guy who's still down on one knee makes this moment more surreal than it already was. "I thought she took a job in Africa."

"She did, but Kai flew there to propose."

"Imagine that." Now I'm the jealous one.

"Hey." Charlie motions to the ring box with a nod. "I'm right here."

I laugh like a two-year-old who's skipped her nap. I used to dream of Charlie coming back, but in real life it's a nightmare. "Of all the days you could have proposed, you pick this one? My job is in jeopardy, and I have a giant cold sore on my face."

He glances at my sore and grunts. "You know that's part of the herpes virus, right?"

"Yes." I've been cursed with the virus since birth. I hid it from Charlie when we were dating for this very reason. Now I'm hoping it will gross him out enough so that he won't want to kiss me, forcing him to rescind his wedding proposal.

His eyes return to mine, but he remains on one knee. "I figured you might not be thrilled to discover you're working with a former fiancé, so I thought getting engaged again could help."

I should have known he wouldn't be deterred.

"Charlie." I cross my arms. If I'm a two-year-old, he's a petulant teenager. "I work with a lot of people I don't like. It's part of being a professional. There's no need to propose."

He mulls it over with a nod, gaze drooping and lips twisting.

I'd think he was here out of guilt, but he doesn't seem to realize he broke my heart. Maybe he just wants someone to cook and clean for him. Or he thinks this will get him free marketing.

"Why do you even want to marry me?"

He meets my gaze, eyes clear and determined. "God wants me to marry you."

I groan. "God hates me." And I'm not sure how I feel about Him at the moment either.

Charlie stands at that. But did he really expect me to accept his crazy proposal?

We face off, and I kind of feel sorry for him. This man is attractive, brilliant, successful, and changing the world, but he's probably better off alone than letting down a significant other all the time.

I can't help wondering if he's capable of empathy. Even his efforts to please God seem selfish.

"What do *you* want?" I demand. That's the real question here.

His jaw twitches. "I want to film a documentary on midwives in the Philippines."

My heart throbs with fresh rejection. You'd think I'd have gotten used to it by now, since I grew up always being second to the church. "Then why are you here?"

His eyes flash with purpose. "On the night before your wedding to the other guy . . ."

"Tim." I don't want Charlie to think of my rebound as "the other guy." Even if I dated him because he made me feel like somebody again after Charlie made me feel like a nobody.

"Tim," he repeats. "I prayed that if God wanted me to marry you, then you wouldn't marry . . . him."

My lips part to let a gasp slip out. I seal them back together.

His gaze darts to my mouth, then back up. Does he think his random prayer means anything to me? Does he want it to?

He shrugs one shoulder. "I forgot about the prayer until I learned from Meri that you'd broken a second engagement."

I close my eyes. I never should have told Meri. Then I wouldn't be in this ridiculous position.

"You see? We should get married."

I form my lips into a derisive smile before forcing my eyes open again. "You could write Hallmark cards."

He gives a nod, completely missing my sarcasm.

I grip the bulge of his bicep and usher him toward the door. Carrying luggage around the world makes his muscles surprisingly firm. "I know you've been out of the country a lot, but here in the United States, women get a say in who they wed. In order to become your wife, I would have to hear from God myself."

Charlie turns at the doorway to face me. "That's fair." He says this hopefully.

Does he think God's going to have a come-to-Jesus moment with me, or does he think he found a loophole to get out of a wedding?

God may not love me enough to protect me from this man showing up in my office, but He's not going to make me marry the dummy. As for Charlie wanting an escape clause, why did he pray that stupid prayer in the first place? Why is he still standing in my office doorway?

"Hmm . . ." He contemplates. "I've stayed in Portland longer than I'd planned, trying to reconnect. Finally God brings us together, and you turn down my marriage proposal."

Morgan spins her desk chair to face us for a better view of the dumpster fire that is my life. And I hadn't thought today could get any worse.

Meanwhile, Charlie verbally pats himself on the back for being a saint. "I've done all I could."

"Except"—I hold up a finger to point out one major inadequacy—"you didn't pray about marrying me *before* taking off to Peru the day before our wedding."

Charlie stills at that, and a golden flicker softens his confident eye contact into almost a caress. "I didn't know I had to choose."

A man always has to choose the woman he loves. Over and over and over again. Because that's what love does. Obviously, Charlie didn't love me. Doesn't love me.

In fact, if he thought he had a choice right now, he would choose to leave all over again.

"Go to the Philippines, Charlie. You're off the hook."

Chapter Four

CHARLIE

Love is friendship that has caught fire. It is quiet understanding, mutual confidence, sharing and forgiving. It is loyalty through good and bad times. It settles for less than perfection and makes allowances for human weaknesses.
—Ann Landers

Since Nicole told me to leave, I'll leave. I don't fully understand how she can be mad that I left, then ridicule me for returning. Obviously, I can't win with her. Which should make me more excited to dive back into work where I know I'll be successful.

I drive my Subaru out of the parking garage into an area that used to be a freight yard along the river but is being revitalized into the hottest new area of the Pearl District. All the old brick warehouses turned into breweries and art galleries are now overshadowed by tall glass skyscrapers, including the monstrosity where Nicole works. I know millennials are supposed to eat up the artsiness of this urban jungle, but it makes me claustrophobic.

I prefer real jungles. I want forests and waterfalls. It's why I live in Oregon. It's also one of the many reasons I love traveling to less populated countries.

My GPS directs in her British accent, "Turn right onto Burnside."

Though I've lived here my whole life, I still haven't figured out the maze of mountains and bridges. I round another giant building on a corner to reveal the greenery of my West Hills and reorient with an exhale. I should be thankful I don't have to keep coming downtown. But I wouldn't have minded so much if it meant seeing Nicole again.

Nicole. I used to feel like I knew her better than anyone I'd ever met. Today she was a stranger. What's changed?

She's always been efficient and used good posture. Her clothes have always looked brand-new, as if she has them dry-cleaned or loves to iron. And she's always smelled subtly fresh. So it's not that.

Traffic flows into a moss-covered stone tunnel, and the console screen of my Subaru brightens against the sudden dimness.

That's what it is. Nicole's light has dimmed. Her warmth has grown cold.

She was poised before, but not standoffish. She listened and cared. The old Nicole would have come up with some plan to help me, even if she didn't agree with what I said. She wouldn't have just told me to leave the country.

This new version reminds me of the one time I joined her kick-boxing class. It's a punch to the gut.

I must have misunderstood God about making her my wife. That prayer was my own doing, not His direction. I'm better off not marrying her. Though I'm sad about not working with her. She's good at what she does.

At least, so am I. Back to business. "Call Meri."

"Calling Meri." The phone makes beeping dial noises over the speaker.

My sister picks up before the first ring ends. "How'd it go?" she asks, though her tone is already low with commiseration.

"Looks like I'm heading to Manila."

"The silver lining," she offers.

"The world will be a better place because Nicole turned me down," I say, but my words are strangely followed by a sigh of resignation.

"I told you to expect her rejection. Women want to be wooed."

I roll my eyes. "I know, but she's a lot different than you. She's more business minded, while you're . . ."

"Emotional," she suggests. "Whimsical, ridiculous, and zany?"

I don't argue. My sister made a career out of such eccentric attributes when she tried following an antiquated list of ways to find a husband for a YouTube show.

She adds, "Also engaged."

"Ouch." The only thing wackier than the YouTube show *Meri Me* is the fact that it worked.

Her chuckle softens the sting. "Should I be more sympathetic that Nicole didn't accept your proposal?"

I'd rather focus on work than discuss the rejection. "Nah." I shrug even though Meri can't see the gesture. "It bugs me that she called me insane, but with that kind of negativity, I'm probably better off without her."

"Perhaps." Meri's vague reply echoes with emptiness.

I narrow my eyes at the curvy road in front of me. "Just because you're getting married doesn't mean it's for everyone."

"I wasn't comparing you to me. I was comparing your new plans with what you believe to be God's will."

"I don't know what else I'm supposed to do." But that's never stopped me before. "I told Nicole I thought God wants us to wed, but maybe I'm wrong." Another infrequent occurrence.

My GPS interrupts. "Take the next right."

I slow to turn off onto the side street that will wind up toward my townhome.

Meri remains silent for a rare moment. "You also told her you love her, right?"

"Not today."

"Charlie!" she shrieks, loud enough to make me jump.

"What?" I've told Nicole I loved her many times, but that wasn't why I was proposing. "Today she felt like a stranger."

"If anyone is strange, it's you."

"Great pep talk, Mer."

She huffs. "I seriously don't think we're related. We must have different dads."

Not a chance. Our father died before I was born, and Mom only started dating again a couple of years ago. "We have the same stepdad now," I counter, as if that's the important thing in our debate.

"You could learn a thing or two from Douglas."

I contemplate my mom and her new man. They play Scrabble a lot.

Nicole and I never played Scrabble, but we used to do everything else together. She'd attend church with me. And movies. We'd go hiking. Visit hot springs. During which we'd discuss all aspects of life, as if trying to figure out the meaning. We never got it all figured out, but there was much peace in trying. We were both wiser for having shared our thoughts. She certainly made me feel wiser than my sister does.

"What could I learn from Douglas?" I ask.

"How to take a woman flowers."

"I think she already has some. She smells of lavender."

Meri snorts. "Good point. Never buy a woman flowers if she loves them so much she smells like one."

The logic makes sense to me, but Meri's tone dips with sarcasm. As if she doesn't blame Nicole for saying no.

"Whose side are you on?" I challenge.

"I'm the only one of us on your side." She clicks her tongue. "You pretty much sabotaged yourself."

I grimace at the idea I could have done better. Nicole isn't the type to be won over by flowers and sweet nothings. In spite of her profession, she's real. It's one of the things I liked most about her. "You've been reading too many 1950s magazines, sis."

"Don't ask my advice if you're not willing to take it."

"I won't make this mistake again." I brake at an intersection and pull the fuzzy velvet box out of my pocket. Doesn't the fact that I've kept the engagement ring for so long mean something? I could have sold it for cash, but I was too sentimental. Now the rock is a symbol of my greatest failure. Besides that time I tripped in fourth grade during the hundred-meter dash.

Other cars at our four-way stop take their turns, and I crack open the box and study the round solitaire in a yellow-gold setting. What would life have been like if I'd never left?

My mom used to say people go faster on our own, but we go farther together. I'm not one to slow down, but I can't help wondering how far Nicole and I would have made it by now. We certainly wouldn't be strangers.

A car honks from behind.

I jolt and slide the box into a storage cubby on my dashboard. I'll take it to a pawnshop before I leave town.

Chapter Five

NICOLE

This is a good sign, having a broken heart. It means we have tried for something.
—Elizabeth Gilbert, *Eat, Pray, Love*

I'm stunned Charlie kept the ring. He's not the type to put off for tomorrow what he could do today. Maybe he figured he'd keep the ring for the next woman he proposed to. Yeah. That sounds like something he'd do.

I wonder what kind of woman will wear it. Probably a flannel-sporting, Subaru-driving nature lover who will be as thrilled the diamond was made in a lab as she will be about accompanying Charlie to the fair for his beard contest. I'm not a fan of the beard, but it probably shielded me from memories and emotions I would have felt if he'd showed up looking like the guy in our engagement pictures.

"Did that just happen?" I ask, mostly as a rhetorical question, though I'm still standing in my office doorway. I'm frozen in shock. Also, I'm procrastinating going to the meeting I don't want to attend.

Morgan leans her forearms onto her desk, work forgotten in the wake of my drama. Or maybe she doesn't have any work now either. "You do get proposed to a lot."

It's not all it's cracked up to be. "If I'd kept that ring, Charlie would've had to buy me a new one. I made it too easy for him."

"Why didn't you?"

I startle. "What?"

"Why didn't you keep the ring he gave you?"

"So many reasons." I'm not going to list them, because I don't want to think about him anymore. Which is, ironically, the number one reason I gave back the ring. Yet here I am thinking about him.

"You understand you could have said no to marrying him but still worked with him, right?"

I snort, then realize how I must sound.

I'm supposed to be poised. Confident.

I hold up a finger. "I sent him away not because I couldn't handle working together, but because he couldn't. When he sets his mind to something, he doesn't give up."

"All right." The glint in her eyes tells me she doesn't buy it.

"You don't know him."

She returns to her computer. "He's ruggedly handsome and he's got amazing energy. I hate people like that."

I look down at the striped carpet tiles put together in a way that forms large zigzag patterns.

My office alone highlights how different we are. I appreciate modern comforts while Charlie purposely left the city to live in grass huts and eat grubs. My stomach spasms at the idea.

"I'm not sure how I thought we would ever work," I say. Though looking back, I can't deny being with Charlie and his annoying energy gave me a tranquility I now have to fake.

"You can do better," Morgan quips.

I shoot her with my gaze. "I'll start now by not talking about Charlie anymore."

"Okay." Her eyes flick my way, as if awaiting a new topic.

What else are we supposed to talk about? Not Dante Sullivan.

William strides down the hall, appearing, as always, as though he just stepped off a cruise ship in Europe. He's wearing a brown tweed sport coat over a white button-up that's not buttoned all the way. He's got a beard too, but his is trimmed neatly and turning silver. His hair, however, has kept its tawny shade and is slicked back as if to show off the way it's receding at his temples. He's the kind of guy who is even proud of his wrinkles, because they come from the perpetual tan he achieves on weekend trips to Hawaii. Funny I've never thought of him as the anti-Charlie before.

He scans the hallway, then locks eyes with me. "Have you seen Charlie Newberg?"

My heart leaps as if jumping off a diving board. My stomach sinks into the deep end. "He left."

William's sniff is a mix of surprise and disdain. "Come with me, Nicole."

I blink a few times to give my eyes something else to do other than gaze upon Morgan's concerned expression as I pass her. I'm concerned enough for the both of us. Not only did I lose a major account this morning, but I turned away another potential client.

I follow behind my boss, the silence of soundproof carpet emphasizing the thundering of my pulse. Should I make small talk? Should I present the argument I hope will save my career? Should I offer some reason Charlie left other than the fact that he proposed and I laughed in his face? Because I'm not laughing anymore.

William's office has the view I aspired to attain. I saw it as representing achievement, but now as he sits across from me, the city skyline behind him seems diminished against the West Hills that are Charlie's home. A pit forms in my stomach at the visual of how the man I sent away could be directly connected to my dreams of success.

No, I refuse to accept such a scenario. I will rise above.

I clear my throat. "It's not too late to salvage the campaign for Slice of Heaven. We can keep the work we've done so far and simply replace Dante with another golfer."

William leans back and laces his fingers. This is usually a sign he's already made up his mind, but he hasn't heard my pitch yet.

"I did some research and found an up-and-coming PGA player who is a real family man."

"Nicole . . ."

"Hear me out." My heartbeat races ahead and I refuse to pull the reins. "Not only do Ugo Alongi and his wife have three kids, but they've adopted eight more. He isn't as charming as Dante, but with his huge heart and his children's wacky antics, he's sure to become a media darling. Plus, he's got an Italian background that lends itself to a pizza restaurant. If we sign him as a replacement, he probably won't be too expensive since he's not as well-known. It'll be a win-win. Dante Sullivan's crash and burn might be the best thing that ever happened to their company."

"Nicole." He says my name with more compassion than my father ever used.

The tone breaks me. William cares about me the way I'd longed for from my own dad. He's become the father figure I needed, and I suddenly feel like I've let him down.

I lower into the seat across from him with all the enthusiasm of Titanic passengers climbing into a lifeboat. "I can make it work."

"I know you could."

His faith in me sounds positive at first. Until I realize the statement is past tense. "Could?" I squeak, remembering the episode of *Myth-Busters* where it was proven that in the movie *Titanic*, Jack and Rose could have both lived.

"It's a brilliant idea." His timbre doesn't uptick the way flattery should.

"But?" I prepare myself.

"As you're the one who convinced Slice of Heaven to sign Dante in the first place, they want to avoid the possibility you might have been one of the many women involved with him."

I clutch my naked throat. "You know I wasn't."

"Yes, I told them you wouldn't let a relationship get in the way of professionalism."

I blink at the impact of his words, then study his shrewd hazel eyes to make sure he's saying what I think he's saying.

He stares with intensity, as if to deepen his meaning. He's not only offering a vote of confidence but a word of warning.

He knows I have a history with Charlie. He knows that if I'd seen him leave, I'd have learned why he was here in the first place. He also knows the only reason for Charlie to go is if I'd told him I refused to work with him.

William is calling me out.

"Thanks." I acknowledge only the part of his statement that I want to at this moment. Though I can't meet his eyes, and I can't look out the window either. I focus on the zigzag carpet, but perhaps I should have been looking to heaven. "How'd the owner respond?"

William pauses long enough that I finally glance up. His lips are pressed together as he waits for my full attention. "If Slice of Heaven is to continue working with us, I have to replace you."

All my effort. For nothing.

I don't even want to know who is taking over the account. It doesn't matter anymore.

My heart plunges. My throat constricts. My vision blurs with stupid tears. They're stupid because I knew to expect this. But that doesn't make it any easier.

"You're lucky Charlie Newberg wants to work with you."

I snort. This is becoming a bad habit.

William lifts an eyebrow at the sound, and I'm suddenly not sure which is worse—crying or snorting. Though snorting at someone else feels better than dealing with my own problems.

"I'll never be that desperate," I say in desperation.

There goes his same eyebrow. "Once you promote Mr. Newberg's next documentary, we can connect you to his Emmy win, and clients' trust will be restored."

There are so many other things I'd rather do with Charlie's golden statuette than connect. For example, melt it down and sprinkle it in his drinking water like Moses did to the golden calf.

But if I don't bow to Charlie's idol, what am I going to do for a job?

Momentum isn't the only marketing company in the area. However, if nobody else is willing to work with me at my current agency, then nobody would hire me elsewhere. I could strike out on my own with less important clientele. I'd have to get a business loan though, and I'm not sure any banks would want to invest in me after all Slice of Heaven just lost. I could sell my condo and move home to Kansas.

Suddenly Charlie is the lesser evil.

I glance up at William and swallow around the lump in my throat. If he knew the situation he was putting me in, maybe he'd have a little more compassion. "Charlie won his Emmy for the documentary he abandoned me to film."

William studies me a moment before sitting up straighter and pulling open his pencil drawer. He withdraws a tube of lip balm and holds it out. "My neighbor started making this for a sore on her dog's nose. Now she sells it at farmers markets. It will help your lip heal."

Not the kind of compassion I was going for, but I take the tube. Hopefully it will be the one thing in my day that doesn't go wrong. "Thank you."

"You're welcome." He leans back, lacing fingers once again. "In the same way, I want you to take advantage of Charlie's Emmy win. Think of it as a tool, like this lip balm."

Can I? That would definitely be a new perspective. Rather than feel like I'm doing Charlie a favor, I could think of myself as using him. Cashing in on a debt. Making the most of his crazy belief that God wants us to get married.

Maybe this is a gift from heaven after all. The Lord doesn't really want us to get married, but He's allowing Charlie to think so in order to save my career.

Accepting God's hand in this might be the only way I survive. Because, no matter what I believe, I can't let my history with Charlie get in the way of my future.

To keep working here, I have to prove to William I'm the woman he claimed I am. Otherwise, I'll be let go to keep the company afloat.

Chapter Six

CHARLIE

*Love is that condition in which the happiness of
another person is essential to your own.*
—ROBERT A. HEINLEIN, *STRANGER IN A STRANGE LAND*

Even though I don't have a contract yet and we won't start filming until January, after the flood season and the holidays, I think I'll head to Manila to start scouting this week. I want to meet the staff and make a list of locations.

I hear the front door thud closed upstairs. One of my roommates is home. I hope it's Kai, because I've been waiting to recruit him to go overseas. He can bring his cameras.

I take the stairs two at a time from the daylight basement up to the main living area. Excitement surges through my veins, and I can't wait to share.

It's Kai. He's carrying a couple of black plastic equipment cases as though he's already got his cameras packed for a trip.

"Hey, great. You're ready to go."

He sets the cases on our coffee-table cubes and glances at me out of the corner of his eye. Meanwhile, my sister, his fiancée, is shoving our leather couch toward the wall for some reason.

They're an odd pair, and I don't just mean because she's short and freckled and he's tall and Polynesian. I mean how they got together when Kai filmed her YouTube show. I'm happy they're happy, but after she literally tried to lasso men on a street corner, I've learned not to ask what they're up to anymore.

"Where am I going?" Kai challenges, as if I could possibly have anything crazier planned for him than whatever Meri's got up her sleeve.

"Manila."

Meri hoots and stands upright from where she'd been bent over the couch. She plants her hands on her hips. "You didn't tell me you plan to take Kai. When?"

I look at my watch.

"Oh no." Meri holds up a palm to stop me. "You can run off on your bride, but you can't get my groom to run off on me."

I think back to Nicole's accusation. Does everyone blame me for our breakup? That's nuts. But it's not my problem anymore. "You've still got two months until your wedding, sis. I only need Kai for a week or so."

Kai glances over. "I thought you were staying in the States until you win Nicole back."

Meri must not have filled him in yet. "That's why I filmed my last documentary here, but I finally got a chance to propose again earlier today. She said no."

Kai has the good heart to guffaw. I appreciate his shock at her rejection. Though when he rubs his jaw like that, he appears to be wiping a smile from his face.

I hold out one arm in a half shrug. "So now I'm free to film in the Philippines. You in?"

"Uh . . ." He kneels and opens his equipment cases. "I've got a lot to do here, man. Wedding plans take work."

I shake my head. "Why are you doing the planning? I thought the girls did that."

Meri pulls some long white PVC pipes from behind my couch and removes a strip of Velcro that holds them together. They drop to the dark wood floor with a tribal beat. "With that attitude, I don't blame Nicole for saying no."

I frown. "I knew you were on her side."

Meri's loyalties are even more confusing than whatever she's attempting to construct in my living room.

Kai plays mediator. "What did you offer Nicole in exchange for her hand?"

I stroke my beard and consider. My roommate's starting to sound as if he stepped out of the 1950s as well, but I do have a response to his question. "I offered to save the career she left me for. I thought that was pretty generous."

"I doubt she wants to give you the pleasure of rescuing her," Kai surmises.

He removes an assortment of pipe connectors and black plastic panels from one of his cases and hands them to Meri, who starts snapping pieces together like they are an Erector set from our childhood. Though this one is starting to take the shape of an oversized Porta Potty.

Meri climbs to her feet and shakes out a large panel of cloth. One side is black and the other side white. "Why does Nicole's career need your help? She seems pretty successful on her own."

I shove my hands inside my pockets. We're supposed to be talking about my next documentary, not my ex. I've been stuck in the past for too long. "Well, she *was* successful. Then she signed Dante Sullivan to a deal with Slice of Heaven Pizza."

Meri whips the piece of material up over the frame of the structure so that three sides are covered, black on the outside and white inside. She spins to face me. "Oh no."

Kai places some sort of camera in the back end of the booth, then leans around it to look at me closer. "I was a big fan of his. I'm so disappointed."

"As is everyone."

Meri holds a hand to her heart. "That just came out today. You proposed to Nicole on the day her career took a nosedive? Your timing just gets worse and worse."

I lift my shoulder. "Her boss called me this morning. I thought reuniting could help us get on the same page."

"She's never going to talk to you again, and I don't blame her."

Meri grabs the now-empty camera cases and totes them inside the contraption.

I remain where I am, pondering. How do I feel about Nicole never talking to me again? That hadn't been my goal, but it frees me to pursue other goals. Only now I have this empty space in my heart that I'd mistakenly thought Nicole would fill.

Meri's hand pokes out of the curtain opening, motioning for me to join her in the strange booth she built in my living room. "Check this out."

I sweep the curtain open wider and step inside the space. On the far end of the curtain, Meri created a bench seat out of the containers. On the paneled side, Kai has set up his camera equipment, so that an iPad displays our image.

Now all the pieces and parts make sense. "It's a photo booth." I drop into the seat next to Meri and give her bunny ears as if we're three and five again.

"Impressive, huh?"

"Why's it in my living room?"

"It's for our wedding."

Of course. The reason Kai can't go with me to Manila.

Kai sticks his head inside the curtain. "We looked at the prices of renting a photo booth and figured, since I already have the cameras, we could just build one. Plus, with the money I can make renting this out, I'll have a way to pay bills between film gigs."

I'm proud of the guy. He used to sit on my couch so much that the cushions had started to form a butt dent. Now the couch is pushed out of the way so he can take the risk of becoming an entrepreneur. "Smart."

The doorbell rings.

"I've got it." Kai's face disappears to the other side of the curtain. "It might be Karson. I wonder if he would want to be our first customer."

Karson is currently dating our other roommate, Gemma. I lift my eyebrows at my sister. "Did Karson propose?"

"You beat him to the punch."

Huh. "Well, I hope he has better luck."

"It's not luck when you're in love."

That might have been the issue. I'd just figured if God is love, then He was all we'd need.

The front door opens with a familiar squeak.

"Is Charlie here?" The feminine voice is familiar too.

That isn't Karson out there. If I didn't know better, I'd say it's Nicole.

Meri spins toward me. She grips my forearm. She mouths what looks like "Nicole." Though she should know better too.

"Come in, Nicole," Kai says.

High heels click against hardwood. My ex is in my house.

Meri slaps a hand over her mouth. I can't tell if she is trying to smother a laugh or in a state of shock. I know I'm in shock.

Kai carries on as though this is normal life. "Did you know Charlie is leaving for Manila?"

The clicking stops. "Am I too late? Has he left already?"

Her questions ring with regret. Maybe God gave her the sign she'd said she needed. Maybe she lost her job and wants to go with me to the Philippines.

My pulse thrums. While I'd been telling myself that working with Nicole was all I'd ever wanted, I want this even more.

I pop up to peer over the top of the booth, a human jack-in-the-box. "I'm still here."

Nicole gives a cute little gasp. Her wide eyes meet mine, and I want to look into them longer, but I'm distracted by my roommate's overreaction.

Kai staggers backward in surprise at my sudden appearance. He lands in his old butt dent, and it's like this photo booth is a time machine that transported us back to the year when Nicole was always over. It feels both weird and right. Until Meri tugs me down to the bench, cutting off my connection to the good ol' days.

"Be cool," she whispers.

"You got sunglasses to be used as a photo prop?"

"I mean be quiet. Let her do the talking so you don't mess everything up again."

Before I'm able to ask if she has paper lips on a stick that I can use as a reminder for keeping my mouth shut, Meri dramatically sweeps the curtain open and steps out to greet Nicole in a completely different tone. "Good to see you again. And great timing. You can help test out a photo booth for the wedding."

Nicole doesn't respond. And her heels don't click. Perhaps she doesn't want to be closer to me after all.

"*My* wedding," Meri clarifies.

I roll my eyes. I'm not the only one who needs to worry about being cool.

"Charlie told us you turned down his proposal."

Nicole chuckles in a magnanimous way that leaves no doubt about how she'd much rather be practicing her kickboxing moves on me than getting a photo taken together.

Just when I don't think my sister can make it any worse, she adds, "I don't blame you."

I close my eyes and shake my head. This moment doesn't feel right anymore. I can't keep quiet.

"Meri," Kai intercepts for me. "Do you want our guest to try out the photo booth or not?"

The curtain sweeps back farther. Nicole eyes the tiny space warily. If she doesn't want to be near me, why is she here? I'm about to question it when she takes a heavy breath and steps inside.

I press my lips together and scoot over to make room on the makeshift bench. We've done this before, and I can't help wondering if she remembers. I arch my eyebrows. Meri didn't prohibit me from asking questions with my facial expressions.

"Sorry, I don't have props yet," Meri calls, reminding us that our privacy isn't complete.

"It's okay." Nicole sits gingerly, facing the iPad screen that captures our images as a very stiff couple. "Charlie doesn't need a fake beard."

I can't help chuckling. As uncomfortable as this moment is, Nicole still makes me smile. I reach for the red circle at the bottom of the screen. "You ready?"

"Wait." She twists toward me. "Okay."

Okay what? I don't ask because Meri told me to be quiet, but I'm thoroughly confused. I knew what okay meant the last time we were in a photo booth together. It meant Nicole was ready for me to kiss her on camera.

She's close enough. I would simply have to dip my chin. I'd considered marrying her earlier today, so how could I not consider kissing her?

Unfortunately, my sister is right outside the booth. Meri would get the pictures of us kissing before we did. That can't be how Nicole wants to rekindle this relationship. If she's here to rekindle it.

I study her dark eyes. She studies mine right back. Is that gold fleck in her dark irises a spark of interest?

Not asking questions feels like not breathing. It intensifies an ache inside my chest. How do quiet people do this not-knowing thing?

"I'm . . ." she whispers. Then she lifts one hand to her lips. She points to her blister. "I'm hiding my cold sore from the camera."

My heart thuds to a stop. I shouldn't be kissing her with an open lesion anyway.

She tilts her head toward the iPad. "You can push the button now."

Right. I waste no time jabbing at the button icon.

The screen counts down. *3 . . . 2 . . . 1 . . .*

I give a closed-lip smile as the light flashes. Our first shot appears on the screen. I'm looking at the camera as she looks at me. It comes across as rude.

I slide my eyes sideways and give a small smirk for the next image. But in doing so, my gaze collides with hers.

Another flash.

I know she isn't meaning to make eye contact. If her blister was on the other side of her face, she'd have her back to me right now. But she's been forced to look my direction. And when she didn't think I was watching, her guard dropped.

She's not poised. She's sad. And even though I'm the one who tried to save her today and got rejected, there's something in her eyes that makes me feel responsible for her sorrow.

I frown, studying her closer. The light flashes, blinding me to all traces of her vulnerability. When I can see again, she's smiling straight at the camera. A little too happy to be real. As the numbers count down for the final frame, she lifts her hand to cover the sore under her mouth.

Then she bolts out of the booth before I've even blinked. So much for letting her do the talking.

I bug my eyes. Is it any wonder I'm lost when it comes to relationships?

The poor guy on-screen bugs his eyes right back.

"Nicole." I call to stop her and follow out into the cooler air of the living room. Meri can berate me later for not keeping quiet as advised, but it would be dumb to let my ex go without asking why she dropped by.

The space is empty except for Nicole, who is staring down at a white strip of photos she's already retrieved from the slot next to the printer. My sister and roommate have disappeared, obviously not as concerned about their little booth as they led Nicole to believe. I'm annoyed, but maybe Nicole will open up now. "What did you come over for?"

She glances at me, flashing the strip of photos just as briefly. "You don't think I was looking for a memento from this horrendous day?"

I extend a hand to take it from her. "If you don't want to keep it . . ."

She shoves the strip in her blazer pocket. Is there something she doesn't want me to see? Or does she really want the photos for herself? If my sister hadn't been so adamant about keeping my mouth shut, I'd question her. I'll wait and ask Kai if the images are saved on his iPad or if he can reprint a strip.

"Charlie." She says my name as though it's the beginning of a letter. It's a formal greeting before she gets to the meat of her message. But nothing follows.

"Nicole." I deserve an Oscar for restraining my thoughts. I've got them locked in straitjackets, but they're ramming into the walls of my brain, and alarms are about to go off.

"Do you think we could work together without our past relationship making things weird?"

So she wants my business, and that's it. I should be offended, but a smile breaks free. "By past relationship, are you referring to when I proposed this morning?"

"Stop it. Stop smiling." Her words are militant, but she says them with a laugh.

"Am I making things weird right now?"

She clutches her throat. "I suppose it's too late not to make things weird. So let me rephrase."

I motion for her to proceed. Meri would be proud.

"If I agree to work with you, can you promise to keep things professional?" She bites her lip above the sore, knowing she's asking a lot.

I allow my thoughts a chance to duke it out, and we both wait to see which one will emerge victorious. It's strange, not expressing my initial reaction. But this gives me time to consider what she needs.

When I realize she's asking for my help, I finally nod. "Yes."

Her shoulders sag in relief. Her hard stare softens with gratitude. In a bizarre way, I'm her hero again. Though she should have been more specific with the question she asked.

Can I promise to keep things professional? Yes. I could promise that.

Will I? Absolutely not.

Chapter Seven

NICOLE

If you love somebody, let them go,
for if they return, they were always yours.
If they don't, they never were.
—Kahlil Gibran

After I get back home to my parking garage, I sit in the car long enough for the security guard to come check on me. I tell Stan I've simply had a long day, but it's more than that.

It's reminiscent of the first time Dad took me skiing in Snow Creek, and I ended up becoming one of those human snowballs normally only seen in cartoons. When the world stopped rolling, I lay there for a bit, afraid to move in case I discovered I'd broken my neck or back. In case it hurt. But when I finally got up, I hadn't even sustained a scratch. My padded gear had kept me safe, and not only was I able to laugh about how I must have looked, but I even felt courageous for having tried something new and challenging.

So after waiting in my car for the shock to wear off and expecting to be overwhelmed with trauma from almost losing my job or the vestiges of PTSD from losing the love of my life, I realize I'm either still numb or I'm strangely at peace. I faced my fears and I've overcome.

I make my way up to my apartment, and the small modern space seems too quiet after the insanity of Charlie's house. Usually, I enjoy the calm. I like the distance from the street noise far below and the serene views of the river. I find solace in not having to share a bathroom or even the television remote. But today my sanctuary feels like isolation. Maybe this is the real reason I took my time coming up the elevator.

I set my shoulder bag on the minimalistic entryway table with its gold stand and wooden top, then I dig inside my pocket for my keys. A slick rectangle of paper slides against the pads of my fingers, stopping my search. I pull out the photo strip, and stare at the images. What should I do with it?

It wasn't that I wanted it so much as I didn't want Charlie to have it. I didn't want him to notice how I looked at him in the third frame. Though maybe those feelings were more in my head than in print. I study the progression of my expression to see if my worries are real or imagined.

First photo, my nose is up high enough to have earned my haughty reputation. Second photo, Charlie is giving me that side smirk that brought back memories best forgotten.

Yep. Third photo, I flat out miss him. Or who he used to be. Who I'd thought he was.

I don't miss who he turned out to be. And that look on my face is definitely not one I want him to mistakenly assume is meant for him now.

For the most part, I think I hid my longing well. Along with the cold sore. That fourth photo is happy and fun and everything I wish I was. Maybe I'll cut off the last photo to give to Charlie if he asks.

He won't ask though. He promised to keep things professional as we work together. Which means I won't be wearing my black pearls for a while. I pull them out of my other pocket and lower them one bead at a time onto the table next to our photos.

I wonder what happened to our old photo strip from college. Not that it matters now.

Closure. That's my word for today. In spite of everything else that went wrong, I finally found closure.

Charlie wanted me back—or thought God wanted him to take me

back (insert eyeroll)—and I got to tell him no. Isn't that what every woman dreams of after having her heart broken? Not to mention, he seemed a little humbled by it.

I went to his house afraid he'd try to talk me into something I didn't want to do. Like go on a date. Or accept a peck on the cheek. Or allow a ring on my finger. But he was so selfless. He listened. He let me set boundaries.

Is he different or am I different? I smile up at my reflection in the big round mirror. Ugh, I still have that awful sore on my face, but it hasn't bled anymore.

Besides that, I appear low energy, as though I just climbed out of a bubble bath or perhaps crawled through a desert, but that means I'm going to sleep well tonight.

Usually after work, I change into sweats and pull out my boxing gloves because my mind won't let me rest unless I completely exhaust my body, but I'm relaxed already. I guess my day already beat me up. How should I take advantage of this feeling?

After wandering into the simple but modern corner kitchen, I pull open the fridge. I usually have a dinner meal prepped, but I'd expected to be out celebrating my campaign launch tonight. There are no leftovers either. I slide open my meat-and-cheese tray for an adult version of Lunchables, then grab a whole carrot for balanced nutrition.

I pause at the island where I normally eat my meals while working, but I don't have the energy to start Charlie's marketing plan tonight. I don't even know what his latest film is about. I'd flat out refused to watch his award-winning documentary.

Glancing at my television hung over the gas fireplace insert, I wonder how I'd feel about watching it now. For the first time, I'm more curious than hurt.

I chomp a bite of crunchy carrot and consider this new curiosity. I guess I could start watching *Dirty Gold* and turn it off if it causes pain.

Settling into all the throw pillows and blankets it takes to make my modern version of a chesterfield sofa as comfortable as it is classy, I click one remote to draw the blinds, thus blocking out the dimming light filtering through my wall of windows, and use the other remote to find the right streaming site.

Though I live in an eco-friendly city and I do enjoy homemade granola, I've never been a tree hugger. I recycle when it's convenient, and that's about it. So I kinda expect a documentary about saving the rainforests to put me to sleep.

Maybe it's my leftover emotional state from the day, but I'm instantly drawn into Charlie's narrative. Not so much the facts about mercury polluting the river or the photos from space that show the deforestation, but about how the cartels are enslaving people and making more money from illegal gold than from drug running. They're rich enough to burn the planes used for smuggling in order to destroy evidence. And they're killing anyone who tries to stop them. Their hunt for environmentalists is referred to as "green blood."

One man, who'd personally planted thirty thousand trees, had two gunmen come onto his property with silencers. He barely escaped, but not all activists were as lucky. Another one lost his son to a hit man. Both men had since hired security companies for protection.

I'm hunching forward in my seat, worried for Charlie's safety even though I know he's already made it home. The presence of an armed bodyguard next to him as he interviews locals keeps me from stress eating the entire wheel of brie. When the screen fades to black, my heart keeps racing.

Had Charlie been aware of the dangerous conditions when he tried to get me to go with him? Would my life have been worth his award win?

I shake my head. Knowing Charlie, it was never about his award. It was about raising awareness. It was about getting the Peruvian government more involved, not to mention jump-starting our own military aid through satellite surveillance. It was about protecting the planet and the people on it. He did that.

I lean back and release a heavy exhale. I'm not hurt by the film. In fact, I feel a little guilty. Because what if Charlie had stayed in Oregon for me? Where would those two activists be now? Possibly dead. Where would that mining community of twenty-five thousand slaves be? Still enslaved. Where would carbon emissions, weather patterns, and crop growth be? Even worse off than they are right now.

No, Charlie didn't handle our breakup well, but I can finally see it was for the best. He needed to go when I couldn't. He found his purpose.

Yeah, it makes my purpose of selling pizza seem rather pointless, but I'm good at what I do. On normal days, anyway. I make a difference for my clients. I help them succeed in fulfilling their dreams. And that's what I can offer my ex.

Charlie and I live two very different lives. And perhaps that's why God allowed Charlie to pray his crazy prayer. It's not because he's supposed to marry me. It's so I will finally send him off with my blessing to go make the world a better place.

Chapter Eight

CHARLIE

*Love does not consist in gazing at each
other, but in looking outward together
in the same direction.*
—ANTOINE DE SAINT-EXUPÉRY, *AIRMAN'S ODYSSEY*

I'm back at Nicole's office, but everything is different now. Well, not everything.

I nod to Nicole's assistant as I stride past her desk. "Good morning. Morgan, was it?"

She gapes up at me, then rises to follow. Perhaps Nicole didn't inform her we're working together now. "Mr. Newberg. You can't—"

Nicole looks up from behind her computer. She's wearing glasses. She didn't wear glasses when we were together, but that's what staring at a computer screen too much will do to one's vision. Which is also another reason I enjoy escaping into nature.

She somehow makes her failing vision attractive.

"You look smart."

Nicole blinks at my compliment. Was it too forward? Or did it imply that she looks dumb without her glasses?

"I don't mean that you normally look dumb."

She slides the black frames off to properly glare at me. She somehow makes glaring attractive too.

Morgan bustles in. "Mr. Newberg, you must wait for me to announce you. Miss Lemaire could be in a meeting or on the phone, and

49

you can't simply interrupt. Even if she *had* accepted your proposal yesterday."

I turn to face the cheeky younger woman. I'll let her gibe slide. "I'm sorry. I thought I was Nicole's only client at the moment."

Morgan's lips press together and her bulging eyes glance past me toward her boss. I didn't mean to embarrass her, but apparently, I was right.

I turn to check Nicole's reaction, as well. She slides on her glasses and turns toward her computer, which I appreciate for more than one reason. The first reason being that I'm hoping she forgot my "dumb" comment earlier.

"Charlie, please allow Morgan to announce you from now on. That's part of her job."

"Oh, of course." I nod toward Morgan. "Go ahead."

Morgan narrows her eyes. "It's too late now." Her inflection suggests she's talking about her introduction as well as my proposal.

I straighten. "There will be a next time." I didn't mean for my response to also have a double meaning, but it fits. This secret thing is kinda fun. I'm practically a double agent.

Morgan's eyebrows draw together in challenge before she pivots out of the room. My nemesis. I almost expected her to do that I'm-watching-you double-finger point.

"Charlie." Nicole draws my attention back to her, though she's still looking at her computer. "Please tell me you didn't go down in these mines."

A grin breaks out across my face. She must be looking up the history of the area where I filmed in Ecuador. The documentary was supposed to have released last year, but it got tied up with government security issues. "Are you worried about me?"

"Yes, I'm worried about you." Her glasses come off again. "You're my client."

I sink into the chair across from her and rest an ankle on my opposite knee. She might mean to put me in my place with the client talk, but it simply means phase one of my plan is complete. I may not be a patient man, but I'm a determined one. "I'm touched."

"And I'm serious." Her gaze lasers in. "I thought Peru was dangerous, but you had a bodyguard to fight off attackers. Nobody could have protected you from a mountain caving in on you in Ecuador."

"I survived." Though many didn't. Not the miners inchworming their way through tunnels so tight their bodies couldn't be dragged out after they'd suffocated, and not sixteen of the kids in the school that had been buried in a sinkhole caused by the mining.

She leans forward. "Has your mom seen your documentaries?"

A chuckle rumbles out. Nicole knows how protective my mom used to be, but Mom's concern for my well-being overseas is nothing new. Nicole's is. "Have you?"

She clasps her hands together. "I watched *Dirty Gold* last night."

I study her. "For the first time?" I'd always assumed she would have watched it back when it won all the awards. Didn't she want to see what she'd missed out on?

"Yes." She takes a deep breath. "You were right to go."

I'd never questioned that. I'd only questioned why she hadn't gone with me. Why she would choose this sterile office, with its zigzagged carpet and a mean assistant who insists on announcing visitors, instead of adventuring around the world.

"But that doesn't mean you have to put yourself in danger." She clicks her computer mouse. "I haven't seen your upcoming film, but I'm getting claustrophobic from reading articles about this mountain town that's disappearing into sinkholes."

She does care. She's not cold. She was only distant toward me yesterday because we hadn't had a chance to reconnect yet. I forget that some people hold grudges rather than say what's on their mind and move on. "I didn't want to crawl in the mines, but I couldn't ask my cameramen to do it. Just wait until you see the footage."

She shakes her head. "What if you'd run out of oxygen?"

"Oh, I had a lantern that would go out if oxygen got too low."

"And you implied I was the dumb one."

My mouth hangs open with that, but I'm not sure whether to laugh or argue. "Hey."

"Yes, you survived this, but what's next? Fire? Volcanoes? Floods?" She holds her hands up in question.

Floods are an option, but . . . "I'm going to try to avoid the rainy season in the Philippines."

She covers her face and moans as if I'm the one making bad choices for myself.

My life may be in danger at moments, but I'm saving other lives. It's like I'm a police officer or firefighter but better, because I'm not fighting alone. I'm uniting my audience to fight along with me. Someone in film school once said that if Jesus had been born today, He would have become a movie producer. He told stories that changed the world.

"You saw what happened as a result of *Dirty Gold*." I shrug. "That's what I want to do with this new film, *Sitting on a Gold Mine*."

"Sitting on a gold mine . . ." She emerges from behind her hands and chews on her lip. The sore below isn't as bright pink as it was yesterday.

Though I shouldn't be thinking about her lips. "Yeah. This film promotes awareness that will hopefully raise the funds to pay for engineers who can prevent further damage."

She sits up straight. "This documentary isn't just about rousing the military to fight crime. This one is about fundraising to protect a city."

Isn't that what I just said? "Yeah, I—"

"Do you still have my engagement ring?"

She wants to marry me now? I glance toward the door, wondering if Morgan overheard. I hope she did. "Not with me."

"That's okay." She waves my answer away. "It's not about the ring, it's about what it symbolizes."

Love? Commitment? God's will for her life? "What's that?"

She taps on her keyboard, and I try to imagine what she's looking up. Venues for our ceremony? "The ring you got me is a lab-created diamond now popular because people like you don't want to pay money for what might be a blood diamond."

"People like me? You mean good human beings?"

"Mmm . . ." she murmurs noncommittally and clicks away on her mouse. "More importantly, the jewelry companies who want to sell to good human beings."

I cross my arms, not liking where she's headed. Because it doesn't sound like it's down the aisle. "What are you thinking?"

"Your film is bringing awareness to the plight of illegal gold mines, so if it takes off, consumers might stop buying gold the way they stopped buying real diamonds."

"Great. Now I'll be hated by both the illegal miners and the legit ones." This can't be good for my campaign.

"Unless"—she pauses in her typing to hold up a finger—"you get jewelry companies on board with you." After a final click to her mouse, she spins the computer screen to reveal a list of the largest jewelry stores in the States.

I lean forward into the momentum of her idea. "We get them to promise not to buy illegal gold? That's good publicity for my film and also good for the environment."

"But there's no way we could police that."

"True. What would keep them from making an empty gesture?"

She angles her body so we can both see the screen, opens a new document, and starts typing. The page already has her letterhead at the top and a watermark that gives weight to whatever she's writing.

Her eyes zip with energy. She's onto something. "We don't only want their promise. We want money for the town in Ecuador."

I nod, considering. "You're asking the jewelers for money? The jewelers who are going to hate me?"

"They're not going to hate you, because you're going to bring them publicity."

I'm still not following. My tone lowers in derision. "Publicity that keeps buyers away."

"Oh no." She grins triumphantly. I always appreciate victory, but I especially appreciate it in her smile. "They're going to agree to pay a percentage of every gold sale to your fundraiser."

My lips part, and I lean back in awe. If a jewelry company agrees to this, it will make them feel as though they are doing a good deed even if they're only doing it for the publicity, which they would have to pay for anyway. Buyers will go to them for the same reason I bought a lab-created diamond for Nicole's ring. They're good human beings. Everybody wins. "I'm setting the gold standard."

Her gaze flicks my way, and our connection is back. The kind that will make it even harder for us to part ways in the future. This is what I prayed for, though the tremor in my chest could be my heart shaking in fear. Because, for the first time, I'm seeing how good she is at what she does, and while she confirmed earlier that it was right for me to go to Peru, what if she'd been right to stay?

She tears her gaze away and clears her throat. "That's what we'll call it. The Gold Standard."

I nod at her brilliance. "Then it won't only be us policing them. If anyone finds out these jewelers are buying illegal gold, it'll be a scandal."

"We simply have to get the jewelers to agree to the Gold Standard." She focuses on her computer screen. "I'll finish up this letter and have Morgan send it out. Then we'll design your whole website around the campaign. Anyone using a search engine to look for jewelry will come across your documentary."

"It could hurt jewelers who don't join," I think out loud. "I don't like the idea of hurting anyone."

Nicole snorts.

I cut my eyes to her, remembering the pain in her expression in the photo booth. Is she mocking me? Does she think of me as the bad guy? "What?"

She avoids my gaze. "You *do* want this to hurt illegal mining."

"True . . ." The wildcat miners will think of me as the bad guy. Because everyone thinks of themselves as the good guy. Even if they're not. That's what makes life so complicated. "Let's focus on helping jewelers feel like the good guys. Before you send out that letter, we should get one jeweler on board as an example of what the Gold Standard has to offer."

She takes a deep breath. "We're kind of on a deadline, Charlie."

She says my name as if I'm the dumb one, and I suddenly don't feel so bad about my glasses comment earlier. I also don't feel bad that my next suggestion is going to take her out of her comfort zone. "Then it's good we have a connection with a jeweler we already know cares about the environment."

Her gaze slides to mine, daring me not to say what she knows is coming. Unfortunately for her, it's another great idea.

"Let's go talk to Alice."

She wraps a hand around her throat. "You can."

She'd said she wanted our relationship to be professional, but apparently that's not completely true.

A grin breaks out across my face.

As bad as I am at hiding my own emotions, I'm even worse at letting others hide theirs. So I say, "If you don't have any more feelings for me, it shouldn't bother you that the last time we went to Alice's jewelry shop was to buy your engagement ring." Even if I didn't say it, my smile would have told her I was thinking it.

She looks away. "I just don't want to make it uncomfortable for her. Since I'm not wearing the ring she sold us."

"I offered to give it back to you."

She throws her hands up. "Charlie. You promised."

Not really, but . . . "I'm only thinking of Alice."

"You're so thoughtful." Her eyes meet mine again, and I can tell she's trying to keep her expression as deadpan as her words, but a laugh escapes.

I win. I love winning.

"Fine." She spins her chair and grabs her purse. "Let's go make Alice uncomfortable for the benefit of Ecuador."

Knowing Alice, she'll appreciate it. This is another win-win.

Nicole and I are a good team. Despite the way our foundation has been eroded similarly to the town I'm trying to save, we work well together. And in the same way I want to raise money to pay for engineers to fill cisterns with cement to secure the land and block the miners, I must somehow do the same for our relationship.

Chapter Nine

NICOLE

*You can give without loving, but you can never
love without giving.*
—ANONYMOUS

The fact that sunstone is the state gem of rainy Oregon is as ironic as my drive to Sunstone Jewelers with my former fiancé. No matter how many times I remind myself that our trip is strictly professional, my memories keep rewinding to our last, very personal trip to what has now become the headquarters of a chain. I shouldn't have allowed Charlie to talk me into this.

"Alice might not be in. We should have called or sent an email." I rub my throbbing temples and look through the rain-blurred windshield at the silver skyline. I usually don't mind the clouds because I know gray brings green, but it also serves to make riding in Charlie's Subaru feel more intimate. I can't roll down a window. I can't invite a breeze to blow away my worries.

I shouldn't have anything to worry about. We're onto something with this campaign. We've struck proverbial—and literal—gold. I'm not simply selling pizza anymore. Besides the philanthropic benefits of having Charlie as a client, this could be even better for my career than Slice of Heaven.

"A visit is more personal than a call, and an email could get overlooked by Alice's assistant." He grunts, and I'm pretty sure he's thinking of my assistant. He seems to have developed a distaste for Morgan rather quickly, though I doubt it's personal. It's just that she's a physical representation of what's keeping the two of us apart.

Even if he's agreed to keep his distance.

"Let's make our unexpected appearance a surprise party. We'll gush energy and get her employees talking. We won't be ignored."

That's Charlie's philosophy for life. He's a man of action, and it's worked for him so far. Except, of course, when he makes surprise proposals. "If you say so."

"I do." He turns into the parking lot of a huge brick building with a striped awning over the corner door. Last time we came here, Sunstone was nothing but a storefront. Now, according to the name painted in white script across one side of the building, they own the entire thing.

He finds a spot, shuts off the engine, and turns toward me. "You know this campaign wouldn't have worked with anyone else. I mean, even if another marketing firm came up with your idea, they wouldn't have been able to visit this shop with me and have the same connection."

I don't want to talk about our connection or view it as a positive in any way. Even if God allows bad things to happen for a good reason, I'm tired of bad things happening. Plus, the common Christian belief can sound like an excuse for the people who did those bad things.

"There's no connection yet," I point out.

Charlie nods in his undeterred way. "Let's go connect."

I laugh at his optimism. Laughing doesn't mean I'm happy. It's more about being dumbfounded.

Before I convince myself of my motivations for sounding joyous, he's at my door with an umbrella. This may seem like a gentlemanly gesture, but I know him well enough to realize it's just part of his plan to get me inside the shop quicker. It fits his agenda. So I won't let it bother me that I'm required to walk close enough to smell his mossy scent or feel his flannel sleeve brush the back of my hand. At least my sleek hairstyle is protected from the rain that would wither it.

A bell rings when he pulls the glass door open for me. Again, the apparent chivalry is just his way of getting me inside faster.

Wow. The interior of the shop has changed since I last saw it. It's bright with marble, mahogany, and, of course, gold.

"Charlie." Alice has not changed. Her white hair hangs in two long braids, she wears no makeup on a face made more beautiful by permanent smile lines, and her wrinkled neck is adorned with leather and turquoise in spite of running one of the largest jewelers in the Pacific Northwest.

It bodes well for our campaign that she's here and excited to see my ex, but I can't help wishing that, just once, Charlie wouldn't get what he wanted.

She glides over. "I love the beard, and I loved your Peru documentary." She pets Charlie's beard like a puppy. "I was so proud of you, though after you won that award on TV, I figured you were too fancy-pants to ever come see me again."

Charlie looks around. "Of the two of us, I'm not the one wearing fancy pants."

Okay, I'm smiling again. But it's not happiness. Dumbfounded, not happy.

Alice waves her hand to dismiss our lavish surroundings. "I have investors now." She turns toward me and takes my hands. My bare ring finger catches her attention. "Nicole, child. Did you lose your ring? Are you here for a replacement?"

I bulge my eyes at Charlie.

He answers for me because he's good at saying awkward things. "We didn't get married."

Her grip tightens. She looks up in horror. "Why?"

I have to say something now. "Peru."

"Oh . . ."

I guess that says it all.

She hangs on to me with one hand and reaches for Charlie with the other, as if she's going to pray for us. "Are you back together? Are you getting a new ring for a fresh start?"

This can't get any worse.

Charlie tilts his head toward me. "Nicole got engaged to someone else while I was gone."

They both turn accusing eyes on me.

Alice *tsk*s teasingly. "And you didn't come to me for the wedding band?"

Charlie's jaw drops as if he's more offended for our hippie friend than for himself. "You didn't get your ring from Alice?"

I should have knocked on mahogany when I'd thought this situation couldn't get any worse.

He shakes his head in disappointment. "No wonder you were hesitant to come here."

I pull my hand out of Alice's grip and reach subconsciously for my pearls. Finding my neck bare, I cross my arms as though that's what I'd meant to do all along. "Tim bought the ring without consulting me first. I would have come here."

"Was it a . . . ?" Alice's voice trails off.

"Was it a lab-created diamond?" Again, Charlie with the awkward things.

I press my lips together, knowing full well they would both be upset by the rock I wore for my second engagement. "I don't think so."

Alice offers a moment of silence.

Charlie, on the other hand . . . "I'm not sure I can marry you anymore."

I do a double take to give him a fully confused glare. "I'm sure you can't."

That has already been agreed upon. So why is his forehead wrinkling in concern?

Alice steps back and claps her hands together. "You're not a couple, and you're not here for engagement rings, so what brings you by?"

Charlie stands up straighter. He does love talking business. And I'm happy to segue from personal topics. "I hired Nicole to promote my next documentary, and she's come up with a brilliant idea I think you'll be excited about."

"Come, come." Alice waves us after her, toward the back office and past her fancy-pants employees.

I take a deep breath and follow. That could have gone better, but at least we got our foot in the door.

Alice's office is filled with plants and lava lamps, and smells smoky like incense, which is how the whole shop used to be. I'm most intrigued by wooden shadow boxes hanging on one wall beside a bulletin board of photos and newsclips. The necklaces displayed inside look more rustic than the pieces out front. More Alice-ish.

Instead of asking about the jewelry collection, I let Charlie launch into his spiel on the upcoming documentary and his latest efforts for saving the planet. Alice climbs on board the campaign train and immediately calls her lawyer to work out the details.

She leans back and laces her elegantly aged fingers. "I don't appreciate all the new changes in my company, but I appreciate that I have lawyers who can take care of the boring stuff for me."

I admire her as a strong, successful woman. "How did your shop expand so quickly?"

She pauses. "What may seem quick to you took a lifetime. In fact, it began before my birth."

Charlie's watch buzzes, interrupting the saga with a phone call. I'm surprised it hasn't buzzed before now. "Excuse me." He steps out. Answering his phone is part of being a doer.

I face Alice again, feeling exposed. This is her chance to ask me relationship questions beyond Charlie's hearing.

Instead, she stands and moves toward one of the shadow boxes. "Do you know the Oregon state motto?"

"Keep Portland Weird." But that's just Portland.

Alice swings the glass case open. "Close." She unhooks a silver necklace and lays it on the desk in front of me.

From the chain hangs a variety of charms. There's a wing pendant, a sunstone, and an engraved bar. I turn the bar to better read it.

"She Flies with Her Own Wings."

I like it. It's very Alice. It's very Oregon. Our state excels at being unique with its lack of sales tax and refusal to pump our own gas. "Is that the Oregon state motto?"

She lowers herself back down across from me. "It's the English translation. The Latin is *Alis Volat Propriis*. Which is where I got my name. Alice."

My eyebrows jump. Her story really did start before her birth. "Oh, wow. Is that how you got into jewelry making?"

"It is." She nods to the necklace. "This is the very first piece of jewelry I ever made."

I finger its delicate ruggedness, contemplating the meaning behind both the words and the piece. They fit Alice's spirit, though she's not flying alone anymore. She's got investors and lawyers now. She has career success. Of course, I know that's not why she would consider herself successful.

She nods at the piece. "I sold necklaces like this one at art shows and fairs for decades. It's where I first met Charlie, and it's all I thought I would ever do."

Small beginnings. She'd been satisfied before her career took off. Not sure what that says for my future, no matter the direction.

"A friend encouraged me to sell my jewelry online, and I started getting requests for designs with precious metals and gemstones. One of my customers offered to fund this storefront. After that, some boutiques on the Oregon coast wanted to carry my jewelry, but the original investor came up with a business plan for a franchise. He took it from there, and now I've got jewelers working for me. It's surreal."

She said it took decades, but it still sounds like a walk in the park. As if she didn't strive for this, but just did her own thing and did it well.

"She flies with her own wings," I quote. Because I'll never forget it.

Her wrinkles make her smirk appear wise. "The 'she' in that quote refers to the Oregon Territory, but I'm going to claim it as my own. And you can too."

"I will," I say, though I'm remembering the old joke, *I just flew in, and boy, are my arms tired*. It would be nice if life offered a Learjet to success.

"I want you to have this necklace."

My eyes snap up. Hadn't she said this was her very first piece? It has to be worth a pretty penny. "I can't take it."

"I'd rather someone wear it than for it to gather dust on display."

I slide the necklace across the scarred desktop, both honored by the offer and offended that she believes I would accept. "Then you should wear it."

She chuckles wryly. "I've developed an allergy to any metal that's not pure gold."

"Then you *are* fancy-pants," I tease because she has to be joking. Her allergy can't be a real thing. It would be too ironic if the metals that made her famous now made her break out in a rash.

"I guess so," she agrees.

I sit back. She wasn't joking. But her faded blue irises remain just as peaceful as before I started name-calling. I need a better argument. "Alice, this is an heirloom."

"I have no heir," she states simply.

I take a deep breath. Because I'm definitely not an heir. We've only met twice. I was honored she remembered my name. With as neat a lady as she is, she must be the mentor to some wonderful young women.

"Why me?" I finally ask.

She looks down at my exposed throat, then her knowing eyes rise to meet mine. "Your neck is bare."

I want to argue, but I'm afraid she remembers my pearls. It's been a long time, and she can't possibly know that I would be wearing them if not for my new client, but I don't want to take the risk of talking about the last time I was here. Especially with the chance said client could reappear anytime.

One corner of her mouth curves up. "Are you going to put it on, or should I have Charlie help you with it?"

My heart thumps hard enough that were I wearing the necklace already, it would be bouncing off my chest. The pounding of my pulse is echoed by Charlie's footsteps heading back toward the office. This place may be bougie now, but thankfully they don't have soundproof carpet squares.

I grab the necklace and fumble with the old lobster clasp. In slow motion, it snaps together, and the pendants fall perfectly between my collarbones. My hands drop into my lap with the heaviness of gold bars. Which has to be about what the piece is worth. Of course, keeping my ex's hands off me is worth even more.

Oblivious, he reclaims the seat at my side. "My entertainment law-yer called. He's going to send over a contract for you to sign, then we'll be able to announce our collaboration in a press release."

Alice turns her smile from me to Charlie. "When you two first came in, who would have ever imagined we'd end up here?"

Charlie flashes his megawatt smile my way. It's all innocence and enthusiasm. And I'm happy for him. But I can't help being sad for me.

"Thank you, Alice," I say, because it's safe to say in front of Char-lie. He'll assume we're all talking about the collaboration, but I'm talking about so much more.

Her gift is something I should treasure, but at the moment it's a reminder of how I fly alone.

Chapter Ten

CHARLIE

*We waste time looking for the
perfect lover, instead of creating
the perfect love.*
—Tom Robbins

I always knew I wanted to work with Nicole, but I never knew how great it would be. I've been glued to the computer ever since Morgan emailed out our press release. I'll focus on signing with the top twenty jewelry chains and let my lawyer handle the rest.

At the moment, I need a bathroom break, something to eat, and a hike along the Wildwood Trail. In that order. Though on my way to the bathroom, I catch a whiff of something spicy like pepperoni and almost redirect my course. "You cooking, Gemma?" I yell up the stairs from the daylight basement.

"Zoodles," she yells back with much more enthusiasm than anyone should ever have for noodles made out of zucchini.

I continue on to the bathroom. Zoodles can wait. Though really, I can't complain. Gemma's gluten- and dairy-free diet is preferable to being a vegetarian. I can't go without my meats.

By the time I bound up the stairs to join her, my stomach is growling. "You know we're going to starve to death after you get married and move out, don't you, Gem?"

Kai is already on a barstool, scooping Gemma's meatballs onto a french roll. "Not me. I'm moving out first, so my death will be on

Meri's shoulders if she doesn't learn to cook anything other than Pop-Tarts."

"Boys." Gemma plants her hands on her hips. She's honestly one of the most beautiful women I've ever met, but more importantly, she's intelligent, creative, and sweeter than Peruvian apple pie. Or as Americans might understand, Kate Upton has nothing on my roomie. "I thought we left the '50s thinking in the garbage, along with Meri's antiquated list of ways to find a husband."

I hold up my palms as if I'm under arrest. "It's not because you're a woman. It's because you're such a good cook that Kai and I never had to learn."

The three of us became roommates in film school when I posted an advertisement to start a Bible study. They were the only ones to show. After I won my first film festival at the age of twenty-one with an awesome short about earthworms, I used the winnings for a down payment on my first condo, and they moved in with me. Gemma's dietary restrictions required her to cook from the very beginning, so my argument could hold up.

Kai takes a big bite of his messy sandwich. "We also don't look as good in your apron."

Her apron boasts a police officer's uniform printed on the front and is, I assume, a gift from her cop boyfriend. Unfortunately, it's unisex, meaning Kai's argument certainly doesn't hold up.

"Hey now," she defends innocently. Then she twirls the towel in her hand and snaps him.

Kai jumps in surprise.

Her lawman must be rubbing off on her.

The doorbell rings.

I chuckle at the idea the cop in question could be on the front porch of my townhouse, here to defend his woman. "Ooh, I bet that's Karson. Kai's in trouble . . ."

"I can take care of myself," Gemma says, but her cheeks still flush when she heads to answer the door.

Kai rubs his arm where she snapped him. "I've been punished enough."

I reach for the bag of bread. "Can I have one of your french rolls?"

"No." Kai snatches it away and glares in retaliation for my taunting. The problem with having been roommates for so long is that we can err on the side of acting like siblings.

"Come on, man," I beg.

Kai narrows his eyes. "Only if you put on Gemma's apron."

I consider wearing the police uniform apron in front of an actual cop. Gemma, Kai, and I took Citizen's Safety Academy from Karson last year, and I'm not sure he's the type to see the humor in it.

I huff and scoop a bowl of slimy green zoodles. But then I hear feminine voices and the *click-clack* of high heels and look up to see Nicole with Gemma. "Ha." I clap my hands in celebration. "It's not Karson. Now I don't have to worry about embarrassing myself. Gemma, hand over your apron."

Kai motions to Nicole. "You're not worried about what your former fiancée will think of you wearing an apron?"

"I'm pretty sure she couldn't think worse of me." I give Nicole an apologetic head tilt before turning to Gemma. "Can I have your apron, please?"

Gemma's chin tucks and her sculpted eyebrows make a V. "Noo . . ." Even with deep aversion to my request, her tone still comes out breathy.

It would have been a cute response if it wasn't keeping me from getting what I want. What's up with everybody telling me no lately? No, Gemma won't let me wear her apron. No, Kai won't give me an extra roll. No, Nicole won't marry me.

The latter watches our interactions with concern and hesitation. I find it rather entertaining how she can be so on top of everything in her world, but the moment she steps into mine, she doesn't know how to respond.

"Gemma?" I prompt, hand out. After accusing me of pretty much being a chauvinist pig for saying I'd starve without her cooking, she should want me to put on her apron.

She doesn't move.

"Aren't you done with the apron?" I ask.

She glances at each of us, then her gaze drops to her white shirt underneath the apron. "I was going to wear it while eating, so I don't dribble any sauce on my clothes."

Kai chuckles. "Like a bib?"

She shrugs. "Kinda."

"That's what they do in crab restaurants. Pretty smart." I look down to see what shirt I'm wearing in case I stain it with delicious sauce. Lucky for me, it's one of Kai's golf polos that I borrowed because I've been too busy to do laundry. I wiggle my eyebrows at him. I might get a piece of his bread after all.

Kai mock glares. "You can have a roll if you take off my shirt."

I whip his shirt over my head and toss it toward the laundry room, then grab a roll and stuff it with meatballs and sprinkle it with mozzarella. The perfect bite of thick bread, gooey cheese, and meaty marinara makes my eyes roll back into my head. I've died and gone to Italy.

Nicole simply stares at me.

"Mmm, Nicole, you hungry? I'm sure Kai will share his rolls with you without"—I motion to my bare chest—"you know."

Nicole presses her lips together and blinks a whole bunch of times. She must not realize what she's missing.

"Here." I step toward her, holding out the sandwich. "Try a bite."

Nicole backs away, hand up. "No thank you."

There's that word again. And I'm not even asking for anything. I'm offering to give.

Gemma retrieves the bowl of zoodles I'd scooped earlier. "If you're watching your carbs, I've made zoodles. They're good too."

Nicole worries her lip. "It's not that."

"Do you want an apron too?" Gemma asks.

"Charlie does," Kai answers for me. "Preferably one with lots of flowers and ruffles."

"Ooh, I know just the one." Gemma stoops to open a drawer.

"Too late, Kai. You already gave me a roll. I can't be embarrassed now." I take another huge bite.

Nicole steps forward and holds out her phone to display whatever is on the screen. "I wouldn't be so sure about that."

The rest of us hush and squint to get a better look. I've seen the shot before. It appears to be the silhouette of a couple in front of a great view of the Willamette River running through the city. On closer inspection, I'd say the couple is on the aerial tram. Which is where I dropped to a knee once upon a time. I thought I recognized it.

"That's us," I announce, then glance up to Nicole's face, unsure why I should be embarrassed. We all knew I'd proposed before. Well, I'm not sure Gemma knows about my second proposal, but I don't think I'd be embarrassed if she did. "Why are you showing me this?"

Nicole's chin is down so she's glaring up at me even though I'm directly in front of her. She reminds me a little of Anakin Skywalker right before he turned to the dark side. Rather than respond, she shoves her phone closer to my face.

What am I not seeing? I take my eyes off Darth long enough to focus on the image.

The frame around the photo identifies it from social media, which is weird because after our breakup, Nicole and I both took down all our photos of each other. I know, because I occasionally cyber-stalked her until she got engaged to the other guy. All that to say, I'm not sure where this photo is coming from. I peer at the name on the account.

"Sunstone Jewelers." I shake my head. "Why would Alice share that? We told her we didn't get married."

"Look at the date," my angry ex growls in a tone that could help her take over voice work for James Earl Jones.

I glance at it again, and my shoulders relax. "It's from five years ago. Alice shared it along with our engagement on her company's business page. That's old news."

"It *should* be." Nicole zooms out on her screen so I can see the shot is part of a larger article about our new initiative. "Someone found it and is using it in connection with your campaign."

"Oh . . ." My lips form an O and remain pursed. I hadn't ever considered this might happen. But I'm not upset about it. "If you would have accepted my second proposal, this wouldn't be a big deal right now."

"What?" Gemma swings her head to look at me, her blond hair flying dramatically. "You proposed a second time?"

Maybe I should have updated my roomie after all.

Her hair swings again until she's looking at Nicole. "I'm glad you turned him down. I love him and all, but—"

"But what?" I demand.

She turns back with less drama than before and softly pats my shoulder. "I've been dating Karson a year now, and he hasn't proposed yet. It wouldn't be fair."

"Right." I nod in understanding. "It would be odd if you were still living here when Nicole and I get married."

Nicole's glare sharpens, giving me the feeling I'll be having a funeral before I have a wedding.

"Apart from that," Gemma allows, though she's scrunching her forehead as if she doesn't know what I'm talking about. "Nicole deserves someone who loves her as much as Karson loves me."

"Perhaps." I stand taller, refusing to be thwarted. "Though shouldn't God's will play into an engagement?"

The girls both remain silent.

Kai shakes his head. "Dude."

I shrug. "We're all Christians. Yeah, this would be a bad thing to say in a room full of unbelievers, but aren't we supposed to be about doing God's will?"

Gemma puts her bowl in front of Nicole, apparently so her hands are free to rub the other woman's arm. "I'm sorry, friend. I'll try to talk some sense into him later. For now, I'll give you the room." She backs toward the steps leading up to her suite. "Eat zoodles. That way you didn't come over here for nothing."

Nothing? I frown after the blonde.

"Oh, hey. Pretty necklace, by the way." Gemma charges upstairs.

"Thanks," Nicole murmurs, sounding like a whole different person from the one who'd been growling at me.

I glance at the necklace around her neck. I hadn't noticed it until now, but it reminds me of the one I bought Mom for Mother's Day a long time ago.

Kai pulls a french roll free from the bag he's been hoarding and sets it next to the bowl of zoodles on the counter. "You'll probably need some carbs to cope with this guy."

Nicole nods, her expression much kinder than when the two of us faced off.

Kai grabs his hoverboard and heads out the front door.

Nicole looks my way again and morphs back into a Sith Lord. Maybe food really will help. She could be hangry.

I grab the pan of meatball sauce from the oven and turn to hold it over her options of zucchini and bread. "Where do you want it?"

Her scowl finally relents, and she points to the bowl. Progress.

I scoop a spoonful of marinara over the slimy green veggies masquerading as pasta. She really should have chosen the sandwich, but if she's not going to eat the bread, I will.

"Charlie." She moans and sinks onto the barstool across from me, face in her hands.

Okay, she can have the bread too. I grab the butter dish and open a cabinet for the garlic powder. I'm not as completely clueless in the kitchen as I let Gemma think I am. "Yeah?"

"I wanted to keep our partnership professional, but now all the promotion is going to become about our past relationship."

I open my mouth to remind her that the relationship doesn't have to be in the past, but she holds up a finger to stop me.

"The photo resurfacing is bad enough, but it's even worse that you're trying to take advantage of it."

Blast my face for being so readable. I spin toward the oven to turn on the broiler and hide my grimace. "Aren't marketers supposed to believe there's no such thing as bad publicity?"

"I believe it when it doesn't involve my personal life."

I guess she's always been more private. In fact, we'd dated for years, and I never even met her family. Though that's probably because after her mom died, all she has left is the father she didn't even invite to our ceremony.

I open a drawer to pull out a fork and knife for her. "I know fancy-pants people like to spin their noodles around the fork tines, but I've always preferred cutting it up. More straightforward. And less messy."

She eyes my bare chest. "You would."

Okay, I can't help smiling to myself as I butter and season her bread then stick it in the oven to broil. Though I don't work out in a gym, I'm extremely active and used to living on a diet of rice and beans in other countries, so there's not much to my torso other than muscle. Or so Nicole used to say.

She takes a bite and speaks around the zoodles. "If you're done eating, you could put your shirt back on."

"You don't want to share your bread with me?"

"No."

There's that word again. I'm tempted to leave my shirt off as payback, but since my whole argument for getting together involves a prayer, I should attempt to keep my behavior prudent.

"All right." I trudge to the open closet, where the turquoise polo landed between the stacked washer and dryer, then pull it over my head. "Satisfied?"

"No."

Grr . . .

"I should have chosen the sandwich over the zoodles. But the meatballs are scrumptious."

Okay, we're on the same page there. I follow the scent of warm garlic and yeasty bread back to the oven and retrieve the french roll for her. With a spatula, I slide the two halves into either side of her bowl, then lean my elbows on the counter across from her. I hope she doesn't eat it all because it smells even better than my sandwich tasted.

I tease. "Did you just pretend to be upset about that photo to get a free meal?"

"I'm truly upset, Charlie." She touches the hot bread a couple of times before picking it up. "Slice of Heaven had me replaced on their account because, after the scandal about Dante broke, the client suspected I might have had an inappropriate relationship with him too. And now this." She uses her roll to motion back and forth between us before taking a bite.

"I didn't know that." I sigh. Her frustration makes more sense now.

When she closes her eyes to savor one piece of bread, I take the other half. The butter melts on my tongue.

Her eyes snap open at the sound of my chewing. "Hey."

"Wanna go on a hike?"

She puts her piece of bread back in the bowl. "I stopped by to talk business."

"For someone who wants to keep things professional, you sure come over to my place a lot."

"I freaked out, but obviously this isn't helping things." She shifts forward on her stool. "Sorry, I won't do it again."

"Wait." My touch seems to freeze her. "I know we have a complicated past."

She presses her lips into a grim line. At least she's not arguing. Though maybe I should want her to argue that our past isn't too complicated. Anyway . . .

"It could be what makes us a good team. And you have to admit, everything we accomplished in the last couple of days is pretty impressive."

"Mmm . . ." she says, as if she's still eating instead of sitting back in a contemplative state. "That's a great way to spin it. If the media asks, that's what we'll say."

I nod in agreement, though I'm not spinning anything. It's the truth. We're a great team. As for the media, nobody is going to care more about our past than we do. This old photo shared in the news article will be forgotten by everyone but us. Nobody is going to ask questions.

Chapter Eleven

NICOLE

We're all a little weird. And life is a little weird.
And when we find someone whose weirdness is
compatible with ours, we join up with them and
fall into mutually satisfying weirdness—and call it
love—true love.
—ROBERT FULGHUM, *TRUE LOVE*

What's with your engagement picture to Charlie being in the news?"

I'm barely out of Charlie's townhome before I run into his sister, who's asking the very question Charlie told me not to worry about. I should have known better than to listen to him. I should have known better than to come over here. If I don't want reminders of our past, I should avoid the home we'd picked out together after he proposed. No matter how great the views are from the West Hills. No matter that when we didn't get married, his roommates followed from their old condo.

"Hi, Meri." I greet her with a sigh.

She's cute and bubbly and undeterred. She's basically the puppy that Charlie's probably glad I didn't talk him into adopting when we were furniture shopping. "Did you see the article?" she asks.

My shoulders slump. "Yes. That's why I'm here."

Her amber eyes widen. "Because you're back together?"

Why, Lord? "Because I wanted to talk to Charlie about how we keep people from making a big deal out of my former fiancé becoming my client."

Meri purses her lips in thought. "Did he happen to suggest you just get engaged again so it's not a big deal anymore?"

My head drops back, and I almost cry the word. "Yes."

"He's a weirdo."

"Yes," I repeat emphatically this time, head lifting.

It's good to be understood. It's good to lament with someone else who's had to endure the man's obtuseness.

"I should simply send an email when I need to talk to him." Business letterhead and all. Though I did get a heavenly piece of garlic bread out of my visit. Next time I have the urge to come over here, I'll go buy garlic bread instead.

"Or call me," Meri suggests. "We can swap Charlie stories."

I clamp a hand over my smile. I'd love to reconnect with Meri, but I should probably avoid Charlie stories. I already have too many.

She leans forward conspiratorially. "Did you know that when I started hanging out with Kai, Charlie was in Ecuador? Because of the time change, he kept calling at four a.m. to check on me."

Okay, that's annoyingly sweet. "The protective little brother."

She howls. "Yeah. He worried about me, but he pushed Gemma toward Karson. Literally."

I cock my head. "You mean he shoved her?"

"That's how Gemma describes it." Meri holds up a hand as if to soften the picture in my imagination. "Granted, Karson was looking for a volunteer in their safety-training class, and Charlie knew she had a crush, so he thought he was helping put her best foot forward."

I scrunch my face. "Poor Gemma."

Meri nods solemnly. "Of course, if you ask Charlie, he thinks he got them together."

I shrug. "Why would he think anything different?" She chuckles, and I can't help but join in.

"I still need to get back at him somehow," she conspires.

"Definitely." I like Meri. She's kooky in a more observant way than her sibling—she knows she's an oddball but doesn't care. I'd been looking forward to having her as a sister. When Charlie left for Peru, I lost her as well.

"Hey." She tilts her freckled face. "We should start hanging out again."

I nod, sincerely. I still appreciate independence and the calm organization of owning my own condo, but after watching Charlie's roommates banter and cook together—and wear each other's clothes—my lifestyle seems a little lifeless.

"Want to come to my bachelorette party?"

My eyebrows jump. She's kooky but not wild, so I'm curious what she means by party.

"Don't worry. It's nothing crazy." She grins. "Kai and I kicked around the idea of having a destination wedding in Maui, where his parents grew up, but we'd rather have all our friends and family attend the ceremony. So instead, I rented a room at a tiki restaurant here to celebrate with a taste of the islands."

"Pupu." I pronounce the Hawaiian term for appetizer like the poo-poo I'd thought my waiter had been referring to on my one visit to the tropics.

"Pupu," Meri repeats, as if excited to hear me speak the language of her fiancé's heritage.

Maui had been perfect. Perfect scenery, perfect weather. And it would have been the perfect honeymoon if I hadn't gone alone. I deserve a do-over.

I smirk but don't tell her my memories. We've already shared enough Charlie stories for one day. "I'm so there."

"Where've you been?" Morgan follows me into my office.

I rub a hand down my face. It's already ten the next morning, and I haven't had my coffee yet. "I stopped at Charlie's lawyer's office to make sure all the paperwork is signed before adding the names of jewelry companies to his website. It took longer than expected."

"Okay. As long as you weren't . . ."

I set my laptop case on my desk and glance up at my assistant's face to gauge her expression. It's blank. "As long as I wasn't what?"

"You know." She taps on her phone screen and turns it around to show me the article about the Gold Standard and the photo of Charlie proposing to me the first time.

"No," I state stubbornly. "I don't know."

She was here when I turned down Charlie's second proposal, yet still falsely assumes I'm coming in late to work because I was too comfortable in Charlie's bed or some such garbage. If my own assistant makes assumptions like that, what will strangers think? This is exactly what I'd been worried about when I went to Charlie's.

But if she wants to make accusations, then she'll actually have to make them. Besides, it's not her job to get all judgy on me. She's my assistant, and this feels like the opposite of assisting.

She pockets the device. "Your reputation affects my career."

She has a point. I stand down. "Rest assured knowing it also affects mine."

We come to an understanding, silent eye contact in place of a handshake.

She lifts her chin. Back to business. "Everything go smoothly with the lawyers?"

"Surprisingly smooth."

I have trouble trusting smooth. If things seem too good to be true, they usually are. Like my deal with Slice of Heaven. But maybe the ease at which everything is coming together for this job is a small blessing in the midst of the emotional upheaval it brings. That's been my experience with God. He doesn't seem to calm the storms in my life, He just holds an umbrella over my head to protect me until the sun comes out again.

I wonder if God still continues to supply grace for Dad after he refused to admit he needed it.

"Good to hear." Morgan's voice draws me back to the topic at hand. "Lance from the website department should be headed over for your appointment soon, then I've got a conference call scheduled with the local film festival after lunch, and I'll need the log-on information from Charlie's email marketing service so we can get his newsletters automated."

I look at my watch. "Yeah, he's coming in for the website design, so I'll make sure to get the newsletter info for you."

"He's here," Charlie's voice announces. He's hanging halfway through the doorway in a ball cap and jean jacket.

With the beard, he looks more like a trucker than a business professional. He's even scruffier today than on his first visit, and it's no wonder Morgan couldn't picture us together. It wasn't until she saw the proposal picture with him clean-shaven and presentable that she started to have concerns.

"Sorry," he addresses my assistant. "Am I supposed to wait for you to introduce me?"

She harrumphs. "Miss Lemaire, that guy who keeps proposing to you is here. Should I let him in?"

My skin warms, and I slide my charcoal blazer off and hang it on the back of my chair. "I believe he goes by Mr. Newberg."

Morgan strides out the door, tossing her stiff curls as she passes the man in question. "Mr. Newberg, I'll let you engage in your business now."

"Engage," he calls after her. "That's funny, because I'm not engaged to your boss anymore."

He's not laughing, but neither is his tone loud with anger nor shrinking with embarrassment. He's just translating Morgan's gibe because he's factual that way. Making sure nobody ever misses an innuendo. And now I want to shrink with embarrassment.

"Charlie, sit down."

He smiles at my invitation and energetically takes a seat across from my desk, as if the whole conversation with my assistant never happened.

I rub my forehead. "I apologize for Morgan."

He props an ankle on his knee. "She didn't say anything that's not true."

Charlie's contention with Morgan is definitely another story his sister would get a kick out of. I think back to my conversation with her last night. "Okay, weirdo."

Charlie laughs. I must have startled it out of him because he's usually too intense to laugh. "Did you just call me a weirdo?"

I'm smiling now too. It's hilarious he doesn't know how weird he is. "Yes."

"What makes me weird?"

I shrug because it has to be obvious to everyone else if his sister jokes about it. "It's weird you don't care what other people think."

He gives a shake of his head, but not with his normal intensity. I'd say he's a mixture of confused and entertained. "Shouldn't we all be weird that way?"

It is what I liked about him to begin with. "Maybe."

"Why maybe? Why not absolutely?"

The thing I liked about him in the beginning is what hurt me in the end. "There are pros and cons to everything. The con to not caring is that you can come across as insensitive."

His face scrunches back up with the normal intensity. "Maybe other people shouldn't be so sensitive."

I try to keep from rolling my eyes. I should have expected him to say as much. "How about we use the word 'inconsiderate,' then? You can come across as inconsiderate. Like you're too focused on getting where you need to go that you don't stop to help the little old lady cross the street."

"Huh." He mulls this over. "What if I'm in a hurry because I'm on my way to a senior center to help a bunch of little old ladies? If I slow to help the one, I won't be able to help the many."

I press my lips together. I'm not going to let him know I feel like I'm the little old lady he left behind in his effort to change the world. I was the one he passed over because I didn't matter enough. If he hasn't figured it out yet, he never will.

But it's not an issue anymore. It's not as though we have a romantic relationship to nurture. He's paying me to promote his films.

His wrinkles smooth and his eyes widen. "Is that how you felt when I left for Peru?"

Goose bumps pop up on my arms, and I consider putting my blazer back on to hide them. This is the validation I used to yearn for. I hate that it still means so much.

Charlie has never been mean. Just unable to put himself in other people's shoes.

I prompt him. "When you left the day before our wedding?"

He holds out a hand. "I didn't even realize . . ."

"I know." I wish I could brush it off as easily as he does. "It didn't mean enough to you."

"That's not true." If he's denying it, he really believes his version of events.

"Charlie, you go after the things you want. And you stopped going after me."

His mouth opens. For the first time in our interactions, Charlie Newberg is speechless. His head tilts, probably from the weight of considering a different perspective. "I thought you were going to run by my side as we chased our goals together."

It's true that we'd talked about me promoting his films from our very first date. But then I'd gotten this job, and I liked it. "Well, I'm working with you now. You got what you wanted."

His foot drops to the floor, and he leans forward. "That's not—"

"Miss Lemaire, Lance Hanselman is here to show you what he's designed for the film website." Morgan stands in the doorway, just a little too chipper about interrupting Charlie.

Unfortunately for her, Charlie doesn't care what she thinks.

I level her with a gaze, then motion Lance forward. "Come on in. I look forward to your proposal."

Chapter Twelve

CHARLIE

To be deeply loved by someone gives you strength,
but to love someone deeply gives you courage.
—Anonymous

Nicole called me a weirdo," I process out loud with my sister. The way Nicole said it makes it seem as though she sees me as Gonzo from the Muppets. But would I rather be Kermit the Frog? He is always so concerned about what people think of him. Of course, if I'd been more like Kermie, I might have gotten the girl by now.

"I've been calling you that for years." Meri doesn't miss a beat of conversation, though she's still struggling along the forested trail leading from the zoo to a summit above the city.

Even though we're surrounded by thick foliage, we can still hear the rush of cars because this is an urban hike named after the four forms of transportation that will loop us back to where we started: trail, tram, trolley, and train. The 4T Trail doesn't completely immerse us in nature, so it's not my favorite, but after Meri saw the photo of my proposal to Nicole in the aerial tram, she lamented that she'd never gotten to ride it, and here we are.

I haven't hiked this since the day I'd proposed. Which could be another reason why it's not my favorite trail and why I can't get my mind off yesterday's conversation with the woman I plan to marry.

"Sisters are supposed to call names," I reason. "While Nicole sounded serious, like she believes it's true."

Meri huffs and puffs. "Oh, it's true." Her comebacks are stronger than her legs.

We emerge above the freeway, and there's a bridge for us to cross over eight lanes of traffic. It reminds me of the first full-length documentary I made on the plight of the mountain lion in Southern California. The state has since begun building a wildlife crossing over Highway 101.

I raise my voice to be heard over the noise of cars whizzing underneath us. "I can't figure Nicole out. After watching my documentary in Peru, she said I did the right thing to leave. Then yesterday, she made it sound like she was hurt I chose to do the right thing."

We reach the end of the bridge, where a wooden post has little metal signs mounted on it pointing the way to Council Crest and counting down the distance for us.

Meri leans over, hands on knees. "Another one-point-two miles? I thought we were getting close."

"That is close." I look between my sister and the mile marker that so offends her, not registering the problem. "You wanted to do this."

"I want the fresh air. I want to burn the calories. I want the views." She stands and reaches for the tube on the hydration pack full of water that I lent her. "I don't want the pain."

That word *pain* stops me. It connects with Nicole's reference to being hurt. "Okay, that makes sense. So while Nicole wanted me to help the people in Peru, she didn't want the pain she felt when I left. I guess you can have both."

"Of course you can have both. It's called emotions." Meri shakes her head as she passes by to set our pace up the trail. "It's what keeps so many people from reaching our goals. It's what almost kept Kai and me apart. Do you seriously not experience the struggle of the climb?"

"Not this one." The most challenging part of this hill is how slow Meri is moving.

She hoots a laugh. "I don't think you ever do. You're too factual. Too driven."

I accidentally bump into her, knocking her forward. Her arms flail. I grab at whatever I can to keep her from toppling onto the railroad-tie stairs that must have stopped her. We end up twisted in a klutzy hug, but we're still standing.

"You just proved my point," she says from where her face is practically smashed into my armpit. She takes a step up and moves toward the side, regaining her balance without my support.

I sniff at my armpit, hoping it didn't gross her out too much. I actually kinda like the musky scent of my own sweat. It smells the way endorphins feel. "What's your point?"

"You can't slow down."

Her critique sounds like a compliment. I'm a racehorse. I get things done. For example, I don't know why we're still here talking about this. "You want me to lead the way to avoid knocking you over next time you stop?"

She sniffs. "So you'll leave me in the dust? You don't think that will hurt me too?"

The word *hurt* gives me pause again. My hurry can hurt others. It hurt Nicole.

But maybe the solution is as simple as taking the lead. I climb the steps two at a time, still contemplating the analogy. "I stayed in Portland for the past couple of years. That's slowing down."

Meri takes a moment to respond, and when she does, it's already from a distance behind me. "You call that slowing down? In that time, you filmed and released your documentary on Gemma's boyfriend's work with the police and pitched investors for your Philippines film."

"That's my job." What does she want me to do? Make a second butt dent in the couch next to Kai's? Not that her fiancé is stuck there anymore, but his laziness almost destroyed their relationship. I don't see how that's better.

Meri doesn't say anything for a while, though I have the feeling it's not because she has nothing to say. It's because she's too busy panting.

I try to enjoy the peace, but my brain has taken on the case, becoming my defense attorney. I did the right thing in going to Peru. And I'm doing what I feel God wants me to do by pursuing Nicole now.

It can't be a mere coincidence that I prayed for Nicole not to get married if God wanted me to marry her, then she broke off her engagement to the other guy. And it definitely can't be a coincidence that her last client's indiscretions left her looking for a new client right when I was about to give up on us. People who believe in God's will don't believe in coincidence.

Yes, I'm going to keep working while I wait for her to come around, but that's what I'm good at. That's who God created me to be. Maybe a few people get hurt along the way, but as Meri said, pain is part of the climb.

A final staircase leads us from the tunnel of trees onto the side of a road. After the coolness of the forest, the heat hits from both direct sunshine above and reflection off the blacktop below. Sweat beads on my forehead as I wait for Meri, but she could get lost here if I'm not patient.

Once again, I'm assaulted with the analogy. If I don't slow down, I could leave people behind. But what about those who need help up ahead?

Finally, Meri emerges. She looks past me, and her face crumples. "A gas station?"

"You look out of gas to me." Lame attempt at a joke.

She narrows her eyes as only an older sister can. "I thought for sure this had to be the summit."

I imagine Moses was treated just as poorly by his sister, Miriam, when leading the Israelites through the desert. Meri is the worst part of bringing Meri on this hike. People are the worst part of helping people.

"Follow me."

I cross the street to a Y in the road. But we don't take the Y. We take the paved trail cutting down the middle of it back into shade. I intentionally block the mile marker with my body to keep Meri from any more whining.

We finally reach the highest point in Portland, and Meri's energy is miraculously restored. She pumps her arms like Rocky, and I pull out my camera to film her because I know Kai could use this footage for their YouTube channel.

We have better weather today than when Nicole and I hiked up here. I'd planned to propose in front of this gorgeous view of the city below. The skyline mingles with rivers, bridges, and so many trees that when the area had first been cleared back in the 1850s, there were enough stumps for people to jump from stump to stump to avoid the muddy, unpaved roads, giving it the nickname Stumptown. The day Nicole hiked with me, it had started drizzling, and she'd been in a hurry to get on the aerial tram, so I'd proposed there instead.

Overhead, the sky is bright blue, but in the distance where the plaques say Mount Rainier and Mount St. Helens should be, a streak of clouds hides them from view. If this doesn't define the Pacific Northwest, I don't know what does. The clouds that keep us from seeing the gorgeous mountains are the very thing that make everything else gorgeous.

Meri runs by, leaping like a ballerina. Or maybe a preschooler who thinks she looks like a ballerina. She's got much more passion than poise. "Come play the piano with me," she calls.

There aren't many hikes where you can play a piano on the top of a mountain, but again, we're in Portland. The musical instrument sits in the center of a paved overlook. It's painted white with the words Please Play Me stenciled in black. I bet Moses would have played with Miriam after crossing the Red Sea if the Middle East had been as accommodating.

Unfortunately for everyone here, the only song Meri knows is "Chopsticks." I join her to prove I'm capable of slowing down. Then I get her going again.

Mostly downhill this time, so she's a little more pleasant. But for some reason, the closer we get to the tram that was built to transport patients to the hospital, the grumpier I feel. I hate feeling grumpy.

These are the stupid feelings Meri was talking about. I'm not sure why she thinks they're so important. They're a waste of time. I bet if I hadn't slowed down, I wouldn't have had the time to notice them.

That's true about physical pain anyway. When your muscles ache, if you start moving, the nerves are too clogged with messages from your brain for your muscles to be able to relay the message to the brain that they hurt.

Meri jogs past me and the sleek hospital. Finally, we're moving, and I'm ready to move on.

Then she halts, arms outstretched as if to hug the view below. I barely avoid bumping into her again.

"Seriously? This is basically the same view we saw earlier." My gaze slides past all the prettiness to the silver pods gliding through the air on cables.

One pod stops at a loading platform. The center doors slide open. I want to push ahead of the crowd to climb on first. I want the five-minute ride over with.

This desire is the exact opposite of what I'd wanted last time. With Nicole, the ride had been the goal. When she'd ducked into the bathroom before we boarded, I'd arranged it with the other passengers to make sure we had the best spot and for them to photograph us when I got down on one knee.

Meri bounces beside me. "It's like that old ride at Disneyland."

The line of passengers files inside the pod until it's packed. We're not in line yet, but we wouldn't have made it anyway.

I grunt. "It's not the Magic Kingdom. It's public transit." I pull out my debit card and approach the ticket machine. The pass will pay for our future modes of transportation as well.

The machine spits out our tickets and we file through the metal stanchions to hop on the next pod.

Meri swoons in spite of my grim commentary. "It's still much more romantic than the second place you proposed to Nicole."

A few faces turn our way.

I smile and wave. "Yes, I proposed to the same woman twice," I tell the crowd. "Third time will be a charm."

Raised eyebrows are chased by nervous chuckles.

Only Meri crosses her arms as if to scold me. "Charles." She sounds like Mom when I first told her I was going to have a female roommate.

"Meredith."

"You're using God's will as an excuse."

I gape. The Bible says family will turn on you when you follow the Lord, but Meri got engaged when serving with a Christian organization in Africa, so she should understand. She loves God and she loves Kai.

"You know about my prayer," I point out. "You're the first person I told."

"I appreciate that you're doing what you think you're supposed to do." She clicks her tongue. "But so did Jonah."

"Jonah? The guy is famous for running away." I'm not seeing the connection.

"Peru," she says.

And I'd thought Nicole's opinion of me was low. "You call that running away? I was risking my own neck to be there. I saved lives."

"That's not the point."

I rub a hand down my face. Nobody else would talk to me like this. Isn't there also a Bible verse about the wounds of a friend? "Not sure your accusations can get any sharper."

"Jonah turned around and went to Nineveh."

Okay, I see some similarities.

"He did what God wanted him to, but not out of love. His heart wasn't toward the people."

That stops me. I want to do the right thing, but I hadn't thought about doing it for the right reason. I'd thought obedience was enough. I don't want to feel the feelings.

"Love is action," I argue. I'm good at action.

"God doesn't only judge actions," my sister adds softly. "He judges man's heart."

My chest throbs. I hate it.

I prefer black and white. I prefer rules and checklists. I prefer facts and percentages.

Procuring a marriage license is much safer than making a relationship work. Relationships are messy. There are no guarantees when love is involved, and it seems more sensible to turn my wedding into a business arrangement.

Another pod slides into place. The doors open. Passengers in front of us file inside. Somehow, Meri and I end up with the best view of the city below. It's a view I've seen before. Before I dropped to one knee anyway.

Had I truly loved Nicole back then? I'd loved being with her. I'd loved the team we made. I'd loved our dreams of the future. But had I loved her for her? If not, is that what God is really calling me to now?

To get my heart in the right place, I might have to give it to Nicole.

Chapter Thirteen

NICOLE

To love at all is to be vulnerable. Love anything, and your heart will certainly be wrung and possibly be broken. . . . Lock it up safe in the casket or coffin of your selfishness. But in that casket—safe, dark, motionless, airless— it will change. It will not be broken; it will become unbreakable, impenetrable, irredeemable.
—C. S. Lewis, *The Four Loves*

I pivot into the roundhouse kick and smack the punching bag with the top of my foot. It stings in the most satisfying way.

Workout Wendy holds the bag from the other side, and though she's almost six feet of pure muscle, I've rocked her back on her heels. The small success propels me into spinning away and switching feet for a back kick. My glutes ignite to power the impact.

But I'm not done. Not when I'm picturing Charlie's expression— the perfect blend of virtue and victory. I follow up with a back elbow and back fist.

Wendy steadies the heavy black bag, keeping it from swinging into the wall and scaring Mrs. Fitzgerald on the other side. "Taking out some aggression?" she challenges.

"Absolutely." I bounce in place and shake out my burning shoulders. Sweat drips into my right eye, blurring my vision. I blink a couple of times, but when it doesn't help, I un-Velcro a glove and wipe the moisture away.

Wendy tosses me a towel from a shelf in the corner. "Does this have anything to do with a guy?"

I swipe the fuzzy terry cloth over my face and behind my neck, then I tuck it under my arm to accept the water bottle she's now offering. I guzzle long and hard. Both to quench my dry throat and to buy time before answering.

My brain must have overheated, because it can't compute fast enough.

"Why do you think that?" I'm curious if I've done something on the outside to reveal what's going on inside.

Wendy grabs her own water bottle, and I'm kind of jealous that she gets paid for working out. We'd met when I attended one of her classes at the gym, but because of my job, I couldn't always make it in time. Now she comes to the home gym I built in my guest bedroom for personal training, and our Sunday morning sessions are the closest I get to church anymore.

I don't have a problem with God, just hypocrites. Thankfully, Wendy's not one of them. She's the kind of Christian I want to be, so I learn from her. If this deal with Charlie goes south, maybe I can take what she's taught me and become a kickboxing instructor too.

"I saw the news about Dante Sullivan," she offers.

Oh yes. Dante. Was I really still working with him last time she came over? "Forget Dante. He's the least of my problems now."

She grabs a mat and unrolls it on the hardwood floor. "So you have a new client you want to elbow in the face?"

I drop onto my back. This is where she'll stretch me out like one of those stretch labs that are popping up all over the place. If only I could always pay other people to do the work for me.

Hmm, maybe I can. If I start pawning Charlie off onto Morgan, he might stop coming around so much. Of course, I'd also have to stop dropping by his house to talk business.

"Remember Tim?" I ask in an attempt to ease her into the shallow end of this conversation.

"You invited me to your wedding." She presses one of my legs up toward the ceiling and the other toward the floor. My hamstring responds like cold Silly Putty, but the longer she holds me in this position, the more my muscles release. "Did he hire you to promote his oral surgery centers? Is he your new client?"

"If only." I roll my eyes toward the wall of windows and look at the gray rain clouds rolling in. The chill offers refreshment after an hour of sweating. "I brought him up because you know him. But remember how I started dating him on the rebound?"

"Uh-oh." She gives my muscle a moment of respite, then pushes it farther. "This is about the guy who left you to make documentaries."

"Yeah, he's back." Kind of like the pain of this stretch. "I'm in charge of promoting the films he left me for."

Wendy leans into my leg with her shoulder, bringing her face toward mine. "Why didn't you say no?"

"I tried." My self-deprecating chuckle shakes us both. "But after Dante, he was the only one willing to work with me."

Wendy stares with the kind of intensity that wins her matches in the ring. The scar in her right eyebrow brightens to stand out against her dark skin. It practically taunts, *You can hit me, but you won't keep me down.*

I'm not trying to hit her though.

"Are you keeping your boundaries up?"

By "boundaries," she probably means not laughing at Charlie's jokes. Not agreeing to attend his sister's bachelorette party. Not going to his house, taking photo booth pictures, and sharing garlic bread. So I don't mention those things. "I turned him down when he proposed again."

"Girl." Wendy springs to her feet.

Without her pressure against my hamstring, my leg flops to the floor, heavy and lifeless.

"The dude finally realized what he's missing."

Off-balance for more than one reason, I pull my other leg up to stretch myself. "I'm not sure Charlie realized anything. He just believes God told him to marry me."

She huffs. "That's the worst line I've ever heard."

I'd thought so too. Mostly. But there's this little part of my heart that has learned the hard way I'm supposed to sacrifice my own desires for the welfare of others. So it's good to have my frustration affirmed.

"No wonder you were punching extra hard today."

"Yeah." My muscles are spent. I let them melt into the mat in well-earned rest.

She tilts over me again, and I expect her to resume our stretching routine. Instead, she unhooks my hands from my leg and tugs to roll me onto my feet. I face her, not quite sure why I'm standing or how I got here.

"The God I know is personal," she says. "Whether you're dealing with a former fiancé or a pastor, God wants us going to Him rather than blindly following what someone else tells us God wants us to do."

I still. She knows about my dad cheating on my mom with his church secretary, because my resentment toward him has fueled many a workout.

She continues her lesson. "God speaks to all of us. If we aren't sure about something, we're supposed to ask Him, read Scripture, and listen for that still small voice of His."

Okay, she's not talking about my dad. He probably wouldn't approve of this sermon anyway, which makes it my favorite sermon ever.

"When someone tries to tell you what to do, they are putting themselves in the place of God in your life. That makes it spiritual warfare."

Her words hit me like a left uppercut. Not because of Charlie though. Charlie is too independent to try to control me. In fact, I wished it had been harder for him to let me go. No, this wound runs much deeper.

Dad loved giving messages on the armor of God. Yet, I'd needed it to stand up against him.

I punch a fist into my open palm.

"This is why we are told to guard our hearts," Wendy preaches, and I'm not sure if we're talking about faith or fighting. Both, I guess. "Guard up."

I lift my fists in front of my cheeks and duck my chin. A moment ago, I'd been ready to shower, but now energy courses through me. I need to defend myself.

I didn't deserve the unfair hits I took in high school, and I wish I could go back in time and protect that teenager.

Wendy draws her guard up as well. "You're on defense. Block and duck. Defend yourself."

I bounce, light on my feet, prepared for her attack.

She fakes right.

I go left.

"Scripture says your battle is not against flesh and blood, so you don't want to attack me, but you do have to protect your heart from me. It's the most loving thing you can do."

Again, I'm sent reeling by her words.

Dad had said if I loved him, I'd keep his secret. He'd said if I loved God, then I wouldn't want Mom to be hurt. It would do more harm than good, and it would be all my fault.

Wendy fakes left.

I go right.

I told Mom anyway. Had telling her been the right thing to do? According to Wendy, it was. Though guilt still twists my stomach.

"Until you figure out what you want and what God wants for you, what do you do when Charlie calls?" Wendy throws a cross.

I whip my arm up to knock her punch away. My forearm stings with success, and I refocus on the man she's talking about. There's nothing I can do about Dad anymore. "Let it go to voicemail."

"Nice."

My pulse surges. I can do this.

Wendy shuffles in a semicircle around me.

I turn with her.

"What do you do when Charlie emails?" She thrusts a front kick toward my core.

I roll my right knee up and out, sending her foot safely past my hip. "Forward it to Morgan with advice on how she should respond."

"And when he shows up at your office?" Wendy regains her balance at the same time she pivots into a hook.

I bob and weave, ducking under her fist and coming up on the other side. "I'll tell him I have to leave for an appointment."

It's simple. I can do it. Why hadn't I tried avoiding Charlie before now? Besides the fact that I wouldn't do it with other clients and I actually enjoy this project? I don't want to avoid Charlie, but from experience, I know this is what I have to do.

Morgan might hate me for dumping more work in her lap, but she'll enjoy keeping Charlie from getting what he wants. And I'll be protecting myself from the pain of my ex's indifference when he leaves again.

Wendy lunges, wrapping her arms behind the back of my knees and yanking them forward. I drop onto my bum, and the mat cushions the blow. I'm sure Wendy planned it that way, but the impact still jars my teeth, and I'm reminded that I'll have to see Charlie at the film festival premiere. No matter what I do, I can't avoid all association with the man.

I flop my arms and legs to the ground, down for the count. While Wendy's bonus lesson had been inspiring, I'm going to be hurting tomorrow. "You're still going to stretch me out, aren't you?"

She looks at her watch. "No can do. Just use some Epsom salts in your bath tonight."

I moan.

She laughs, giving me a low five on her way out the door.

I'll eventually make it to my soaker tub. At the moment, I'm still soaking in all Wendy's wisdom and feeling like a failure in body and soul.

I watched my mom obey Dad as if he were God, and now she's gone. I refuse to let the same thing happen to me.

Chapter Fourteen

CHARLIE

Love is like the wind.
I can't see it, but I can feel it.
—Shane West as Landon, *A Walk to Remember*

As if to spray my wound with the sting of antiseptic, God reinforces Meri's lecture on slowing down with the actual "day of rest." I'm not a big fan of the Sabbath because I don't know what to do when I'm not working. I just tell myself if God is my maker, then the Bible is an owner's manual, and I'll stay in better condition if I follow its instructions.

I start my day with church, of course. Then Mom invites me out for prime rib at the oldest steak house in Portland to celebrate her first wedding anniversary with Douglas. With its plaid carpet, low-beamed ceilings, and stuffed fish hung as decor, it looks like a lounge where my grandpa might have once smoked cigars, not where I would normally picture my bright-blazer-and-scarf-wearing mother with her Princess Di haircut. Though she would fit in better at a tea house, the steak house's sizzling meat doesn't disappoint, and they offer a relish tray to tide patrons over until the main course is served. Probably so the delicious smells don't make anyone drool all over the table or assault waitresses out of hangriness.

Kai and Meri join us and are so busy talking about their wedding plans that I let my mind wander to Nicole. I'm looking forward to going over our newsletter campaign, but it's more than that. I kind of wish she was with us at this table right now. I think we could be a good family for her. I think she'd fit in.

Douglas fits in. He and Mom eloped in Cannon Beach last summer. Clean-shaven with salt-and-pepper hair that's receding above his temples, he's the exact guy I would have picked for a stepdad if I'd ever imagined Mom would date again.

As it was, I was out of the country when Meri told me Mom had a boyfriend. It threw me for a loop at first. But after I came home and played Scrabble with the two of them a couple of times, I was glad Mom wasn't stuck playing Sudoku by herself for the rest of her life.

Meri kicks me under the table like she used to do to get my attention when we were little. I look up to find tears in her eyes, though I'm not sure why she's the one crying when I'm the one getting kicked.

She tilts her head toward Douglas. What'd I miss?

"Douglas?" She turns his way in a much more mature approach to getting someone's attention than the kick she gave me. "I have a question for you."

I stroke my beard, wondering what she's going to ask. Does she need more money for her reception? Because I could help her out with that.

"What's up, hon?" he asks.

He may be our stepdad, but he didn't raise us. Most of our interactions with him involve Mom, church, and Scrabble. In that order.

Meri blinks her watery eyes. "I was wondering if you'd want to walk me down the aisle at our wedding."

Douglas doesn't respond right away, but he can't be more stunned than I am.

I sit up straighter. If I'm ever going to be in a wedding, it should be the one between my sister and roommate. "You don't want me walking you down the aisle anymore?"

Meri does a double take to frown at me. Then her eyes bulge Kai's way.

Meanwhile, Douglas adjusts his tie and shoots my mom a look of panic. "I don't want to interfere . . ."

Meri holds her index finger up in front of Douglas. "Hold on." She snaps the fingers on her other hand at Kai. "I thought you said you talked to Charlie."

Kai scratches his cheek and scrunches his face. "I said I was going to talk to Charlie the other day, but then Nicole came over, and things got . . . stilted. That's when Gemma and I left the room."

I'm not sure what's happening, but it's not fair Nicole is being blamed. I like the fact she came over.

Mom pats Douglas's arm while shooting the rest of us warning looks. "What's going on?"

Meri groans. "Kai. Ask him now. Hurry."

Kai blows out a breath. "Charlie?"

Wow. He's off to a great start. "Yeah, man?" I need him to spit out whatever he's trying to say so we can get back to this walking-Meri-down-the-aisle business.

"I'd like you to be one of my groomsmen."

Ahh . . . The picture comes into focus. "Did something happen to your cousin or coworker? They can't make it to your ceremony, so you need me?"

"No." His eyes slide Douglas's direction, then he cups his hand around the side of his mouth, as if such a gesture will keep everyone else from hearing what he has to say to me. "I would have asked you right after I proposed, but your mom hadn't remarried yet, and we expected you to walk Meri down the aisle."

Got it. I'm not being replaced. Douglas and I are both being up-graded. "Hey, Doug." I turn to my stepdad. "You're not interfering. You're one of us now. You should give Meri away. You know, since Mom's going to be so weepy that if she walked Mer down the aisle, guests might expect her to not let go."

"Dude," Kai admonishes.

I shrug. "What? Mom said that's why she eloped. She didn't want to cry in front of people."

Mom wipes a tear. "It's true," she admits, even though it's already obvious.

"See?"

Meri kicks me again. I think she just likes kicking as much as Mom likes crying. She did play soccer in high school.

Douglas clears his throat. Then he clears it again.

Meri reaches for his hand. She's much nicer to the newer members of our family.

His wrinkles deepen and his voice cracks when he tries to speak. After a couple of tries, he finally chokes out, "I'd be honored, Meri."

Since Douglas's first wife died before they had kids, this will be the only time he gets to give a daughter away. Knowing his history makes me happy for both of us.

Meri starts crying for real. Mom's crying is contagious. But at least they're happy tears.

Maybe emotion isn't so bad after all. This moment is downright beautiful.

Life was much simpler when it was only the three of us. Me, Mom, and Meri. The bigger our family, the more possibilities for miscommunication. But also the more possibilities to share in each other's joy.

I can't wait to call Nicole on my way home to tell her about this.

My call goes to voicemail. Nicole's recording greets me over the car stereo.

I wonder what she's up to as I merge onto the freeway. She could be beating up a punching bag. Exercise might be considered work by some, but for her, it's more like play.

Does she work on Sundays? I'd be jealous if she's working without me. Especially if it's on my campaign.

Maybe she's hiking. Silver Creek Falls used to be a favorite spot of ours. And now I'm jealous all over again.

Her smooth greeting segues to a jarring beep. My turn.

"Hello, Nicole. This is Charlie." Would she know it was me if I hadn't said my name? Are there other men who leave her voicemails? Even if there are, I'd like to think she'd recognize my tone. "I'm looking forward to finalizing the newsletter promos. They look great so far."

Blah, blah, blah . . . That's not really why I called her.

"But that's not really why I called." I think back to dinner. To all the happy tears. A chuckle rumbles from my chest. "I'm not sure if you know my mom got remarried. My stepdad's name is Douglas. He looks like Tommy Lee Jones in *The Fugitive*, so you'd probably love him."

The Fugitive was Nicole's favorite movie. Okay, she has other favorite girlie movies, but this is the one I approved of. It has a powerful message about the dangers of pharmaceuticals.

"I have more to tell you, but I want to tell you in person."

I pause to pass a semi. And to let Nicole feel the weight of my statement.

But in that moment, I'm transported back to our wedding plans. Nicole didn't want her dad at the wedding, but she had nobody else to walk her down the aisle. She'd claimed it was an antiquated tradition, and she was fine without it. In light of Meri asking Douglas to give her away, I'm sad for my former fiancée. Of course, I know she won't want to talk about that.

So instead, I say, "Call me when you get this."

If Nicole and I had gotten married, I bet Meri would have asked her to be in the wedding too. Now that I'm seeing so much of Nicole, I have lots of these kinds of thoughts. It's like one of those Choose Your Own Adventure books, and though I finished it, I'm going back to check out my other options.

I would have liked that life with Nicole, but I'm also glad I went to Peru. Now we're being given another chance, and this time we can have it all.

I jab the icon on my dashboard screen to hang up, already looking forward to her response.

Monday morning, I still haven't heard back from Nicole. This is out of character. She's very thorough, especially where work is involved. Between compiling a list of reviewers and reaching out to my contacts with film festival venue options for the premiere, I shoot her a quick email.

> *Nicole,*
> *I think you might have missed the last part of my voicemail because I was driving when I called you, and I paused to pass a truck. You must have mistakenly assumed my message was over. I hope you're not having problems with your phone.*
> *I'd like to get together today to start planning the premiere. We could leverage the glitz and rich history of the Hollywood Theatre and incorporate some jewelry raffles as part of the fundraiser. When are you free?*
>
> *Professionally Yours,*
> *Charles K. Newberg*

The thing about a jewelry raffle came to me out of the blue as I typed, so I immediately begin preparing a form letter for all the jewelers who've already signed up for the Gold Standard. I've barely opened up a new document when my email chimes to alert me of an incoming message.

Eagerly, I click my mouse. The address lists Momentum Marketing as the sender, but it's not Nicole's name. *Morgan?*

I cringe. Does the starchy assistant want to announce my emails too? Or maybe Nicole is out of the office. I hope she's not sick.

Nah, even if she was sick, she'd still be there.

> *Mr. Newberg,*
> *At your request, I have scheduled an appointment at 3 p.m. Pacific to discuss plans for the film premiere of* Sitting on a Gold Mine. *You may come to the office or join on the Zoom link.*
>
> *Thank you,*
> *Morgan*

Fine. I'll go and just talk to Nicole. She's the one I'm paying to do this job. And also, if we're going to fall in love again, like Meri suggested, then it would be a lot easier to do in person.

I have my normal checklist in mind for promoting the documentary, but as the elevator rises to the sixteenth floor, I have a second checklist compiling in my brain. It consists of things I want to tell Nicole. Besides the fact that Meri asked our stepdad to walk her down the aisle, I think Nicole would also like to hear about the piano at the top of the 4T Trail. She doesn't play much anymore, but I know it was one of her favorite things to do with her mom.

Also, Meri took off with Kai's Pop-Tarts last night, so this morning he made some amazing french toast stuffed with cream cheese, strawberries, and bananas. I bet Nicole would love the recipe.

The elevator chimes and the doors slide open. Nicole stands on the other side, looking like a cloudless summer sky in her light-blue business dress and matching blazer.

My face breaks into a grin. "Hey."

She looks up from her watch, dark eyes much too serious for the fun we've been having. Maybe she doesn't realize I've been calling and emailing. Her phone really could be on the fritz, and Morgan might have intercepted my email like the overbearing assistant she is. Now's our chance to reconnect.

I step off the elevator to join her. "Did you get my messages?"

She moves past me onto the elevator. "Yes."

I turn to face her again. "Where are you going? We have an appointment."

If she received my messages, then she must have some kind of emergency. That's why she's so serious. Did she get another concussion from kickboxing? It would explain why she's been avoiding screens.

Nicole pushes the elevator button, and the doors start to slide shut. "Your appointment is with Morgan. I have to go."

I turn sideways to squeeze back onto the elevator without getting squished. I'm not letting Nicole drive herself to a doctor's appointment with a concussion.

She steps back in alarm. "You'll be late for your appointment."

"I'm sure Morgan won't miss me." I lean closer to peer into Nicole's eyes. Last time she had a concussion, her pupils were really dilated and her irises wiggled. They seem steady at the moment, but the elevator doesn't have the best lighting.

She takes another step backward. "What are you doing?"

I reach to stabilize her. I don't want her to hit her head a second time. "Did Workout Wendy knock you out again?"

"What?"

Nicole's confused.

Not a good sign.

"Wendy gave you a concussion?" It's the only reason I've known Nicole to miss work.

She twists her arm and pulls it away. "No."

Okay, I'm the confused one. "Then where are you going?"

She clutches her angel-wings necklace and takes a deep breath. "I'm meeting up for a late lunch with a reporter from the *Oregonian*. He can get you some interviews."

I reel back on the heels of my leather hiking boots. "He?" I sound like a jealous ex. It's the opposite of how I want to come across. It's the opposite of how I want to feel. But she's leaving an appointment with me to go to lunch with him.

Her gaze sharpens. Her chest rises and falls. She doesn't say anything. And she shouldn't have to.

I have no claim to her. But I just blew my cover of keeping things between us professional.

The elevator dings for the first floor. My mind scrambles for the right words to stop her from leaving, which is the only way to explain what comes out of my mouth.

"I'd offer to take you to lunch, but I'm still full from french toast," I say. Of all the things I wanted to tell her on my mental list, that one's the least important.

Her guffaw melts into laughter, and I expect her to call me a weirdo again. In this case, she'd be right.

She steps off the elevator and turns to face me. "We're going different places," she states simply and with enough intention that I know she'd planned this.

She doesn't have a concussion. She purposefully ignored my call. She forwarded my email to Morgan. And she double-booked herself during our appointment.

The elevator doors threaten to separate us, and I lunge through them.

She retreats farther into the lobby. It's a big open space framed with glass, chrome, and slate. The sparse decorating consists of nothing but the most uncomfortable-looking square chairs you can imagine. There are only a few business types milling around, and they glance warily at our jerky movements.

I block it all out and step closer to focus only on her. Her rigid posture. The purse clutched to her chest. Her stormy expression, warning me away. She doesn't remind me of a cloudless sky anymore. But if she's lightning, then I'm thunder.

We face off, and I hate it. We're supposed to be on the same side.

"We're a good team," I gruff.

Her lips part. Her words falter, but her gaze does not. She says, "Let's divide and conquer," as if to let me down gently.

"I'd rather work with you."

Her head tilts. A sigh escapes. "I know."

If God really wants me to love Nicole like Meri suggested, then why is He making it so hard? Our issue isn't miscommunication. Our issue is that she knows I want to marry her, and she doesn't want the same. Despite how well we work together. Despite the way we can be real with each other. Despite the way she makes me feel both relaxed and energized at the same time.

A male voice calls her name from a distance. It doesn't resonate until I hear it a second time. "Nicole?"

She blinks before nodding at the newcomer by the entrance. Then her face turns back toward mine, but she keeps her gaze lowered as if in guilt.

Could this guy be her other former fiancé? Or someone else she's dating? He's wearing a suit and is as clean-cut as one can get. "Wow. He makes me feel like Sasquatch," I say aloud.

One corner of her mouth curves up. She speaks softly. "I have to—"

"Go," I finish for her. Or dismiss her. She doesn't *have* to do anything. She's choosing to.

Her eyes snag on mine once again, almost in apology. Then she turns and strides away.

I retreat, keeping my eyes on Nicole as I push the button to call the next elevator.

Mr. Perfect nods at me over her shoulder. "Who's that?"

"My client," she responds a little too lightly.

I look at him once more, but instead of his clean-shaven face, I see Travis Escalante from fourth grade accepting his blue ribbon for the hundred-meter dash at field day. I'd won that blue ribbon every year prior. There's no doubt I was the fastest in the class. But that year I tripped on a shoelace and fell. Even the slowest runner beat me, and it haunts me to this day.

I'd always loved winning, but that's the day I learned to hate losing. Meri said it's important to feel emotions, but this emotion makes my stomach churn.

Why would I put myself through that again? I can't win if I fall for Nicole.

I pivot on my rubber heel and step through open elevator doors. Looks like Morgan's going to have to deal with me after all. Then I'll be making more phone calls to the Philippines.

Chapter Fifteen

NICOLE

There is always something left to love.
And if you ain't learned that,
you ain't learned nothing.
—LORRAINE HANSBERRY, *A RAISIN IN THE SUN*

With as many questions as Aaron asked about my relationship with Charlie, I should have known he wasn't only interested in a newspaper interview. But I put up with his questions for a few reasons.

First, I was trying to do my job and get Charlie the local story, along with an interview on a national affiliate.

Second, I was flattered. Aaron's attention took my mind off the man I was trying not to think about . . . even if it meant we were talking about him.

Third, I never imagined Aaron had taken a photograph of me with Charlie and we would end up in the gossip column of the newspaper's website.

This is the photo I woke up to on Tuesday morning. It came in a text from Morgan.

> **Morgan:** Charlie seemed
> subdued in our meeting
> yesterday, however he looks
> anything but subdued here.

I study the shot. It's our stare-down outside the elevator. When Charlie gazed at me so intently, I thought he might care about me as much as his documentaries. And I'm gazing at him with hope, even though I'd been the one trying to escape. Of course, that was before he told me to go.

The photo is very personal. It's so raw I don't even want to touch it in case I get salmonella. But why do others care?

My phone dings in notification of another text because, besides the readers of the biggest newspaper in Oregon, my assistant cares way too much.

> **Morgan:** What happened
> between you two?

I tear my eyes away and stuff my face against my silk pillowcase to muffle a moan. (I don't want Mrs. Fitzgerald to think I'm dying and call an ambulance like she did for her other neighbor.) I also kick my feet against the tangle of sheets for good measure. Finally, I've vented enough to respond reasonably.

> **Me:** Charlie said he would
> invite me out to lunch if he
> wasn't still full of french
> toast.

> **Morgan:** ?

Her question mark sums up my thoughts exactly. But while Charlie's weirdness seems to vex her, I can't help smiling.

> **Me:** Charlie takes his french
> toast very seriously.

I giggle at the ridiculousness of my life. It's a better option than moaning and kicking. Once I get out of bed, those aren't options anymore, so I might as well move forward.

I laugh because I'm dumbfounded as usual. Charlie dumbfounds me.

> **Me:** He also mentioned
> that he felt like a bigfoot
> compared to Aaron.

> **Morgan:** He's a charmer,
> all right.

I close my eyes and shake my head. Charlie will probably die from a snakebite in one of his foreign countries, since he possesses such an inability to charm.

> **Me:** He's not though.
> So why is he making the
> gossip column? Why do
> people care about a photo
> of us?

Dots appear underneath my text, but Morgan's response doesn't immediately come, so I whip back my covers. After stepping into my furry cross-band slippers, I retrieve my kimono from the hook in the bathroom, and flip on lights on my way to the kitchen.

All this french toast talk made me hungry. I can't remember the last time I made french toast, but Kai did mention that I need carbs to deal with Charlie. I'll just have to burn off the calories in an extra-hard kickboxing session tonight. With the energy already thrumming through my veins at this early hour, that's probably going to happen anyway.

I stop and stare at my espresso machine. I might not even need caffeine today.

I wonder if Charlie is awake and has seen our picture. I'm not going over to his house to vent this time, but I expect a text or call.

My phone vibrates in my bathrobe pocket. My heart follows suit. I retrieve the slick device.

It's only my assistant.

My shoulders sag.

> **Morgan:** In case you forgot, you recently made the news with Dante Sullivan. Not to mention, Charlie is an Emmy winner. Now the two of you are starting a glitzy promotional campaign involving the top jewelers in the country, and you have a romantic history. But if none of that were true, people would still care about this photo. Because every woman dreams of having a man look at her that way. Even if it's Charlie.

I sink onto a barstool, pulse throbbing so hard I can feel it in the bend of my elbows. Morgan's facts make sense, though I didn't expect that last part from her. She's not Charlie's biggest fan, so I'm surprised she had anything nice to say, let alone for it to sound swoony. But she can't be right. She must have misinterpreted the image.

I hate how my fingers tremble as I scroll up to the shot she'd sent earlier. Charlie looks intense. That's all. Viewers won't know how intense he is, so they'll mistake his everyday appearance for passion.

If he was passionate, it's because he cares about his films and their promotion. It can't be about me. Yeah, he wants to marry me, but only because he thinks it's the right thing to do. There's no affection there.

He'd said we make a good team, and I can't argue with that. There are remnants from our previous friendship. We have the freedom to speak our minds to each other. And he did express some jealousy over my lunch with a man, though he's self-centered enough that it could have been nothing more than the shock of realizing I might have another suitor in my life other than him.

Not that I do. Not that I want one. *She flies with her own wings.*

My chest tightens, remembering the part from our elevator interaction that really got to me. Charlie became protective when he mistakenly assumed I had a concussion.

As if a concussion would be the only reason I didn't return his calls or his email.

But if he'd been right, it would have been nice to have someone take care of me for a change. It's been a long time since Dad pushed me out of the nest.

Still contemplating, I abandon my phone on the counter and pad down the hallway toward the front door. I flick on the wall sconces and blink at their bright reflection off the mirror above the entryway table. Then I grimace at my own drab reflection. At least the sore below my lip is gone, but I didn't wander over here to look at myself. Not in the mirror, anyway.

I pick up the photo strip and focus on the third image. Thankfully the media didn't get ahold of this pic. I take a deep breath and try to exhale any of the remaining longing from my captured expression. It was a moment of weakness, and I won't let it happen again.

My phone buzzes from the kitchen counter.

I drop the strip and slipper-slide back down the hallway to find out what Charlie thinks of making the gossip column. But it's only my assistant following up her previous statement with a disclaimer.

> **Morgan:** He does kind of
> look like bigfoot with that
> beard.

I set my phone down and stare at it.
The ringer remains silent.

As it does for the rest of the week.

Charlie doesn't call or text. We're still working together, but all emails go through Morgan. Which is what I'd wanted.

I set boundaries, and Charlie is respecting them. This hurts more than I want to admit, but not as much as it would if I married him and came in second to his true love—his job. Or, as he sees it, saving the planet. I can't compete with that, and I won't try.

I vowed a long time ago to never again put myself in a position to be sacrificed. Then Charlie sacrificed me.

Charlie doesn't call, but his sister does. I'm dripping with sweat from working on my jump kicks when my phone buzzes in the corner. Meri's name flashes, and I'm torn over whether I want to talk to her or not. My boundaries might need to extend to his family if I'm going to get him out of my head, but I did agree to attend her bachelorette party.

Plus, I wouldn't mind a workout break.

I grab a towel to mop off my face while sinking onto the exercise mat next to my phone. Pink clouds outside the wall of windows brighten the room with their reflection of the setting sun.

I swipe my finger over the old-fashioned phone icon and look out at the view to help me keep my peace no matter what Charlie's sister has to say. "Hi, Meri."

"You sound out of breath. Are you hiking?"

I twist the mouthpiece of my cell away from my lips to keep from huffing and puffing in her ear, but I have to pull it back in to answer her question. "I don't hike anymore. I kickbox."

"Oh, I remember that. Charlie tried it with you once and failed to block your blow to his gut."

I'd felt horrible at the time, but now I smile a little. "Preemptive strike."

She laughs, thank goodness. Some sisters wouldn't be okay with their brother getting beat up. "I saw the new photo," she says.

I know exactly which one she's talking about. The same one everyone at the office has been talking about. "I don't want to talk about it."

"Sorry."

I appreciate her apology.

"I've been hanging out at Kai's, hoping you'd stop by again. It was fun running into you there last time."

Yeah. That's not happening. "I need to work on my jump kicks."

"I hear ya." Her pause tells me more than her words. She's letting the subject drop with a TKO—technical knockout. "So you're at the gym?"

I lean against the wall, releasing the tension in my lower back. "I turned my guest bedroom into a kickboxing studio."

"You're so classy. You don't even work out in a gym—you work out in a studio."

I glance at my reflection in the mirrored wall. I've pulled my chin-length hair into two tiny pigtails, and my skin isn't only shiny with sweat, but some of that sweat has dripped into one of my eyes, turning it red. "You wouldn't call me classy if you could see me right now."

"Funny you mention it, because I'd love to see you right now. I'm in the Pearl District, and thought I'd stop by."

I glance out the door toward my kitchen. I did the dishes after cooking garlicky shrimp zucchini boats, so my house shouldn't be too messy. Though it will probably smell a little fishy. I'll have to pull out the candle Morgan gave me for my birthday. I don't remember the scent, just that it reads, *Having me as your assistant is gift enough, but here's a candle anyway* on the front.

I rarely light candles, because I rarely have anyone over. My place is not like Charlie's, with roommates and an assortment of significant others. I do appreciate my condo, but I miss the friendships.

I smile at the sweaty woman in the mirror. "Come on up."

"Why don't you come down? This sunset on the river is spectacular."

I glance out the window at the cotton-candy clouds. My apartment faces east, so I can't see the sun from here, but if the clouds are that pretty on this side, then the view of the sun sinking behind the West Hills must be even prettier.

Unfortunately, I'm not pretty. I frown at the mirror. It's not the image I wish to display outside this room. "I've been kickboxing," I remind Meri.

"Perfect. The breeze will cool you off."

I roll my eyes. The woman once pretended to drown in order to be rescued by a man for her YouTube channel. She won't understand that I'm not as eager to look like a wet rat. "Fine."

"Yay."

I pull a dry T-shirt over my sports bra and slip on my favorite slides. While I don't get out on the waterfront as much as I'd like, there are lots of people who bike and jog. So at least I won't be the only one in workout gear.

I take the elevator to the lobby and am looking forward to seeing the sunset when I push open the door to the greenbelt side. But it's not the sunset that takes my breath away.

"Surprise!" yells Meri, along with three other women all sporting heart-shaped sunglasses.

One of them has to be Gemma, with her unmistakable long hair and even longer legs. But I don't know the other two. Why are they surprising me?

Meri steps forward, a bouquet of pink balloons in one hand and bubble bath designed to look like a champagne bottle in the other. This is the oddest surprise ever. I feel as though I'm expected to put the pieces together, but they aren't matching up.

Meri and company. Heart sunglasses. Balloons. Bubble bath. It's rather Valentine-ish, but Meri already has a Valentine.

Ahh . . . The wedding. I close my eyes.

"Nicole, would you be my bridesmaid?"

I open my eyes and force a smile. I love Meri to death, but we haven't been close for a while. If I'd married Charlie, her invitation would make sense. She would've been in my wedding. We'd be sisters-in-law now. But she wasn't, and we're not. We're old friends. Acquaintances.

I glance at the trio behind her. "It looks like you already have bridesmaids."

Meri's been engaged for a year, so she's had plenty of time to recruit the bridal party. I'm an afterthought. Or worse. She's going to make me walk down the aisle with Charlie.

Wait. Charlie said he's giving Meri away in place of their dad. I exhale, feeling a little safer.

Meri shrugs. "Something happened, and I have an opening."

My stiff smile softens with compassion. Because she's in such a celebratory mood, I don't want to ask what happened. If she's lost a bridesmaid, that something can't be good. Perhaps a friend moved away, or they had a falling out. I should be honored to be offered the position. I was just thinking how I need more friends.

"Who's the maid of honor?" I turn my grin to the women, pretending to share in their excitement when, really, I want to make sure I'm not being saddled with all the responsibility.

Gemma raises her hand, and I try to keep my smile from slipping. As a screenplay writer, Gemma often disappears into her own world. She'll have beautiful ideas for the perfect ceremony and reception, but then they'll trigger her to start planning a wedding for one of her characters, and she'll forget all about the real one.

A woman with curly hair holds out a pair of heart-shaped sunglasses for me. "Gemma and I are sharing the job. She's the dreamer, and I'm the doer."

I take the glasses even though I'm not really a heart-shaped shades kind of gal.

"I will do Meri's makeup though," Gemma adds, not an ounce of offense in her breathy voice. "I can do yours too."

I'm sure I look like I need a makeover. "Thanks."

Meri claps. "So you'll do it?"

"When is it?" I know it's coming up, but so is Charlie's movie premiere.

"You didn't invite her?" booms a deeper voice.

My stomach plummets as I look toward the sound and find Kai behind a video camera. I really should have asked more questions before agreeing to come outside while dressed as if I'm attending middle school gym class. I slide on the sunglasses to hide my bloodshot eyes and hope Kai's footage is only for a personal wedding video and not for their YouTube show.

"I still have to send out invites," Meri informs Kai, as if I was always on the guest list. She beams back at me. "I'm going to Bridal Veil Falls this weekend to mail them. Just to get the postmark that says Bridal Veil."

Gemma stares off dreamily. "I wonder if Karson would want to have our ceremony at Bridal Veil Lakes."

The blonde isn't engaged yet, according to Charlie, but I let her dream.

"Kai and Meri's wedding is October nineteenth." The curly-haired woman answers my question, since everyone else is too excited to think straight. "It's at Kai's golf club."

Meri beams. "We've started playing FootGolf together. It's super fun."

"Oh." I picture FootGolf as something similar to soccer and have trouble imagining it as a setting for a ceremony. Though they could use the pun "you're a keeper" in their vows.

"Don't worry, there's a normal golf course, as well. It's beautiful." The curly-haired woman comes to my rescue again. "I'm Roxy. And this is Anne."

The other woman sports a cute blond pixie cut. "Sorry I'm so low energy. I'm preggo."

"Congrats." I have no such excuse. I'm more of the opposite— running from men and babies. As much as I appreciate Meri's wackiness, I'm also going to appreciate Anne's chill.

"So?" Meri holds her arms wide in question.

A smile creeps onto my face. It's hard to say no to a friend in heart glasses. Plus, Charlie's premiere is over a week later, so it should be doable. "Yes."

Meri jumps and squeals. Gemma clasps her hands to her chest. Roxy gives an affirming nod. And Anne rubs my arm as if to say, *There, there. We'll get through this together.* She'll make a great mom.

Then we're looping arms around each other in a semicircle to face Kai's camera. I'm squished between Meri and Gemma but feeling lonelier than ever.

I've been in Meri's shoes before. I've had bridesmaids. I've had a dress. I also drove to Bridal Veil to mail invitations.

Bridal Veil was named after a nearby waterfall that resembles a veil. The town was established in the 1880s during a logging boom, but it's since been abandoned. Only the post office is left to fuel the hopes and dreams of brides-to-be.

Once upon a time, Charlie and I hiked to the falls for our engagement photos. Now all that remains of our relationship is a ghost town. And I'm haunted by the memories.

Chapter Sixteen

CHARLIE

When we love, we always strive to become better
than we are. When we strive to become better than
we are, everything around us becomes better too.
—Paulo Coelho, *The Alchemist*

I know my interview in the *Oregonian* is online, but I also know Mom will want to keep a copy, so I walk to the convenience store on the corner and buy a newspaper. Carrying that thick bundle feels more official too. Strangers will have photos of me on their kitchen table, and I won't only be something they scroll past if I don't capture their attention in the standard two-point-seven seconds. Plus, if they're interested in supporting the cause, they won't have to try to hunt down the website but rather hang a clipping on their refrigerator, old-school style.

My stomach churns with excitement as opposed to the nauseous way I felt last time I saw Nicole. I'm still trying to reconcile what I'd thought was God's will for my life with the relief I feel from not pursuing her anymore, but I don't have any clear answers. I'm just waiting for God to give me a sign.

Riffling through the different sections, I pull out the Local News and spread it artlessly across the counter. It's bigger than a computer screen and much bigger than my phone. It's also printed on dead trees, which makes me feel a little guilty, so I'll make sure Mom recycles what she doesn't keep.

Sadly, my photo is not on the front page of Local News. The story of saving a town in Ecuador has been beaten by the celebration of a guy in a pickle costume. He's the mascot for our minor league baseball team, the Portland Pickles, and it's his birthday, but still. If Portland is going to be weird, I wish it was in the same way I'm weird—in a way that makes a difference.

The paper crinkles when I turn the page, and it's so thin it folds in on itself. I smooth the layer and focus on what I hope to be my photo. Instead, it's a shot of a group of women wearing heart-shaped sunglasses. I shake my head. Meri would like it, but . . .

I pause. The woman in the middle has Meri's freckles. The blonde with them must be Gemma. Curly hair is Roxy. The one with short hair is Anne.

My brain pauses before registering the final woman in the photo. What reason is there for Nicole to be wearing heart sunglasses in a photo with Meri's bridesmaids?

"Kai?" I shout.

Even if my roommate is here, I can't wait for an explanation. I hunch over the tiny newsprint.

Local YouTube star, Meri Newberg of Meri Me, *invites marketing director Nicole Lemaire to be a bridesmaid in her upcoming wedding.*

"Kai!"

I turn to find he's already bounded up the stairs. "What?" He looks around as if expecting a fire.

I jab at the newspaper.

He frowns on his way over to see what I'm making a big fuss about. He glances at the photo and his confusion dissipates. "Oh, hey. They took a still from my YouTube show. That's great."

Facepalm. Not only am I going to have to walk down the aisle with the woman I'd wanted to marry, but I can go watch footage of her being asked to walk down the aisle with me.

As if her trying to escape our last appointment wasn't rejection enough.

I cross my arms. "Was it Meri's idea for you to invite me to be your groomsman so I'd have to escort Nicole at your ceremony?"

Kai straightens. His face goes blank. "Uh . . ."

"You're not innocent." Not only is he the one who took this photo, but it became another story beating out my interview. Apparently, if I want my picture in the news, I have to be pining after Nicole outside an elevator.

I'll bet this article references our recent exposure in the media. I hadn't minded the photo from our engagement, because I'd seriously thought we were going to get engaged again. But now that I've decided to let my ex go, I don't want reminders of my failure popping up for all to see. I don't want my mom calling with questions. I don't want Nicole's assistant sending screenshots and gloating. I don't want my sister's pity and sad attempts at matchmaking.

Kai shrugs. "Meri truly desires for Douglas to give her away."

I snort. "But she didn't mention the idea until Nicole started showing up at our house?"

"Well . . ." Kai rubs his jaw in contemplation.

Perhaps he believed the way she'd spun it. But I'll tell him the truth. "I wasn't upgraded. I was ensnared."

Kai swings a leg over a stool to sit on it like a saddle, settling in. "I'm sure Meri thought she was doing you a favor. If I'd known what she was up to, I would have figured you'd be all for it." He shrugs. "Meri can toss the bouquet to Nicole, and I can shoot the garter to you."

"If only following God's will were so simple." Not that I believe getting married is God's will for me anymore. If it was, wouldn't He have told her too?

Kai grimaces. "Believe me, I know."

I study my roommate. I've never considered asking for his advice before. Of the two of us, I've always been the successful one. But here he is, preparing to put a wedding ring on my sister's finger while I'm planning to sell the engagement ring I own.

Ironically, in Kai's scenario, he was the one who didn't want to get married. He'd been as determined to remain a bachelor as Nicole is to avoid me. Even though I've decided to move forward with my Philippine documentary, I'm curious as to what wisdom he could offer if I were to woo Nicole.

"You didn't used to want to get married." It's why I'd warned my sister away from him. "What changed your mind?"

He blows his cheeks puffy. "I didn't fear marriage—I feared failing."

My head jerks back in surprise. In all the years I lived with Kai, he'd seemed to embrace failure. He'd made an art form of it.

"I feared my best efforts wouldn't be enough," he explains, as if he'd read my thoughts.

I'm not good at hiding what I think even when I don't speak. "Okay, that makes sense." We'd both had the same fear and simply ran from it in different directions.

He chuckles at my response. "I'm still afraid. But my greater fear is Meri feeling as though she's not worth my effort. So I will try for her, even if it means I fail."

While I hadn't expected Kai to have a fear of failure, the fact he's still scared is even more unexpected. Only out of love is he willing to face his fear. "Wow, man. Welcome to the family." I'm moved.

But at the same time, I don't want to be. This isn't about my fear. I'm the one willing to get married.

"You think Nicole is scared to try?" I ask.

Kai gives a low hoot and slaps the newspaper. "Nicole doesn't have a butt dent in her sofa. Nicole kicks life in the butt."

He's right. "She must have some other fear holding her back." I squint to better examine the situation, though it just gives me a better view of Kai's eye roll. "What? You don't think Nicole loves me enough to overcome her fear? Meri said something like that the other day on our hike."

Kai sighs. "I don't think Nicole's love is the issue."

"Really?" I lean forward, pulled by my heart lurching in my chest. "You think Nicole still loves me?"

He runs a hand through his hair. "Dude. Didn't you see how she looked in the photo?"

I study the picture in the newspaper. She's wearing heart glasses, so how am I supposed to be able to tell? Oh, wait. "You mean the photo on the internet?"

Kai's right eyebrow drops. "I don't know about an internet photo.

I'm talking about the photo booth. Didn't the strip of pictures print out?"

I tilt my head. I'd seen the image on the iPad screen for a moment, but that was it. "She took the strip."

His mouth opens. "Ahh . . ."

What does he think he understands? I'm not the best at reading expressions, but maybe Kai can translate. "How was she looking at me?"

He holds up a finger. "I'll go print you a copy."

He leaves, and I face the newspaper. After licking my fingers, I reach for the corner to turn the page and find my interview, but my eyes snag on the shot of Nicole again.

She's wearing gym shorts and has her hair up in pigtails. I'd forgotten she styled her hair that way when kickboxing. It makes her look years younger. Cuter. Sweeter. As if I could pick her up and take her out for ice cream at that one shop we used to go to where they have swings instead of chairs. Life had been so simple back in college.

As for now? I have to read about her in the newspaper to know what's going on in her life. I pick up reading where I'd left off.

Lemaire would have been Newberg's sister-in-law had director Charlie Newberg not left her at the altar to film his Emmy Award–winning documentary, Dirty Gold. *Now the pair are working together to promote his upcoming film, and perhaps they'll be walking down the aisle together at his sister's wedding. Their tainted history doesn't seem to be stopping the pair from career success, nor from believing in true love. Congratulations to the happy bride and her husband-to-be, Kai Kamaka. For more on Charlie Newberg, see page 4.*

The story gives new meaning to the term "fake news." I didn't leave Nicole at the altar. I'd suggested we elope. She chose not to come and gave the ring back. They make it sound so dramatic, like a scene from *The Princess Bride* or something.

It's also old news. The stuff between Nicole and me happened years ago. Just like the engagement picture that resurfaced.

Though how is Meri's wedding party even news at all? It's the kind of photo that gets taken every day in Vegas and Nashville. I suppose Meri was kind of a celebrity for a while, but Kai's YouTube show isn't about her trying to find a husband in outlandish ways anymore. It's simply about their wedding plans. Doesn't the general public have better things to do with their time than watch strangers pick out their cake, playlist, and flowers?

I could give viewers some suggestions. In fact, that's what I'm trying to do through my documentaries.

I shake my head at Nicole's image, then turn the huge crinkly page to find my article. Really? They ran the photo of me holding my Emmy rather than the photo from South America.

My phone chimes. *Morgan*. Could this day get any worse?

> **Morgan:** What's black and
> white and read all over?

> **Me:** That joke doesn't
> work in writing. If you spell
> out the word "read," it's
> not a pun, and there's no
> misdirection.

> **Morgan:** You're the joke.

That might be funny were it not true. But if Morgan's going to give me a hard time, she'll also have to learn to take it.

> **Me:** You're working for me,
> so what does that make
> you?

> **Morgan:** Touché.
> Besides texting to rip
> on each other, I need to

let you know Nicole set
up an appointment with
the Hollywood Theatre
tomorrow at noon.

Perfect. The sooner we get the premiere over with, the sooner I can head to Manila.

Me: See you there.

Morgan: Ms. Lemaire
handles event venues
personally.

I set my phone down and stare at it. I guess I'm going to see Nicole again.

"There she is." A black-and-white photo strip slides into my line of sight.

I glance up and nod a thank-you to my roomie without seeing him. I look back at the strip, and my eyes are drawn to the third picture as if it's the only one in focus.

I know Nicole was simply looking at me to hide the sore on her face, but what matters is how she's looking at me. The tough, independent woman has let down her guard. She's open and vulnerable. There are no pigtails, but she comes across as even younger here than the newspaper photo.

My heart hitches in a way that I try to avoid, but the twinge of pain I feel is not for myself. It's for her. I want to protect her, only it appears as if I have to protect her from me.

Chapter Seventeen

NICOLE

A lady's imagination is very rapid;
it jumps from admiration to love, from love to
matrimony in a moment.
—JANE AUSTEN, PRIDE AND PREJUDICE

As if having the *Oregonian* speculating on my relationship with Charlie wasn't enough, stepping into the Hollywood Theatre brings back memories of dating. The place was built in the 1920s and still offers glamour from the past with its Spanish colonial exterior that makes it look a little like a castle. There's also a newer lighted sign, vertically spelling out HOLLYWOOD, for which the whole neighborhood was named.

The theater runs another free little cinema in the airport that shows shorts. They gave Charlie his start back when he was fascinated with earthworms. I'm pretty sure no other cinema in the world would show a documentary on worms, no matter how beautiful the close-ups of dewdrops on bright-green leaves. He's forever grateful and happy to bring them business with his premieres.

The interior of this Hollywood Theatre invites guests into an intimate alcove with antique chandeliers and rich, red carpet. The buttery scent of popcorn mingles with a subtle scent of aged wood. I know it's practical that the huge seating area, which once held almost fifteen hundred viewers along with an orchestra pit and organ, has been renovated into a multiplex, but if I ever discover a time machine, I'll come back here to experience the golden age in all its glory.

As it is, Charlie and I used to come here on Sundays when it was too rainy to hike. This is where I first saw *Jaws*. As it was an old movie, it affected me more than I expected. Charlie took full advantage of my fright by holding my hand, letting me hide my face in his shoulder, and kissing me for the first time afterward. When planning to come here with him today, I hadn't considered that little factor from our past. Charlie is going to bring it up for sure.

Sunlight enters the lobby along with the man in question. He's wearing his trademark plaid, but today it's in the form of Bermuda shorts rather than a flannel. That alone would be unprofessional for a meeting with our venue coordinator, but he's topped it off with a straw hat and shades. As though he's leaving directly for a vacation afterward. Knowing him, he's just being Charlie. The man doesn't do vacations.

He nods at me, looks around, then turns back toward me and slides off his sunglasses to hook on his T-shirt. This is the first eye contact we've had since the fateful photograph almost two weeks ago, and it's still as intense. I was hoping separation would've cooled whatever's been simmering between us.

"I just remembered this is where we had our first kiss." He weighs my reaction with his gaze. "I hope it doesn't make things weird."

I press my lips together, trying to keep my smile demure. "*That's* not what's making things weird."

His eyebrow arches and he tilts his head. "Are you calling me a weirdo again?"

He's questioning his weirdness while dressed like a tourist in the tropics. I can't keep my laugh inside. "Asks the man in a straw hat."

"Hey, I'm an artist," he defends. But then he takes off the hat. "Actually, I forgot I was wearing this. I picked it up for Kai's bachelor party at the tiki lounge."

"Suuure." I try to keep things light, so he doesn't start talking about kissing again, but my heart shoots sparks of panic down to my toes. Are Kai and Meri having their bachelor and bachelorette parties together? I hadn't thought to ask when she invited me. But if so, it will be one more point of connection keeping Charlie and me from going our separate ways.

Hat in hand, Charlie studies me seriously. "I saw Meri asked you to be a bridesmaid."

I shake my head at the whole situation. I mean, who else besides Meri would have made it in the news with her bridal party? And I'd been concerned about showing up on Kai's YouTube channel. "I'm as honored as I am stunned, though I would have said no if I'd known it meant I'd have a photo of my pigtails in the newspaper."

"You look cute in pigtails." Charlie compliments me without hesitation, using the same tone he used when he told me the blister on my lip was herpes. He has no filter, but also no agenda. My cuteness is simply a fact to him. He believes it, which makes it more of a compliment than his "God-willed" wedding proposal.

I press my mouth closed and look around for the manager we're supposed to be meeting. As it's the middle of a workday, the place is dead. I suppose we should be searching for a back office, though I'd expect someone in there to hear us talking out here.

"Did Morgan tease you about the article as much as she teased me?" Charlie's question draws my attention back in time to see his grimace.

I twist my lips. I'm afraid to ask how Morgan teased him. She's all business when I'm around. "I got a lecture."

"On your pigtails?"

"Among other things." I chuckle at the extent of Morgan's horror over the possibility of Charlie being my escort to his sister's wedding. "I had to explain the article didn't get everything right, and you'll be walking Meri down the aisle, not me."

"About that . . ."

My eyes zip to his. They are clear and serious. He's not kidding. Did he plan this? And pull Meri into it? He's gone too far. I could punch him.

He holds up a palm as if he knows he's going to need it to block my right cross.

"Sorry to keep you waiting." A big man with longish curly hair, a crooked nose, and close-set smiling eyes comes out of a back room with the worst timing ever. "It took me longer than expected to set up your reels on the projector to give you a glimpse of it on the big screen while you're here. Most people use digital now."

"Thanks for doing that." Charlie's face turns toward the man, but his gaze remains on me, as if unsure I'm going to be able to transition into business mode.

I'm only here to do business, so of course I can, but I take the opportunity to shoot him a scowl first.

He should consider it a warning of things to come.

I step past him to shake the manager's hand. "It's nice to meet you. I'm Nicole Lemaire, the marketing director for Charlie's documentary *Sitting on a Gold Mine*."

His shake is firm but fleshy enough to keep from pinching. "Ace McCourtney." He releases his grip and turns to greet my client. "And you're Charlie Newberg. I'm a huge fan. I admire your talent as well as your determination for truth."

I barely hold back a snort but let myself level a glare on Charlie from behind Ace's back. Okay, I'm struggling with the professional thing. But that's because Charlie isn't keeping his agreement to make our relationship strictly professional.

This whole time I'd thought he was respecting my boundaries, he was simply regrouping. I should have known. He doesn't give up. He always achieves what he goes after. He got me to take him on as a client, and next I'll be walking with him down the aisle of Meri's wedding. For all I know, he's been sending our photos to the newspaper.

"I try," Charlie responds with his humble brag before he notices the daggers I'm shooting and does a double take. He tips his head in an expression that's probably as close as he'll ever get to penitence.

Ace says something else. More raving over Charlie's genius, I'm sure, but I'm not able to hear through the steam coming out of my

ears. He leads us through the lobby, pointing at black-and-white pho-
tographs hung on the walls.

Charlie follows along, nodding and making small talk. I trail behind, unable to keep up with the conversation. I try, but their words
fade in and out like a cell phone call with bad reception.

Regarding phones, I pull my cell out of my pocket, open my mes-
saging app, and type in Charlie's name.

> **Me:** I can't believe you're
> using your own sister's
> wedding to manipulate me.

He's deep in conversation over the upcoming one-hundred-year
anniversary of the theater, but his smartwatch lights up, so I know
it's alerting him to my text.

He laughs at something Ace says, then flicks his wrist to see his
message. His questioning gaze rises to mine.

I know I shouldn't be doing this. We're in a meeting with a client,
and he isn't good with multitasking. But I'm not going to be able to
finish any tasks at all until I get some personal business out of the
way.

He holds up a finger to Ace. "Excuse me a moment." He taps his
phone and says, "I'm not," into the receiver before tapping again.
"Sorry. What were you saying about seventy-millimeter film?"

My phone buzzes.

> **Charlie:** I'm not.

Ace leads us through another arch and up a wide stairway lit by
wall sconces. "We're one of the only theaters in the nation that can still
show the older wide format. It's why Quentin Tarantino premiered a
film here. I'll show you the projection room."

Okay, so they aren't talking business after all. They're playing
movie trivia. I don't feel so bad about texting as I climb the stairs.

> **Me:** Are you escorting me
> down the aisle at Meri's
> wedding? And was it your
> idea?

The staircase rounds a corner, so the men are out of my view when I hear Charlie say, "Yes and no."

My phone buzzes with his words typed out for me to read. Yes, he's walking me down the aisle, and no it wasn't his idea. I grit my teeth, hating that I believe him. He's too direct to lie. But even if it wasn't his idea, he must have gone along with it.

I pause where I am to demand more answers. My fingers fly over the keyboard, letting him have it. I'm not marrying him. In fact, I'm ready to drop out of Meri's wedding, quit my job, and change my name, if that's what it takes to free myself.

I hate being this upset. I hate how Charlie can have such a powerful effect on my emotions. If the opposite of love is indifference, then that's where I need to get. I need to opposite-of-love him.

At the moment, he seems to be the indifferent one. He's palling around with his new buddy, Ace, as if they've known each other longer than the two of us have, yet he says he wants to marry me. It's maddening.

"Hey, Ace, do you mind if I run to the restroom really quick?"

Charlie's words barely register as I jab the exclamation point one more time for emphasis. Though this might be one of those messages better left unsent. I feel a little better now that I vented. My phone was only a digital punching bag for my thumbs. I'll read over my text once before deciding whether to hit Send or not.

"I'll be right back." Charlie's footsteps thud closer, and I realize I'm in the way of his trip to the bathroom.

Before I even have time to look up, Charlie is beside me. I expect him to pass, but he sweeps his arm around my waist and ushers me down the stairs. He releases me in the small alcove outside the restroom entrance, but he doesn't go through the door.

Instead, he pops his silly hat on his head and grasps my shoulders with both hands. Then he leans closer to warm my insides with laser vision. "Meri asked our stepdad to walk her down the aisle, so Kai asked me to be a groomsman instead. I didn't know she invited you to join the wedding party until I read about it in the newspaper." Charlie's voice is low and rushed but sincere.

His words douse the flames of my anger, and all kinds of other emotions rush in to take anger's place. First comes joy for his sister. She has a dad to give her away.

Next comes embarrassment. I threw a huge fit over thinking Charlie was still trying to get back together with me when the only reason I'd been offered a bridesmaid position was due to an uneven number of attendants.

"Oh."

His dark eyes study me. To avoid adding "exposed" to my growing list of feelings, I take the moment to admire his eyelashes. Not the top ones but the bottom ones. They are dark and long and as masculine as eyelashes can be. From a distance, they add definition to his features, like eyeliner does for a woman, but up close I can see each lash defined.

Lower lashes are a strange thing to find attractive. They're just hair. Like the scraggly growth along his jaw and over his lip. It's not as if I find that attractive. Or I didn't before anyway.

"I'm not trying to manipulate you." He pauses. "Yes, I'd hoped working together would bring us closer, but you've made it very clear you don't want that. I'm doing my best to respect your wishes."

Right. Yes. Good. I say these things in my brain and hope my expression says the same thing. Is it possible to want different things in your head and your heart?

He blinks and his grim expression softens. "I never wanted to hurt you, and I'm sorry that I did."

It's a good thing he's holding onto my shoulders because the shock of his apology could have knocked me over. I've deserved an apology for a long time and finally accepted it would never come. Not from the Charlie I knew.

Who is this man? He might be one I'd want to get to know. You know, if I weren't trying to opposite-of-love him.

There's too much history between us now. Too much pain. Not that I want to admit I was hurt. No, I am better off. But still. I deserved his apology.

"Thank you," I whisper, voice thick.

He gives a small, sad smile. "This may be a weird time to ask, since I just told you I'm respecting your boundaries . . ."

I should've known the oasis would turn out to be a mirage. I reach for my necklace, and the movement must have made him realize he's still holding my shoulders.

He releases his grip, dropping his arms but not his gaze. "I arranged with Ace for a private screening of my documentary, if you want to watch it."

It's a respectful offer. It will be good if I know what I'm promoting. And he did go through the trouble of setting up a screening.

Can we watch a film together in the theater where we first kissed without there being any expectation of a sequel to our romance? Believe it or not, I think we can.

I huff. This is not how I thought our meeting would end, but there are worse things. "Throw in some popcorn, and you've got yourself a deal."

Even if Charlie hasn't changed, I see him in a different light. He apologized for hurting me. He's proven he can respect my boundaries. He might even care for me as a person and not only about what I can do for him.

Also, if he's going to be my escort at Meri's wedding, it would be good to give this alliance a test run.

Chapter Eighteen

CHARLIE

I think love can save the world.
—ANNE RICE

The magical thing about sitting in your own film premiere is getting to see and hear the audience respond to something you created. In film school, one professor assigned us to sit in the front row of a theater but face backward and watch the crowd. I picked a movie I'd already seen, so I knew what parts everyone reacted to.

It was fascinating and empowering, and only one woman called the cops on me for being a creeper. Of course, the experience didn't compare to my very first film showing. So I'm actually surprised when, as thrilling as it was to see viewers get sucked into the importance of earthworms on the ecosystem, my debut wasn't nearly as intoxicating as watching Nicole gasp and point and bite her lip as my story of Ecuador unfolds.

I've learned the hard way not to stare, so I only look over at her when she moves or makes a sound. When she's quiet and still, I munch on buttery popcorn and try to see the documentary through her eyes.

Not so long ago, I also watched *Jaws* through her point of view. I knew exactly when Bruce—the shark named after Spielberg's lawyer—would pop out, so I expected every one of her jumps. Seriously the best date movie ever. I didn't have to put any effort into making a move, because she was clinging to my arm so hard I was forced to hold her hand to keep her from cutting off my circulation. As for the kiss, I'd only been turning my head to whisper in her ear that she had nothing to be scared of, but she was so close my lips grazed her temple. I tried to explain, but at that point, she turned and kissed me back. I was too much of a gentleman to stop her.

Before Nicole, I'd always made it a point to ask permission to kiss a woman. With Nicole, everything happened naturally. Well, until now.

Thankfully, I was able to calm her down about the bridesmaid debacle. She seems okay with being paired with me for Meri's wedding now that she knows I'm not the one who put us together. Her anger must have come from assuming I still had expectations of making her my wife.

Perhaps I should be offended she hates the idea so much. But it seems that once I gave up the goal of becoming more than friends, we were freed to be friends again.

On-screen, the credits roll. The final folk song plays strings of a bandolin and a panpipe's lonely call. I look over at Nicole to find projector light reflecting off shiny tear streaks.

She holds a hand to her heart before turning toward me. "Charlie."

This is a big difference from the way she kissed me at the end of *Jaws*, but somehow it feels even more intimate.

Maybe because we're seated in the center of an empty cinema.

I've died and gone to Hollywood. "You like it?"

"Like it?" She wipes her palms across her cheeks to dry them. "I want to go hug that mom who lost her two-year-old down a sinkhole in her back yard. And I want to help rebuild the school." She sits up straighter and crosses her arms before tilting her head in a similar warning look to the one she gave me earlier. "And I definitely want to use my kickboxing gloves to help drive the illegal miners away."

"That can be arranged." I consider. "Well, except for the kickboxing part. Fighting the gold lords could get you killed."

"Oh." She collapses back into the leather seat, causing it to rock. "We are so safe here in the United States, aren't we?"

I lift a shoulder. "Comparatively." There's danger everywhere, and sadly Americans can be our own biggest threat.

Nicole rolls her head my direction, still flopped against the seat as if she's recovering from battle. "You do important work."

"I'd like to think so."

"You're going to win another Emmy."

I harrumph. Award-winning movies are not always the ones that bring in big bucks. "But am I going to save the town?"

"We are." She rises and retrieves her purse from the seat next to her. "I may not have been in Ecuador, but I'm going to help you fundraise all the money you need."

My heart stills. I've already accepted the fact the two of us won't be together, but it's kind of sad to think we're a better team this way. The world benefits because we never got married.

Maybe God allowed me to think proposing to Nicole was His will simply so we'd reconnect for this reason.

I stand and say with full confidence, "I know you will."

She smiles at the floor, then glances hesitantly up at me through the dim light. "I'm sorry for earlier."

I hate miscommunication as a general rule, but Nicole was kind of cute when angry. Very unprofessional, but cute. "You don't normally send angry texts to your clients during important meetings?"

She closes her eyes. "There's nothing normal about how I've treated you."

I study the way her lashes fan out above her high cheekbones. Despite her fair skin tone, she has a few features resembling Persian women from a documentary I watched. Its focus was on why so many women in Iran get nose jobs. Her nose isn't large, but it's wider at the base than my sister's. I wonder what Nicole's heritage is and also how I don't know this.

"Well." I'd like to think I'm not her normal client. "Is it because I proposed on my first day in your office? It's probably because I proposed."

She peeks one eye open. "Yeah, let's blame you."

I chuckle. It's a rare occurrence when I enjoy being blamed, but I'd made it clear I thought I was doing the right thing when proposing.

Of course, that might have been the problem. Not that it matters anymore. "Now that we've both apologized, we can start fresh."

Her eyes meet mine with a softness of appreciation. "Meaning you won't propose anymore, and I can stop hiding behind my assistant?"

"I'm sure Morgan would appreciate it." This is the kind of thing Kai would deadpan, but it comes out of my mouth with my usual zest for life.

The lights flick on overhead, and I tell myself it's why Nicole's smile looks so bright. "Don't take Morgan's put-downs personally," she advises. "They're her love language."

"Then she must really love me." I turn to make my way down the aisle with a hoot. "Does this 'no proposals' rule apply to your assistant too?"

"Actually . . ."

I pivot and walk backward to see Nicole's face when she answers.

"I'd find Morgan rejecting your wedding proposal very entertaining. Especially since she's married with children." She holds up her half-empty bag of popcorn. "Just let me know before you do it, so I can bring popcorn into the office that day."

I pause at the end of the row, reach into the bag, and snag a couple of the remaining kernels for myself. "I'll probably wait until after my premiere, because we have a lot of work to do right now."

She nods in mock somber approval. "I suppose that's wise."

We head into the lobby together. A lot has happened since we entered the theater. Some good, some not so good. Finally, though, we found neutral ground.

My watch vibrates that I have an incoming message. I glance down to find Morgan's name lit up on my wrist. "Morgan's calling right now. It's like she knows."

Nicole wrinkles her wide nose in a fun way, then pauses as if waiting to hear what her assistant has to say.

I tap the square screen to answer. "Hi, Morgan. I'm with your boss. You're speaking to both of us."

"Ms. Lemaire." Morgan completely ignores me. "Where are you? I've been trying to get ahold of you for hours."

Nicole's eyebrows pinch together, and she leans forward over my wrist to answer. In spite of my agreement to stop pursuing her, I find her lavender scent more appealing than popcorn. "I'm still at the theater. I was watching Charlie's documentary. Everything okay?"

"Better than okay. The anchor for *World News Today* called. They want to fly out tomorrow to interview Mr. Newberg."

My pulse surges and my mind begins listing all the things I must mention on national TV. "That's big," I say. "I've never been on WNT. How did they find out about me?"

"The article in the *Oregonian*."

I guess people read it after all. Maybe even people who weren't simply curious about me from the story on Meri's wedding.

Nicole widens her eyes and covers her mouth. She lowers her hand to talk. "Book it."

"One more thing . . ." Morgan trails off ominously.

Nicole does a silent handclap to cheer for me without interrupting her assistant.

"What's that?" I ask. Not sure how her call could get any better or worse. This one interview could be all I need to sell my documentary to a network.

"They want you both."

Nicole's hands stop clapping. They fold together as if in prayer. "Why me?" she squeaks.

I'm confused as well. Nicole possesses the poise to be great in front of a camera, but she only just watched the documentary today. She can't answer questions about Ecuador.

"It has to do with the Gold Standard."

Okay. I nod. That kind of makes sense. Nicole was the mastermind behind the campaign.

"They want to go with the angle that you once returned a gold engagement ring to Mr. Newberg, but now you're working together to stop illegal gold mining."

Nicole's arms drop to her sides. Her head falls backward. We've just decided to put my proposal behind us, and now we're supposed to tell the nation about it.

My stomach churns. It's as though we're back where we started. I'd told Nicole I didn't want to hurt her, but not doing this interview will hurt me. As for what she'd said . . .

"You said you wanted to help me save the town." I run my free hand through my hair, knocking off my hat. *Please say yes. Please say yes.*

She takes a deep breath and stands straight. "I can't say no."

Morgan launches into the details of where and when. I try to listen, but I'm still reeling from the fact that I've been given such a great opportunity, and that I only get to accept because of Nicole's self-sacrifice.

"Thank you," I mouth.

"Mmm . . ." She gives a wry smile, and I appreciate her more than ever.

I'm still confused on her *mmm* thing as it doesn't explain why Nicole agreed to the interview. It could be out of compassion for Ecuador. It could be to benefit her career. But I'd like to think it's for our friendship too. This fresh start.

I just hope the rest of the world doesn't read more into our relationship than we've decided to.

Chapter Nineteen

NICOLE

When someone loves you, the way they talk about
you is different. You feel safe and comfortable.
—Jess C. Scott, *The Intern*

I knock on my boss's open door and swallow the trepidation in my throat. "You wanted to see me?" Every time William calls me in, I feel a little like a kid going to the principal's office. It doesn't help that the last time I was here, I almost lost my job.

My boss motions me inside without looking up from his computer.

I stride to the rigid white leather chairs across from him and sit primly, legs crossed, fingers clasped over my top knee. There's nothing to worry about, except maybe for how uncomfortable this chair is despite the price I'm sure he paid for it. But Charlie's campaign is going well. Maybe too well, since I'm about to be interviewed on national news with him in a couple of hours.

I shift to keep from sliding forward.

William looks up and taps the corner of his mouth. "Your lip looks better."

Oh, yeah. It's been a few weeks, but my sores used to last that long. Every time I yawned or smiled too wide, they would crack open and bleed, creating a new scab that would take even longer to heal. "Yes. I'm not sure what's in the lip balm you gave me, but it worked wonders. Thank you."

William rests his forearms on the desk and leans over them. "You're welcome. I'm glad it worked considering you're going to be on TV."

I should've known he would hear about my interview with Charlie. And I should've run it by him before accepting. I didn't even think about it because this kind of situation is unprecedented.

"Oh . . . yes." I clear my throat. "*World News Today* is going with the angle that I once gave Charlie back his gold engagement ring, and now we are fighting illegal gold mining together."

William nods. "How do you feel about being interviewed?"

I smooth my black pencil skirt and look down at my crisp white button-up. I hope the red belt and heels aren't overdoing it. At least they don't match a cold sore on my face. "I think I'm ready. Is the red too much?"

William chuckles. "You look fine. I'm asking how you feel about being associated with your ex. Last time we spoke, you almost gave up your job to avoid him."

I paste a pleasant smile on my face. It's practice for being in front of the camera. "Charlie and I have come to an understanding."

William circles one hand inward toward himself repeatedly in a gesture for me to continue. "Is this the kind of understanding your employer should know about?"

"What?" I jerk straighter, leaving my pleasant smile behind. I expect these kinds of assumptions from Morgan, not him. "No. We've realized we make a good team marketing-wise. He's a brilliant director, and I am thankful I get the chance to help him change the world."

William rests his chin on his fists. "So you're not paired up together for his sister's wedding?"

"Oh, that." I brush the issue away with the back of my hand. "Yeah, but only because Meri asked their stepdad to give her away, making Charlie a groomsman." I blink back the threat of tears. Since I heard about Douglas walking Meri down the aisle, that became the only part of our situation that matters. I'd happily accompany my ex during the ceremony if it means Meri has a father figure in her life.

"Uh-huh."

William watches me, so I crank up the wattage of my grin. By the way my eyebrows jump and cheeks burn, I might have cranked a little too hard. Whereas my cold sore made me feel like Two-Face, this expression is going to scare people like I'm a whole different Batman villain. I dial it down a notch.

"Well, kid." William leans away, looking much more comfortable in his chair than I am in mine. "I'm happy for you."

The stiffness in my smile melts into something more authentic. All this time I'd thought I was in trouble when William simply wanted to share my success. "Thank you, sir."

"Remember when you suggested losing Dante Sullivan could be the best thing that happened to Slice of Heaven?"

"Yes," I answer, because I'm supposed to. Though the conversation he's referring to seems like a lifetime ago. I haven't given Slice of Heaven another thought since I'd left his office.

William spins his computer monitor to show me what looks like a billboard ad with Ugo Alongi's family all eating pizza around a table at a golf club. "I wanted to let you know I passed on your suggestion for switching out golfers in their campaign, and the pizza place took you up on it. Test markets are responding positively, and the new commercials will air tomorrow."

"Oh." I grip the arms of my chair, unsure how I'm supposed to feel about this.

The campaign was mine. The new idea mine. But the credit won't go to me.

Unexpectedly, I'm okay. Maybe even pleased. While I'd thought my career was over and my client's reputation tanked, things haven't only worked out, but it appears they've become a blessing for Ugo's family as well as the pizzeria.

I turn back to William in awe. "That's great."

"I'm glad you think so." My boss studies me. After finding whatever he's looking for, his hazel eyes glow amber in amusement. "Though I suspect it's because losing Dante Sullivan was also the best thing to happen to you."

My mouth drops open. I'd expected the Slice of Heaven ad campaign to make my career and losing it felt as though it would ruin my life. But I've since been handed an even bigger opportunity. This isn't something I ever would have planned or worked for. I'm humbled.

"All that to say . . ." William slides off his glasses and pins me with a knowing smile. "I don't have a problem with you and your client coming to another new understanding."

I'm back at Charlie's house, but despite William's approval, this visit is absolutely not personal. It's where WNT wanted to hold our interview.

The reporter, Adeline Guzman, wanders around, fascinated with Charlie's movie-themed decor and looking for the best camera angle from which to capture it. I'd always just considered it as a basic bachelor pad and felt bad for Gemma who had to put up with it. The entryway displays black-and-white photos from classic movies, the overhead lighting resembles spotlights used on set, and his throw pillows are shaped like clapper boards.

The two of us sit side by side on the modern camel-colored leather sofa between clapper board pillows, adjacent to where Adeline takes her place on the love seat. She motions for a makeup artist to powder her face.

I touch my forehead to see if it's slick with sweat from all the hot lights glaring on us. It is. "I might need some of that."

The artist steps over and tickles my skin with a different feathery brush.

Charlie watches. "Nervous?"

I lock my fingers together in my lap to keep them from trembling and force my shallow breathing to go deeper. "Why, Charlie, are you learning to read body language?"

"I don't have to when I have Gemma here to translate for me." He nods toward his roommates, watching from barstools. "She told me to comfort you."

I wave a thank-you to the woman. Her mind is usually in her imaginary world, so I get the uneasy sensation she's watching us for ideas for her characters.

I wonder what the old me would think if she could see me today.

She'd probably be both confused that Charlie and I are not a couple anymore and that we're working together. It's likely the same thing all of America will think, since it's why we got this interview.

If I could, I'd explain to young Nicole that we're in a good place. We may not get to live happily ever after, but that doesn't mean we can't be happy.

Charlie shrugs. "I wouldn't have known you needed comforting because you look poised to me."

"Thanks." I accept his compliment with the grain of salt needed as seasoning for all his perceptions of emotion.

"I like your belt." He plucks the front of his oatmeal Henley. "Should I have dressed up more?"

"You dressed up?" I tease. At least he's not wearing a plaid flannel.

He elbows me. "Gemma picked this out. Though she did complain that I don't own a tie."

While his roommate has fashion sense, she apparently doesn't know Charlie as well as I do. "You would've felt strangled in a tie. Then you'd fidget enough to make me even more nervous."

He slaps his leg. "Exactly."

"Is she dressing you for the premiere too?"

"She wanted me to wear a tuxedo, but the rental company from Meri's wedding won't let me keep it that long." He grimaces like a teen when his mom tells him holey jeans are not holy enough for church. "I agreed to wear a sport coat if she'll let me wear a beanie with it."

It's as good as we'll get. Also, it's unique enough to make him stand out. "Sounds fair."

Adeline reaches across the arms of the sofa set to tap Charlie's arm. "We go live in ten seconds."

"All right." Charlie rubs his hands together.

I hold a hand over my churning guts. Even though I'm going on air in front of an average of eight million viewers to promote the documentaries my former fiancé left me to film, I realize that's not what makes me nauseous. I'm at peace with Charlie. I'm excited about saving the small town in Ecuador. I'm skittish because of the fear my dad could be watching.

My gaze jolts to the camera. I don't want to do this anymore.

The man standing behind it holds up five fingers, counts down to one, then points our way.

Adeline beams at the camera, all startling white teeth and perfect Michelle Obama hair. "Welcome to the living room of Director Charlie Newberg. He lives in the Pacific Northwest, but his documentaries take him around the world, and you may recognize his name from his recent Emmy win. With him today is the marketing director for his next film, Nicole . . ." She checks her notes. "Lemaire."

"Hi." Even if I'm not greeting my dad for the first time in twelve years, someone back home will recognize my name and tell him about seeing me. There will be rumors and speculation.

"Charlie, tell us what drew you to Ecuador."

I listen while Charlie sums up his adventures and his message. It's an important message, but the congregation from my old church won't judge it to be as important as Sunday morning sermons.

Adeline clicks her tongue. "Such a harrowing tale. Now tell us your plan for saving the town and how Nicole plays into the campaign."

Charlie turns my way, excitement energizing his movements and tone as he gives me credit for coming up with the Gold Standard.

I'm going to be seen as the prodigal daughter, running off to seek my fortune. I wipe my forehead.

"Nicole." Adeline leans forward to better view me around Charlie. "Is it true you came up with the idea from the engagement ring you returned to Charlie after ending your engagement?"

A laugh bursts out. I knew this was coming, but I hadn't thought about how everyone from my old hometown would view it. How I'm not good enough to keep a husband.

Well, too late to worry about that. Time to do what I advise all my clients to do and focus on my intended audience instead of my haters.

"Yes." I share a smirk with Charlie. "The diamond Charlie proposed with was lab created, not only because we were poor college students at the time, but because he didn't want to buy a blood diamond. I realized there's no equivalent to purchasing legally mined gold."

"It's time we do something about it." Adeline nods. "Though I'm sure all our viewers are wondering how you ended up working together on this when you're not a couple anymore."

I shrug nonchalantly. "We're both good at what we do, but we have to do it from different sides of the world."

Charlie narrows his eyes in a mock glare. "I tried proposing again recently, but she turned me down."

I hold out a hand as if to ask why. "We could have left that part out."

"It's the truth," he states.

I nod at Adeline. "Telling the truth is part of what makes him good at his job."

She lifts her chin, knowingly. "And challenging for others."

"Like illegal miners," I finish for her.

"Yes, that's who I was talking about."

We share a chuckle.

The reporter tilts her head, assuming a more serious position. "With a history like yours, I can see how working together might come with unique challenges."

"Absolutely," I agree. "Though we're not going to tell you all of them, are we, Charlie?"

Charlie crosses an ankle over one knee as if getting into a comfortable storytelling position.

"Charlie?" I warn.

He shoots me a mischievous grin before turning back toward our interviewer. "It also comes with unique benefits. For example, Nicole knows me, so she can redirect me when I'm headed for trouble."

I guffaw at his unexpected answer. "Though he can still surprise me."

He wiggles his eyebrows before sobering, his countenance continuing to face mine. "I believe we were brought together for a reason. I mistook that reason at first, but there's no doubt we were meant to help save the town sitting on a gold mine."

Our eye contact remains as solid as my heart is jittery.

Chapter Twenty

CHARLIE

*If you wish to be loved, show more of your faults
than your virtues.*
—EDWARD BULWER-LYTTON

Nicole disappears the moment our interview ends. I look around for her but can't leave the crew to see themselves out of my house. Hopefully she simply had to go to the bathroom.

As far as I could tell, the interview went great. Nothing for Nicole to be upset about.

"How do you think it went?" I ask my roommates, mostly for Gemma's female perspective.

Gemma clasps her hands in a swoony way. "I couldn't have written it any better." She wanders toward Adeline. "Did you know I'm a screenplay writer? I have a romantic comedy in development. Maybe I could do an interview with you sometime."

The reporter looks for an escape. "Let me know when you write a script involving world politics."

"Okay." Gemma stares off into space, obviously plotting a political thriller. I pity Karson for the questions he's surely going to have to answer on law enforcement after this.

Meanwhile, Kai is having trouble keeping his hands off the camera equipment. "Need any help with that?"

The photographer turns his body to block Kai from touching anything. "I got it."

Finally, the crew leaves, but Nicole still hasn't returned.

"Nicole?" I check the bathroom. Empty. For good measure, I run downstairs, then up to Gemma's suite to check those bathrooms as well. She's gone.

I'll have to call her. Something must be up.

I'm charging back downstairs to grab my phone when I notice movement on the balcony past the living room.

A female figure leans against the railing, watching the white peak of Mount Hood turn pink in the reflection of the setting sun. No drama necessary. She's simply taking advantage of the view.

I exhale and open the door to celebrate with her in the cool evening. "You were great," I rave.

She stays in place but gives me a small smile over her shoulder. "See? You had nothing to worry about."

"Mmm . . ." Normally that's the sound one makes when eating something yummy, but she always seems to hum it vaguely. Like she doesn't agree but has no energy to argue.

I cross my arms and lean back against the railing. I can't see Mount Hood, but I can see her face. "Why'd you say 'mmm'?"

She remains quiet. Doesn't even say *mmm* this time.

"Are you bothered by something I said?"

"No, Charlie." She straightens and turns sideways to rest her hip on the railing. "You did great too. I'm sure you'll be getting more interviews from this one."

My chest puffs out. "Really?"

My watch buzzes.

I glance at it to see the name of the critic who trashed my earthworm short. *Now* he's interested in my work.

"See?" she says.

I grimace. "I don't care what that guy thinks of our interview."

She sighs. "I wish I felt the same."

So she's worried about what others thought of us. Is she worried about everyone or a particular someone? My eyes narrow. "Are you concerned about what your ex thinks? I mean your other ex?"

She never talks about him, but maybe he's the reason she turned down my second proposal. He could be the reason she's out here pining over a sunset. I'd always thought she didn't marry him because of me, but maybe it's the other way around.

She rolls her eyes but with a smile. "No."

Her vague answer makes me even more curious. "I never asked why you broke up with him."

She laughs wryly. "You were too busy assuming it's because I was still in love with you."

She has me there. "I'm asking now."

She sighs. "Where I had to vie for your attention, he lavished it on me. But being the center of his world turned into a burden. I started to feel smothered."

"Huh." She is pretty independent.

"When he bought me the Porsche, I ended it."

"Wha-what?" I choke out. "He bought you a Porsche? Who is this guy? Timothy Boyle?"

"Who?"

"CEO of Columbia Sportswear." Nicole's sense of style apparently went out the window when she stopped hiking. "Never mind. Obviously, he's not your ex."

She chuckles. "Tim is an oral surgeon."

I knew surgeons made good money, but wow. "What kind of Porsche? Not that it matters. What matters is how the company is making their cars recyclable and cutting down on emissions. I might have married him for a Porsche."

She looks out at the mountain, dreamy in a Gemma way. "I want to buy my own Porsche. And pick out my own ring. And take myself to Peru."

She wants to go to Peru? She could have gone with me. But maybe that's her point. Does she not think she's worth those things? "We accept the love we believe we deserve."

Her eyes cut to mine, though they are glassy, as if she's looking through me. She reaches for her necklace. "She flies with her own wings."

"*Alis volat propriis.*" I translate the Oregon state motto into Latin.

I learned it from Alice when I bought a similar necklace for my mom. "You can fly with your own wings, but you don't have to fly alone."

She looks down at the necklace and lets the three different charms fall through her fingers. "I flew the coop."

She must mean her family. Her dad. I never met him, but I know he was a pastor who cheated on his wife. "Have you talked to your dad since I left for Peru? Was he going to walk you down the aisle when you married Mr. Moneybags?"

She shakes her head sadly but stares at the skyline. "I'm afraid to find out that he likes his life better without me."

What a horrible thing to fear. Maybe that's why Nicole really keeps canceling her weddings. She's not afraid to love but afraid she won't be loved in return.

"Would you like to reconnect with him? Are you hoping he reaches out first?" I try to understand. Waiting around for other people has never been my style.

"Mmm . . ." she hums before meeting my gaze. "I quit hoping for that a long time ago."

I know she's talking about her dad, but the way she's looking at me makes me wonder if she's talking about us too. Either way, a glimmer of gold in her dark eyes gives the impression there's still a spark left, and I don't want to see it put out.

"Where are you going to church now?" She used to attend with me, but that ended when we ended.

"I'm not," she states defiantly.

I'm not sure whether I'm more surprised by her words or her attitude. I scratch my head. "You don't believe in God anymore?"

If she's not a believer, then I totally misread God's will about marrying her. Being "equally yoked" is the one directive for marriage where He's perfectly clear.

"I believe in God." She bites her lip. "I don't believe in people."

That makes sense with her career as a marketer. She's sure to have seen some shady salesmen. It also makes sense with her upbringing.

But it doesn't make sense with what we're doing.

"You believe in *saving* people," I counter, nodding at her necklace. "It's what we're uniting to do in Ecuador."

She looks down again, considering. "That's different."

"It might not be why everybody goes to church," I amend. Even if her dad became a pastor for the right reasons, he was misled and likely misled others. He used his position for selfish gain. "But it's why I go to church."

Her eyes meet mine. Pure. Contemplative. Lonely.

"Come with me again this Sunday."

She motions inside my townhome, where Gemma seems to be trying to teach Kai to cook. He's in her police officer apron anyway. "Your roommates might think—"

"Who cares?"

She studies me. "Weirdo."

I grin and plan to pick her up.

Just like I once watched *Jaws* through Nicole's point of view, I'm trying to see our church service from her perspective, as well. She's a pastor's daughter, so she has a lot of experience with corporate worship. Unfortunately, her first pastor, her dad, turned out to be a bad example of Christian living. As for my pastor, she knows and seems to like him, so maybe she would have kept attending our church if not for me.

Or maybe she only came because of me.

"If you don't stop staring, I'm never coming back," she whispers out the side of her mouth over the sound of guitars and a keyboard.

I hadn't even realized I was staring. Realigning my body with the stage and the words to a song projected onto a screen, I focus on singing along.

I used to spend worship dissecting the lyrics and what they are supposed to mean. I thought that was the act of praise, and I wanted to do it right. Then Gemma told me she came up with her best ideas for writing during worship because it's like the doors to heaven were opened and she could create with the Creator. Since then, I've granted myself permission to problem solve while singing, and God has given me answers to all kinds of issues, from logistical to financial to directional. These are answers I don't think I could have come up with on my own, and I give credit to the connection formed when believers unite. In this way, worship shouldn't only be about music but a way of life.

Except today. Today I'm considering what the songs might mean to Nicole. I'm judging the musicians based on their performance. If I'm able to stop staring at her, is the music good enough to make her want to keep coming?

Art in the Christian world is tricky. The musicians on our stage aren't paid, they're volunteers. It's hard to say no to volunteers. On one hand, we're supposed to care more about their heart than their skill. But on the other hand, Jesus called us all to excellence.

I see excellence as effectively getting out of the way of the art form. When an audience looks at a painting and doesn't see brushstrokes or reads a book and doesn't get tripped up by grammar, that's when the artist is most successful. In the same way, worship is best when the drums aren't too loud, the transitions meld smoothly, and the singers stay on key. Otherwise, it detracts from the experience.

Today's experience seems pleasant enough. I refuse to peek at Nicole, so I rely on imagining what the lyrics mean to her as we sing them.

They all seem to be about love, which, as her former fiancé, would not have been my first choice. But maybe it's what she needs. The girl broke up with a man for buying her a Porsche. She doesn't seem to think she deserves that kind of love.

It's the lyrics about God's "reckless love" that give me pause. I prefer order and predictability. It's one of the things I appreciate about nature. There's beauty but there are also scientific explanations for why things happen the way they do. Recklessness makes me think more about how civilizations destroy nature. How humanity can selfishly value mining gold over the people who are dying from their digging.

But maybe God's reckless love is the exact opposite of that. He values people over appearances to a degree that confuses us mere mortals.

Noah got drunk. David committed adultery. Paul held coats while a disciple was stoned. The Bible is certainly R-rated, as Mel Gibson once claimed, but that's what makes it powerful. It doesn't sugarcoat. It's real.

Perhaps that's the meaning of reckless love. God still loves us at our worst.

"You can look at me now, Charlie."

The music has ended, and by the way our congregation is shaking hands and conversing, it appears the worship leader has directed us to greet each other while Pastor Greg takes the stage.

I smile at Nicole. It's a relief to be able to look at her without bearing the threat of her never returning to church. She's wearing a dress as usual, but this one has polka dots and straps that show her shoulders. There's a dimple in the back of her shoulders next to her shoulder blades, which she's self-conscious about. I'm glad she feels comfortable enough in our service to show off what she considers to be an imperfection. Or maybe she's expecting to be so uncomfortable that she didn't want to add the discomfort of being hot during the sermon. I'm going to do my best not to add to her discomfort.

"I didn't know all the songs would be about love today. I didn't plan that."

She blinks. "I didn't think you did."

I shrug. "You'd thought I planned to escort you at Meri's wedding."

"Were you afraid I was going to angry-text you during the service?"

I hadn't thought that far ahead, but I could see it happening. "I wouldn't have been able to talk-text back until afterward, so I figured I'd let you know now, just in case."

"Okay, weirdo."

I laugh at what has become her common response to what I consider common sense. I was only being proactive. If that's weird, then I'll own it. "So you didn't mind singing about love while sitting beside me?"

"We were singing about God's love," she answers nonchalantly. "I didn't even think about you, because that's not how you loved me."

"Ouch," I say, which is becoming my common response. Though I'm not offended since I know what she's talking about. The New Testament used four different Greek words for love, two of which differentiate God's love from romantic love. "Speaking of love, here comes Gemma and her man. Have you met Karson?"

Gemma pulls Karson up the aisle after her. When she lets go of his hand to hug Nicole, he crosses his brawny arms and gives me a stern nod. This is Karson being friendly.

"Hey, Lieutenant," I greet.

Before he has a chance to say anything, Gemma grabs his hand and continues pulling him up the aisle. "We're on our way to teach kids' church."

Nicole and I watch them go. "He seems . . ."

"Intimidating?" I suggest. "I hope he doesn't scare the children too badly."

"I bet they climb on him like a jungle gym."

Somehow the image fits. The students won't see Karson as scary but sturdy. He's a cop to protect them from bad guys. Only the bad guys need to fear him. Same as our fear of the Lord.

"Welcome," a voice booms from the pulpit.

Nicole and I settle back down, and once again I'm putting myself in her shoes. When Pastor Greg launches into a sermon that continues the theme of love defined as God's leaving the ninety-nine sheep to rescue the one, I'm thankful Nicole and I already discussed how the subject of God's love doesn't make her uncomfortable. Though that doesn't explain why she's digging her fingernails into her own arm the way she once did to mine when watching *Jaws*.

Chapter Twenty-One

NICOLE

*You will find as you look back upon your life
that the moments when you have truly lived
are the moments when you have done things
in the spirit of love.*
—HENRY DRUMMOND

As I stare at the ad on my computer for Charlie's campaign, I can't shake yesterday's sermon about the lost sheep. My goal is to get this ad in front of the biggest audience possible. It's the opposite of the message Jesus taught. If I targeted my ad to only one percent of my target audience, it would be a failure.

The whole parable about leaving the ninety-nine sheep to find the one is not a new concept. I learned about it in Sunday school before I even started kindergarten. Gemma and Karson probably taught it to a bunch of preschoolers yesterday, with Karson giving sheep rides on his back as a related activity. But in the light of all I've learned since I was four years old, it doesn't make sense.

The story that makes sense to me is the one where the train track operator told his son not to play on the tracks. His son disobeyed, and one day his dad had to make the decision of whether to direct the train down the track that would crash and kill all aboard or down the track that would have them running over his son. Out of his great love, he chose to save the people on the train.

My dad used this as an illustration about Jesus giving His life for us, and how we are supposed to be like Jesus. I don't like the story, but I can relate. I've been sacrificed.

This belief is what makes me okay with Charlie's decision to go to Peru. It's also what makes me determined not to walk that track again.

So, if that analogy is true—and in spite of it coming from my father, I believe it is—then how does the lost-sheep thing work? Why would a good shepherd put his whole flock in danger like that?

"Miss Lemaire?"

I jump.

Morgan stands in the doorway, judgment hardening her dark eyes and pressing her lips into a thin line. "Are you daydreaming about Charlie Newberg?"

Ha. Not even close. "I am contemplating the love of God," I say, and as the words are leaving my mouth, I realize in our society this subject is more taboo than desiring the love of a man. Hanging out with Charlie and listening to all his awkward honesty must be rubbing off on me. I try explaining. "I went to church yesterday for the first time in a long time." Still awkward. "Do you go to church?"

"I attend a Unitarian church."

"Oh." All this time the two of us have worked together, and I didn't know my assistant went to church. I think Unitarianism means they don't claim to know the truth, but they are searching together. Is that better or worse than thinking I know the truth but not talking to anyone about it? It's more honest. "Do you believe God is love?" I ask.

Her eyebrows twitch. "I believe love is the perfect blend of truth and mercy, and if there is a God, I'd like to believe that describes Him."

I rest my elbows on my desk and my chin on my entwined fingers to take that in. If God is a blend of truth and mercy, then both the stories I've heard could be true. The truth is we put ourselves in danger by disobeying God's direction, like by playing on the train tracks. The mercy is when He comes after us. My heart twinges because I have yet to feel Him come after me.

I don't say all this out loud because I still have more of a filter than

Charlie. Rather I sum it up in a politically correct way. "I'd like to believe that too."

She nods. "God might actually exist, because it's a miracle who is here waiting to talk to you right now."

I bolt upright.

My dad?

No. I tamp down all expectations. I haven't received so much as a Christmas card from him since I moved away for college. And besides, Morgan wouldn't care about his arrival. "Who?"

She fights a smile, which is not normally a battle for her. "Gordon Scott represents a national radio affiliate and wants to talk to you about doing a public service announcement for the Gold Standard."

My lips part. This had been my hope when making the Gold Standard a nonprofit, but the kind of publicity this could get us on the radio can't be measured with gold. It's priceless.

I watch through the sound booth window and listen through a headset as radio DJ Pete Peterson reads the PSA I approved. Not only did the affiliate agree to air information on the Gold Standard, but it also offered an interview opening for Charlie.

Apparently, they'd slotted the time for Dante Sullivan and somehow missed the memo that he wasn't the spokesman for Slice of Heaven anymore. In a panic, the station reached out to me because I'd been the one to schedule Dante's interview, and they offered the PSA as a bribe to get Charlie down here today.

He enters the station looking as professional as ever in a gray T-shirt and backward baseball cap. Though his beard appears less bushy, like he trimmed it on the sides.

I pull the headset off and rub my cheeks, nodding toward his face. "What's this?"

"What—my beard?" He grimaces. "Meri said I was going to look like a homeless man in her wedding photos, so I'm trying to find a compromise. What do you think?"

I won't tell him how much I look forward to being able to see his dimples when he smiles. He might get the wrong impression, though the truth is I probably wouldn't find dimples so attractive on anyone else. "You should braid it and add an eye patch, like a pirate."

"Who wouldn't want a pirate at their wedding?"

I nod, even while knowing Meri will kill me if Charlie dresses up. Maybe he should play Jack Sparrow before the ceremony. "A pirate costume fits the island theme of the bachelor and bachelorette party."

He strokes the long part of his beard. "Even better than the Bermuda shorts and straw hat?"

"Anything is better than that straw hat."

Pete, the small-statured DJ, peeks his graying head out the studio door and speaks in a surprisingly deep and smooth voice. "Charlie Newberg?"

Charlie strides toward him, hand extended. "Thanks for offering to do a national PSA for the Gold Standard. It's going to change lives."

"We're happy to do our part." Pete takes credit as if they weren't desperate for content.

The two men go inside the booth, and I put the headset back on. I don't have to be here, but since the interview isn't live this time, listening in gives me the opportunity to request they cut anything especially unrefined that comes out of Charlie's mouth. It's not that I expect him to do something dumb like Dante, but as the opposite of Dante, he tends to be embarrassingly authentic.

I claim a stool and pull out my phone to check my emails, ready to multitask, but the little redhead from the front desk joins me, pulling on a headset of her own. I smile hello, but she's not looking at me. I follow her gaze to see what has her so enraptured.

Charlie. He's drumming with pencils on the table, and Pete reaches over to stop him.

My chest twinges. I've never been a jealous person, I have no reason to be jealous now, and even when Charlie and I were together, he never gave me any reason to be jealous. The twinge has to be heartburn. I did stop at a food truck for tacos on the way here.

I grab my purse to dig for some Tums, then pop one of the chalky, minty tabs in my mouth. Problem solved.

Pete introduces Charlie, and they fall into a rhythm of questions and answers, except more surprising and fun than most radio interviews because Charlie is the one answering the questions. So far nothing too scandalous that needs to be cut.

"Tell our listeners where you got the idea for the Gold Standard," Pete prompts.

I hold my breath, waiting to hear what he says about me. "It was my former fiancée's idea. She's my marketing director now."

"Real-ly?" Pete's deep tone conveys interest, but not as much as I see in the redhead's hypnotizing blue eyes when she turns my way.

She removes the headset from one ear and waits for me to do the same.

I came here to listen to Charlie, but I oblige.

"Is he talking about you?" she asks, as Charlie continues to discuss our complicated dynamic in my other ear.

"Yes." I'm ready to slide the earpiece back over my ear.

"Are you getting back together?"

"No." Hopefully she's as done as Charlie and I are.

"Is he seeing anyone else?"

I pause, because I'm not sure. It isn't likely since he only proposed to me last month, but I suppose if he thought God told him to get married, then he could be looking elsewhere for a spouse. "Not that I know of."

She nods, and as her gaze returns to the man in question, her incredible eyes light with intention. Maybe she's the kind of woman he needs. Redheads are known for being earthy and nature-loving, right? She looks fit enough to keep up with him on hikes. Her office assistant skills can benefit his career as a director, and from her position here, she could have lots of great contacts for him. She also doesn't seem to mind the scraggly beard.

As if reading my mind, she asks, "Did the beard tickle when you kissed?"

It's a totally inappropriate question to ask a stranger, which implies she's even more perfect for Charlie than I originally assumed. The two of them can travel the world, making everyone around them feel awkward together.

My heartburn flares anew, and I rub my chest. I might have to leave early to treat the issue with exercise. I'm not positive physical activity will ease the discomfort of acid reflux, but I have the distinct urge to kick my punching bag. Until then, I have to respond to the future Mrs. Newberg.

"I don't know," I admit. "He didn't have the beard when we were together."

She licks her shiny, plump lower lip. "Fascinating."

"If you like eating grubs for dinner in foreign countries and taking a back seat to his career," I say before I can stop myself.

"I see." One of her sculpted eyebrows arches, implying she sees more than I want her to see. Or maybe she just enjoys eating grubs. One never knows with redheads.

As for me, I need to get out of here. The words coming out of my mouth are a bigger issue than the words coming out of Charlie's. Not to mention this heartburn.

Tugging the headset completely from my head, I slide off the stool. "I have to get back to the office."

I wave at Charlie to let him know I'm leaving, but he's too engrossed in his conversation to notice. If that's not a sign, nothing is.

"Bye," the redhead says a little too sweetly while focusing through the window as though I'm already gone.

I secretly hope Charlie's beard hair gets stuck in her lip gloss.

Chapter Twenty-Two

CHARLIE

*You know you're in love when you can't fall asleep
because reality is finally better than your dreams.*
—Dr. Seuss

If my sister wasn't known for trying to catch a man with a lasso, I might be going too far with this pirate costume for her bachelor-bachelorette party. Of course, it's not her reaction I'm looking forward to.

Gemma finishes the last touch of eyeliner, tickling my eyelids. I tried to get out of the makeup, but she insisted, and she is the expert. I also let her pick out my puffy white shirt and put an itchy wig underneath my tricorn hat. She leans back to study her handiwork.

"Savvy?" I ask.

"I should have been a costume designer." She claps her hands, looking the part of Malibu Barbie in a sundress with shades atop her head.

"Is Nicole going to think she's died and gone to the Caribbean?" I don't only say things that embarrass others, I say things that embarrass myself.

Gemma's hands settle to her lap. "This is going to make Nicole so happy she's in the wedding, so she'll have an excuse to tuck her hand in the crook of your elbow."

Her answer makes me puff up my chest, for which this shirt comes in handy. "Gemma, I think I like her."

Gemma tilts her head, eyes squinty. "You didn't know that before you proposed?"

I suppose I'm doing this all backward, which could be why I'm so confused. But Gemma writes romance, so if anyone can help me figure things out, she can. "I asked her to marry me because I thought God wanted me to. When she said no, I figured I must have heard wrong, so I told her I wouldn't pursue her anymore. That's when we became friends." I shrug. "Maybe I just like her as a friend. That would make things easier."

"Maybe." Gemma purses her lips thoughtfully. "Though men don't normally wear puffy shirts and makeup for their friends."

I look down at my outfit. Too late for that. So, I counter with . . . "Men don't normally wear puffy shirts and makeup at all."

"You've got me there." She holds up a finger. "One question. Do you like being with her more than anyone else?"

I consider my options. There's Kai. He's a cool buddy, but now that he has my sister, I'm not his favorite person to hang out with. Same kind of thing with Gemma. As for my family, I like them but not in an I'd-wear-a-pirate-shirt-for-you kind of way. Work friends are some of my faves, but I don't miss them when we're not working together. Citizens in underpriveleged areas fill me with purpose, but rarely can I even pronounce their names correctly.

I nod slowly. "I think I do."

"That makes it official then. You like her."

"Uh-oh." My stomach fills with dread. "What do I do?"

Gemma shrugs as if the answer is obvious. "You enjoy your time with her."

This weight in my guts is not in the least bit enjoyable. "What if she doesn't enjoy being with me?"

"When have you ever cared about that?"

I sulk. I've never had to worry about it before, because I'd never promised not to pursue anyone before. Relationships shouldn't have to be so complicated. It would've been easier if commitment had come first, like I'd wanted. "Since now."

Gemma stands, hands on hips. "It's about time."

Meri hugs me the moment I step into the private chieftain's lounge, with its bamboo-beamed ceiling, dim bottle lanterns, lush foliage, and thatched walls, each spotlighted a different color. The strumming of a ukulele accompanies the buzz of voices, and the air smells both sweet like pineapple and smoky like pork.

"You look incredible. This is the best costume ever. Did you buy it on . . . sale?" My sister laughs uproariously, and I only have to stare at her a few seconds before comprehending she thinks she told a joke.

"Sail/sale. Funny."

"Thanks." She removes my hat with one hand and loops a lei over my head with the other. Then she uses it to pull me down and whisper menacingly, "If you show up to my wedding with your beard in braids, I will strangle you with these flowers."

"You sound like *you're* the pirate," I retort, "though I guarantee I won't ever braid my beard again."

Kai strolls over, hands in pockets, no idea he's interrupting a death threat. "Ahoy, matey."

Meri releases me and smiles innocently.

I would warn Kai about what kind of woman he's marrying, but I don't want to ruin his party.

Plus, he might be the only man in the world chill enough to handle her.

I pluck my hat from her murderous little hands and plop it back on my head to scan the rest of the faces in the room. "Is Nicole coming?"

With the way she disappeared from the radio station, maybe I shouldn't be expecting her attendance. Something could have happened. Like her fancy-pants former fiancé offered her another Porsche, and after Sunday's sermon on love, she was finally able to accept.

"She's here already," Kai assures. "You just can't see her through all your eye makeup. Did Gemma talk you into wearing that getup?"

"She's here?" I do another scan. I'm still not seeing her.

The bathroom door swings open, and Nicole emerges wearing a

long flowing dress with big flowers printed on it. There's also a big flower behind her ear. I think she's looking at me, but it's hard to tell in this dim lighting. At least she heads our way.

That's a good sign, right? Nicole wouldn't head my way if she didn't enjoy being with me. Unless she's only coming over to congratulate the bride and groom.

Instead, she looks me up and down in disbelief. "Charlie? Is that you?"

"Sword of." Kai slaps me on the back. "Get it? Sword?"

With the happy couple's love of dad jokes, it probably won't be long before they start having children.

However, I'm still focused on Nicole. I hadn't considered she might not recognize me. "I took your suggestion of dressing up. What do you think?"

"No eye patch, but you look better than I imagined."

Shiver me timbers. She imagined me in a pirate costume. I'll make the most of it the way the bride and groom seem to be. "Arrr . . . you looking for someone to sit with?"

Nicole looks around. "You didn't bring a plus-one?"

I don't remember Meri mentioning I should bring a date, though that could be because she knows I don't have time to date. I glance at my sister. "Was I supposed to?"

"Only if you wanted to," Meri answers.

Nicole holds out a hand in a half shrug. "That little redhead from the radio station seemed interested in you, and I thought maybe you ended up asking her out."

I nod with new understanding. "So that's why she was acting strange."

Meri snorts and pulls Kai away. She mock glares over her shoulder. "It's okay for women to do strange things to attract men."

"You're strange to begin with," I call after her like the good little brother that I am. Turning back to Nicole, I realize it's just the two of us. Though she could have a date here somewhere. I scan the room for the kind of man who gives sports cars instead of chocolates. "Did you bring a plus-one?"

"No." She smooths her hair. "That's what this flower behind my right ear means."

And I'd thought I was confused about relationships before. As for flowers, the only ones I know about are the ones Meri threatened to strangle me with. "What?"

"In Hawaii, right means single. Left means taken. Like how you wear your wedding ring on your left hand."

Interesting. "I've never been to Hawaii, so I didn't know that."

Nicole crosses her arms, chin lifted. "You would know if you went on our honeymoon with me."

Moment ruined.

Except Nicole's chuckling. "Come on, Captain. I'll introduce you to poké and short ribs."

We sit together like a couple. Everyone stops by our table to speak as if it's National Talk Like a Pirate Day. The food is amazing. There are even hula dancers and fire jugglers. "Is this what I missed out on in Maui?"

"Not all you missed out on." Nicole pops the last of her mini pine-apple upside-down cake in her mouth and licks her fingers.

I'm mesmerized.

"You're right." I'm only able to tease about this stuff because we're friends now, but for the first time I really do feel like I missed out. "I would have gotten to . . ."

She arches an eyebrow as if expecting me to say something that will make everything stilted between us again.

" . . . put the flower behind your left ear."

She throws her head back in laughter and said flower slips out, floating down to our red leather booth seat.

I pick it up and roll the stem back and forth between my fingers, releasing its soft, powdery scent and a desire for more than friendship.

But what can really happen between us? Would she travel with me for work this time? Or would she expect me to stay in the States all over again?

"Hey, guys." Gemma *clip-clops* over in her heels that almost make her taller than her boyfriend. "Karson's ex is Hispanic and taught him how to salsa dance."

Nicole and I glance at each other.

I shrug because *why not?* My sister's getting married. I'm dressed like a pirate. Anything can happen. "I've heard all the toughest police officers salsa dance."

"You know?" Nicole plays along. "I've heard that too."

Gemma giggles. "He may look tough, but he's a jellyfish in armor. Anyway, I've talked Kai and Meri into going salsa dancing with us tonight. Do you want to come?"

It would be an excuse to hang out with Nicole longer. Maybe we can't be more than friends, but we can dance. "Okay."

"Yay." Gemma *clip-clops* away.

Nicole turns completely toward me, chin jutting. "Okay?" she challenges.

Wow. If this is how she feels about spending time with me, then it's a good thing I started with an invitation to dance before asking her out on a real date. "We'll be dancing at the wedding, so it's not as though the suggestion is anything scandalous."

"Charlie." She plucks her flower from my fingers and tucks it behind her right ear. "Salsa dancing isn't regular dancing. You have to be able to"—she rolls her shoulders and sways side to side—"move."

So that's what she's worried about. My dancing skills. Not about being seen with me or held in my arms. I don't know enough about the dance to be worried. "Have you done it before?"

"Well, yeah."

Another man took her dancing. I wonder if it was Tim. Salsa-dancing Tim.

She grimaces. "But I had half my big toenail kicked off, and it hasn't grown back normal since."

Maybe Tim bought her the Porsche to make up for it. "Are you worried I'll kick off your other toenail?"

"A little, yes."

I can't be that bad. And I've got to take advantage of this opportunity. "Girl," I say with much more confidence than I feel, "I can dance."

Chapter Twenty-Three

NICOLE

Lust is easy. Love is hard.
Like is the most important.
—CARL REINER

The Crystal Ballroom was originally built in the early 1900s as a cotillion hall. Over the years, the ornate third-floor venue went from hosting jazz to square dance to homeless, in which case, Charlie would normally fit right in with his scraggly beard. But both the building and the man have been refurbished.

The way Charlie's beard is braided with beads changes his look drastically. Gemma did a good job. I'm sure the redhead would approve had he asked her out.

As it is, he invited me to go salsa dancing. Not that he knows how to dance. Naturally, I couldn't miss the opportunity to see him try.

After removing his hat, wig, and vest, Charlie appears more artsy than anything in the smoky-eye look he's got going on. I never imagined I'd be attracted to a man in eye makeup.

And I'm not.

We're just having a good time.

The colorful disco lights wash over him as he watches the dancers from our spot underneath one of the many arches along the wall. The rare floating floor gives extra bounce to each step beneath a huge chandelier. I'm sure its design will come in handy when Charlie gets up the nerve to take me for a spin. One of us is probably going to get hurt, and I'm going to make sure it's not me this time.

"Salsa is the same three quick steps over and over," I explain above the rise and fall of live trumpets and drums.

Charlie's eyes narrow, and his gaze drops to focus on people's feet. His head nods with what I assume are the counts in his mind. They're not even close to being in time to the music.

I learned to salsa by following the lead of a little Latino man who had to stand on his tiptoes to kiss my cheek when he proclaimed, "I must dance with you again." I made sure to avoid him outside these walls, but when the music played, he became the best dance partner I could ask for.

Charlie won't have the same benefit of letting a partner lead. I'm going to have to teach him the basics, then follow along. I should have eased him in by bringing him earlier for the lessons, though we would have had to leave Kai and Meri's party before it ended.

Karson glides past, twirling Gemma under one arm. Her long hair flies in a circle, then spills wildly over her shoulders when he pulls her close. Other women might be jealous of both Gemma's dance partner and her looks, but I'm happy for them. She's a darling who deserved a man to sweep her off her feet.

Personally, I'm hoping to stay on my feet tonight.

"They're not doing the same three steps," Charlie argues. "They're rotating."

I grin at his choice of wording, but when he turns to me with studious intensity, I let my humor dissipate. Probably also not the best time to bring up how he'd assured me, *Girl, I can dance.* Though I'll be laughing about it in my heart for a long time to come.

"Take my hands," I instruct, extending my palms between us.

Facing me, he grasps my fingers with his firm, warm ones.

My belly flutters.

I didn't think this through.

And I don't want to. Even if the last time we held hands was when we went to the courthouse to pick up our marriage license, that doesn't matter now.

"Okay, you're going to step your right foot toward me, then step back together quick-quick."

He follows directions, albeit rigidly, and I match his movements, stepping backward with my left foot when he comes my way.

"We did it," he announces proudly.

It's going to be a long night. But for some reason that thought makes me smile. "Yes, now do the opposite on the other side."

He steps back while I step forward. It's slow and stiff, but I keep him going, and eventually we're moving to the music.

"This is the basic move. But you can take it all different directions."

I get him to circle a little bit, reminding me very much of the first middle school dance I snuck out to attend. When my parents saw a picture of me dancing in the yearbook, I was grounded for the summer. I never understood how that was a fair punishment—especially after I learned Dad had an affair. But they'd always insisted dancing was looking for trouble.

I've since learned all kinds of different dances from ballroom to country swing, and the worst thing that ever happened was the broken toenail. Until now.

Trouble put on a pirate costume for me.

"Good job," I encourage. "Once you get a feel for it, you can add a spin to the same beat."

I let go of one of his hands and lift the other overhead, so I can twirl underneath our arms. I count, so he realizes the steps haven't changed. "One-and-two."

"Oh, cool. Do it again."

I repeat the move. "Three-and-four."

"You make it look good."

My heartburn is back. Apparently, physical activity is not the cure.

"Then . . ." I hang on to both his hands as I do the turn, ending up with his arms wrapped around me, one over my shoulder, the other beside my hip. It's been too long since I've felt this satisfied. This connected. I keep talking so he doesn't realize I'm savoring the solid wall of his chest pressed against my spine. "If you don't let go, we can do the steps together, facing the same direction."

He doesn't step back into the next move.

I bump against him. The force of impact knocks all sense out of me, and I forget to rock away. His heart thumps in rhythm with mine.

"Sorry." His apology rumbles in my ear. In my chest. "I got confused."

"It's complicated," I allow, turning my ear toward him, but keeping my lashes lowered. If we make eye contact over my shoulder, he could read in my expression that I'm talking about more than dance moves.

His nose brushes my temple like it did the first time he kissed me.

My toes curl in fear of much more than a ruined pedicure.

"I forgot how sweet you smell," he says. "Like spring in the Canary Islands."

I'm pretty sure that's a compliment. Though I'm not going to respond in kind by telling him his scent reminds me of a hike in the forest. I don't hike anymore.

Onstage, the song clashes to an end. Applause follows.

Then a sudden silence emphasizes the rasping of my breath. I break from a trance and twirl away.

Charlie hangs on to one of my hands and reels me back toward him in a dance step that can't be taught. I catch myself before we collide again.

A guitar strums a slow intro to my favorite fast merengue song. The couples on the dance floor prepare for a series of new steps. I need to get us out there, so we're surrounded by a crowd rather than getting cozy in the corner.

I pull on his hand, tugging him toward the floor. "This is a merengue. It's simpler than salsa. You just march."

Charlie follows, eyes on me as if I'm the only one in the room. So much for the crowd. "You just march?" he repeats.

"Well, yeah." I'm going to rotate my arms and hips and even roll through the balls of my feet, but it's nothing more than a right-left, right-left pattern. The dance is as easy or as complex as one makes it, and we really don't need more complications.

"Okay." He salutes and proceeds to march in place like a soldier.

I freeze, trying to figure out what is happening. Charlie is following my directions literally. I told him to "just march." But who in the world would think that's what I meant?

Karson spins Gemma our way, and though her gaze is supposed to remain on her dance partner, she spots Charlie marching like a G.I. Joe while wearing a pirate costume in the middle of a dance club, and her face remains focused on us, mouth agape.

Kai and Meri also merengue past. Kai's keeping it basic, but he's actually dancing rather than pretending to be in the military.

It's too much. I cover my face to hide my laughter. I don't want to hurt Charlie's feelings. Again, he's doing exactly what I told him to do.

I told him to dress like a pirate, and he dressed like a pirate.

I told him to march, he marched.

I told him salsa wasn't easy, and he said, *Girl, I can dance.*

My head falls back, and my amusement explodes. He's doing all this for me, and I adore him for it. I can't remember the last time I felt so joyful. I'm too joyful to catch my breath.

This is good. This is what I needed. It's safer than being in his arms anyway.

"Hey." He stops marching, but the confusion on his face makes the whole thing even funnier. "You told me to march."

I grip the very biceps I was thinking it was good I escaped. But I'm trying to calm him . . . while also calming myself. "I know. I . . ." I can't stop laughing long enough to explain. "I'm sorry. It's my fault." Another peal. "What do you think this is? Boot camp?"

He lets a chuckle escape. "That did seem like a weird way to dance."

I wipe my eyes, glad to be laughing with him and not at him. Being able to take a joke is one of the best qualities in a person.

"You did it anyway," I point out, trying to imagine what all the other dancers thought when they saw him. Another giggle fit overtakes me. "You could have looked around to see if other people were marching like Father Abraham before you began."

He flicks his gaze to the roomful of dancers as if surprised they're still here. Then he grins and shrugs. "You know I don't care what they think."

I lean forward, hands on his shoulders, sharing my mirth. "Okay, weirdo."

His hands circle my waist, and all the air I've been fighting to breathe rushes straight out of my lungs. I straighten except for this little smirk in my lips that won't go away.

See, part of marketing is knowing where and when a buyer is most likely to make a purchase. For example, in the grocery store, people naturally gravitate toward the walls first, so that's where all the healthy things are. The shoppers use their willpower to make good choices in the beginning, but that determination can only last so long. By the time they get to the chip aisle, they're running out of the emotional energy it requires to make healthy choices. And once they've gotten to the checkout stand, they've depleted their last reserves and cave in to the desire for a chocolate bar.

Willie Wonka got it right. Charlie is my chocolate factory.

His face tips toward mine, lips hovering. "I'm going to kiss you next time you call me a weirdo."

I lift my gaze to his, and it's the vulnerability in his searching eyes that does me in. This man doesn't care what anyone else in the world thinks. He only cares what I think.

"Okay, weirdo." I've held out as long as I could.

His mouth lowers to mine, and the warm, firm touch sears shut the wound he'd left on my heart. The rest of my body goes slack, like a patient recovering in a hospital bed after surgery. There is hope of healing.

But at the same time, I know things are going to have to change. A heart attack victim can't leave the hospital after surgery and go back to the same lifestyle if they want to survive.

I kiss Charlie as if he's the drug that will keep my pain away. Needy, hungry, intoxicated. It's different from how we first kissed in college. His beard is fuzzy against my face, yes, but it symbolizes how this time I'm kissing a man.

I'm kissing Charlie. My client. In a public place. Where anyone could take a picture and sell it to the tabloids. We've kissed in public before, but that was back before it could ruin my career.

I pull away, the pounding of my heart rivaling the bongos onstage.

He rocks toward me, and I plant my hands on his shoulders to hold him back. If he didn't look like Jack Sparrow before, he does now.

"That was a really good kiss," he says because he's still Charlie.

His kissing is definitely better than his dancing. Though both are trouble.

"What does this mean?" I yell over the beat. Because that's what really matters. I want to keep kissing him, but it might make him think we're going to get married, and that idea didn't work out so well before.

He grins. "It means I like you."

I like him too. If only it could be that easy. "This isn't part of a plan to propose again?"

He shakes his head. "I just enjoy spending time with you."

I bite my lip. It's not like Charlie to do anything without a plan. But maybe in the same way he cares what I think of him, I'm the exception.

His earlier vulnerability eases my fears. I'm not at his mercy. He's at mine.

"Good." I smile, giving in to the ease of being together.

Chapter Twenty-Four

CHARLIE

*Falling in love is not at all the most stupid thing that
people do—but gravitation cannot be
held responsible for it.*
—Albert Einstein

Funny how all my sister wanted from a man was a wedding proposal,
while it's my vow *not* to propose to Nicole that has her wanting to
spend time with me. After a week of hanging out, she even agrees
to come on our family day trip to Hood River to pick apples. I don't
understand her, but I like her.

Driving through the Columbia Gorge on this crisp, fall day, I turn
off on the winding highway that leads toward Portland's iconic mountain peak. Mount Hood is one of the few places in the world high
enough to allow skiing during the summer, and now that we're near-
ing winter, the tip of white is starting to expand.

If it were up to me, I'd keep driving this road until we climbed
through the forest high enough to need snowshoes for a hike. But
picking apples in the valley has been a long-standing tradition in our
family, and I guess that tradition is even more important to Mom now
that Meri is getting hitched. Plus, Meri said something about apple
pie bringing her and Kai together, so it seems to be a romantic thing
for them.

Mom and Douglas rode with Meri and Kai in her Jeep, giving me a
little alone time with Nicole. Not that we're doing anything important

with our alone time. She's just picking songs on the radio and telling random stories of past clients and gasping at nature, but it's relaxing and peaceful and something inside me wishes this could become one of our traditions. Though unmarried couples don't normally have apple-picking traditions, do they?

We round a corner, revealing Mount Hood framed above a valley of orchards. The trees are all lined up as if they would dance the merengue the same way I did.

Nicole gasps again. "It's beautiful. Can you believe I've lived in Portland for twelve years and never been here?"

She's missed out on a lot by staying in the city limits. "Mom makes us come every year. I'm surprised I didn't bring you."

"I think you invited me, but I had a conference in Vegas that weekend."

"Makes sense. Except for the part where you chose Vegas over this."

She rolls down the window as if to make up for lost time by breathing in the rush of air. It's cold enough to be invigorating, though the sky is bright blue and the sun brighter. Everything smells fresh like dew.

I've also been in the city too long. I need more of this, and I don't understand how anyone could live as close as Nicole does and not take advantage of the area's natural splendor.

"Your other fiancé didn't bring you to Hood River either? You could have driven your Porsche. On these roads, it would have been like you were in a car commercial."

"I'll keep that in mind if I ever sign a marketing contract with a sports car company."

I wish I could cut her a look, but I'm too busy maneuvering around rivers and bluffs. "You avoided the fiancé part of my comment."

"Not expertly enough if you're still asking." She digs through her purse and retrieves a pair of sunglasses. Is she wanting to hide from the sunshine or from my perusal? "He wasn't an outdoorsy guy."

I narrow my eyes, not sure what that means. It's an oxymoron in my mind. "What did he do?"

"Oral surgery."

I shudder at the idea of putting my hands inside other people's mouths. "I know that. What did he do for exercise? Enjoyment? Escape?"

"He took spin classes and swam in a pool. We attended fancy fundraising dinners and the mayor's ball. At home, he cooked. He was a great cook."

Just the description of such a lifestyle gives me claustrophobia. I momentarily take a hand from the ten-and-two position to tug at the collar of my flannel. "Is that what you wanted?"

"Yes," she states. "He was the opposite of you."

"I see." This is a weird place to be. She likes spending time with me, but she wanted to spend the rest of her life with someone who's the opposite of me.

"He was safe." She shrugs. "He would never leave the country to risk his life crawling through mines to save strangers."

I take a deep breath of air icy enough to sting my lungs. Because I will never be that man. "I will never be safe."

"Apple picking is safe."

She seems to find satisfaction in this moment, even though the family she's picking with might never be hers.

Of course my mother beams as if she's seeing a long-lost daughter when we pull into the gravel parking lot by a whitewashed barn. Mom waves from the giant doorway, apple-red scarf around her neck, a mug of cider in one hand. Douglas stands next to her, holding a paper bag full of produce she's already purchased. She's in her happy place.

Meri is in her happy place too. I don't mean frolicking in front of the trees for Kai's camera, though I don't think there's anyone else in the world who could have as much fun while frolicking. I mean she's with Kai.

Nicole peers through the windshield as she gathers things from her purse to stuff inside her jacket pockets. "Is that your stepdad?"

I look back to the man in question. "Yes." He's wearing a red sweater to match Mom's scarf, carrying her bags, joining her for family traditions, and willing to both hike through an orchard and walk Meri down the aisle despite having a bad knee. He's sturdy and reliable, much like the kind of guy Nicole wants. It's weird to think that's one of my favorite things about him, as well.

"I'm happy for your mom."

"Me too." Though I'd struggled at first. I'd been the man in her life for twenty-eight years before she met him.

Mom hands Douglas her cup so she can run toward my car.

She runs right past me.

"Nicole. You haven't changed a bit. How are you?"

I don't hear Nicole's answer, but they hug for a long time.

Meri and Kai join me to watch the reunion.

"Your mom has never hugged me that way," Kai quips.

"Would you want her to?" Meri asks.

"Nah." Kai chuckles. "I've got my own mom."

I look back at Nicole in my mom's arms. She doesn't have her own mother anymore. For the first time, I wonder if losing my family had been hard on her when we went our separate ways. Maybe it's because we're at an orchard, but I feel my Adam's apple grow larger inside my throat.

Uncertain yet protective, I stroll toward the emotional women. "Can you believe Nicole has never been here before?"

Mom pulls away, cheeks almost as rosy as the fruit. "I'm so glad you're here now. Make Charlie carry the basket for you because you deserve all the fun."

Before Nicole can even look my way, Kai thwaps me in the chest with a basket. "This is why we're really here, huh? We're the pack mules."

Nicole grins at me. "You carry the basket, and I'll make you a pie."

I didn't know she could bake, but I'll take her up on it. "Sold."

Meri skips by. "Just don't let Gemma make it. She uses crushed nuts in place of flour."

We follow Meri down a row between trees, but it's her light heart that leads the way. The warmth of the sunshine balances out the chill in the shade, the sweet harvest perfumes the air, complementing the earthy scent of wet dirt. The view of my favorite mountain is matched only by the glory of Nicole's smile.

Mom surveys an apple before plucking it and placing it in the basket Douglas has waiting. "Charlie used to carry the basket for me before he could even get his arms fully around the thing. How old were you when we started coming here?" she asks.

Nicole turns her beam my way in wonder, making me wish I had a more impressive basket to carry for her today.

"It was a kindergarten field trip, so I must have been five."

Mom pauses to glance over her shoulder at me in surprise. "I didn't realize it had been a field trip, but I guess that's how I learned about this place." She nods in agreement with herself before strolling along beside Nicole.

Douglas and I follow dutifully, though Kai and Meri have disappeared far ahead.

Mom reaches for another apple. "I was a single mom back then, so I didn't have much money for fun things."

I frown. As a kid, I never thought of Mom's struggles. I just figured she'd be fine because she had me. Though . . . Meri and I both got jobs in high school to pay for our own activities. "We did fun things," I say.

Mom laughs. "You played in the park, attended story time at the library, and hiked to waterfalls. All free stuff."

"That's the best stuff." What else do kids do?

Nicole sets an apple in our basket. "Is that why you love hiking so much?"

I shrug. "I've just always loved to hike." Funny how we're shaped by our experiences without even realizing it. I'd assumed my childhood was normal despite losing my dad before I was born.

"Good. I'm glad you didn't feel like you missed out." Mom nods proudly. "I was pretty careful with money, though there was one year where I probably shouldn't have brought you guys here. I'd cut back my hours to stay home more with you through the summer, and I barely had enough money for gas and apples. Then we blew a tire. You remember that?"

"It's one of my best memories." I tilt my head to better recollect. "It felt like an adventure because we had to stay in a hotel overnight until the repair shop opened. We ate hamburgers, swam in the pool, and watched cable TV. That's the only overnight vacation I remember."

Nicole strolls beside me. "Maybe that's why you like to travel now too."

Hmm . . . I did sign up for study abroad the first chance I got.

Mom lifts a hand to rustle leaves of the tree she passes. "I missed an electricity payment because of that. When they shut off our power, I had to take a second job. But I'm glad you had that experience."

I stop in my tracks. "What? How did I not know this?" I remember opening the refrigerator and the light not turning on. Then Mom made a phone call, and it worked again. I don't remember her having a second job except when . . . "You told me you were working at Walmart on weekends because they needed help for the holidays."

She smiles sadly. "We both needed help."

"Mom." I drop the basket as if there's something I can do now and I need my hands free to do it. "I could have helped you."

"You were eleven."

"Yeah, so? I could have mowed lawns."

She passes Nicole to veer back toward me. "It was autumn. Nobody needed their lawns mowed."

"I could have raked leaves."

She takes my hand. Hers feels so delicate, as if it's made up of bird bones. These are the hands that worked two jobs so I could watch Animal Planet one time in a Motel 6. To make matters worse, she says she's glad she did it. "Honey."

With my free hand, I rub my fuzzy jaw—what's left of my beard. "I should have known." I'm angry with myself. I'm angry with the kid who took advantage of his mother. This doesn't sit right.

"God provided."

I throw my hands up in the air, inadvertently knocking away her grasp. "I'm supposed to help Him provide."

She presses her lips together and levels her gaze. "In a perfect world, your dad was supposed to help provide. Though the truth is we should always rely on God."

I feel chastised even though I'd only wanted to do the right thing. Again, it's like that time I tripped during the hundred-meter dash. I should have been there. I should have won. I don't want to have to rely on God when He's already given me the gifts needed to succeed. But I suppose nobody does. "Sorry, Mom."

She reaches for my hand again and gives it a satiny squeeze. "I'm sorry too. I'd thought staying single would be the easiest thing for you kids, but I can see how it made you feel like you had to be the man of the house."

Mom sacrificed herself for us. I hate it at the same time I'm grateful. This is what it means to be loved. "You gave us a good childhood." I swallow around my stupid inflamed Adam's apple. "I'm glad you have Douglas here for you now." I give him a quick nod in appreciation.

"And I'm glad you have Nicole." Mom reaches for Nicole with her free hand, connecting the three of us. "Now we're all in good places."

I take a deep breath. Yes, Mom's in a good place. And Meri's in a good place—wherever she's at. As for Nicole, she's become a kissing friend. Certainly not what I'd imagined when I felt as though God told me to marry her, but I'm not sure what I can do about that. "Nicole and I—"

"—are going this way to get a good photo of Mount Hood." Nicole lets go of Mom's hand and swoops down to pick up the basket I'd dropped.

I hope the apples aren't too bruised. Bruised apples would make me feel like an even bigger failure.

Nicole heads up a different row of trees and looks over her shoulder. "Coming, Charlie?"

"Yes." I guess. She's probably going to want to talk about hard stuff now too. What happened to easy?

Mom watches Nicole go and lowers her tone. "I hope that wasn't too much for her. I really want things to work out between you two this time."

"Me too," I say, rather than stopping to explain. Also, I don't know how to explain.

I wrap Mom in my arms for a hug. She used to hold me this way, and now she's the tiny one. I'm glad she has Douglas to take my place when I can't be there for her.

I let her go to chase after Nicole and catch up easily, because she's stopped at the end of the row, taking pictures like she'd mentioned. "Hey," I say to the back of her head.

"Hey." She doesn't look at me.

We could simply pretend none of this happened and force laughter until it becomes real again. But that's not my way. "Sorry about that."

"Mmm . . ."

"What does 'mmm' mean? It's supposed to mean something tastes delicious, but you say it at the weirdest times."

She turns but holds out her camera as if she's going to take a selfie with the mountain behind her. She motions me to join her. "It means I'm pondering."

"That's 'hmm,' not 'mmm.'" I step behind her and wrap my arms around her waist to lean my cheek in against hers. "What are you pondering?"

She clicks. "Where your love of hiking, your love of travel, and your desire to rescue others comes from."

She lowers the camera, but I stay there with my arms around her because I can. Because I don't ever want to let go.

As for our conversation, yeah, my love of hiking originated from cheap family outings, but as for the other things, aren't we all supposed to support each other? "We're all called to help the hurting. To change the world."

"Yeah." She turns to face me, her arms looping around my neck. "But we're not all called to save cities in poorer countries. I mean, where would we be without the farmers who planted these apple trees right here?"

I look around the beauty surrounding us. "We'd still have a great selfie with Mount Hood."

She smirks and gives a little shake of her head. "Without orchards, you never would have come here as a kid. Your mom never would have blown a tire and gotten a second job to stay in a hotel overnight. You never would have fallen in love with travel and might never have made your documentary. Without the farmers who planted these orchards, you wouldn't be saving the town sitting on a gold mine."

"Touché." I give her that one because it helps a little to think that Mom's sacrifice played a part in rescuing a foreign town. God used the bad for good.

Nicole continues, rubbing her nose against mine in a way that almost distracts me from her words. "That means the migrant workers who moved here to support their families by picking fruit have helped change the world. Your mission isn't any greater than theirs."

My heart thuds to a stop with that statement.

I risked my life. I won an Emmy. Not to look good to the world but to make a difference. To feel like I'm doing great things for God. All the while, the people I went south to save are the very same people coming north and helping save me. Yet they receive no recognition. They probably struggle to get by the way my mom did. It's kind of mind-blowing.

Now I'm pondering too. "That reminds me of my earthworm documentary."

"Me too," she teases. I know she's teasing, because worms gross her out.

So I'll explain. "Farmers don't want worms in their apples, but earthworms benefit the soil structure and eat the dead leaves that reduce fungi. In the same way, even hurtful things can be used for God's purpose."

"My thoughts exactly." Nicole's nose nuzzles my earlobe.

Her outlandish claim tickles my funny bone while her touch tickles in a different way. "Are you sure you're not trying to shut me up?"

"What makes you think that?" she whispers, her nose against my neck.

The warmth of her breath sends a shiver down my spine. And I can't tell if she kissed me or not. I don't want to make the same mistake she made in the movie theater while watching *Jaws*. Or maybe I do.

I drop down to capture her lips with my own. Then I feel another shiver up my arm, and it takes me a moment to realize the vibration is coming from my watch.

I rub my hands up Nicole's back and peek one eye open to check the incoming message over her shoulder. It's my contact in Manila asking me to call him immediately.

"Mmm . . ." Nicole murmurs against my mouth, using the sound correctly this time. And I completely forget the text.

Chapter Twenty-Five

NICOLE

*The real lover is the man who can thrill you by
kissing your forehead or smiling into your eyes or
just staring into space.*
—MARILYN MONROE

I'm still thinking *mmm* when I wake up in bed the next morning and decide to hit the snooze button. And when I add extra creamer to my coffee. And when I take a bubble bath instead of doing my kickboxing routine that night. And when I bake a pie for Charlie the next. The list could go on and on.

Charlie's got me out of my routine and forming bad habits. It's especially damaging behavior the week before I'm supposed to fit into a bridesmaid dress. But in his weirdo way, I've started to care less what others think.

I knew Charlie was bad for me the first time he walked into my office, but since I'm not sure how long he'll stick around, I'm going to enjoy these delicious moments while they last. Kind of like eating all the carbs in your house before a diet.

Joining his family at the orchard might have been a mistake, but it helped me better understand why the two of us will eventually go our separate ways again. He felt the weight of providing for his mom as a child, and now he feels the weight of providing for the whole world. I would only get in the way of that mission.

I have him with me until at least the movie premiere. And tonight is the wedding rehearsal.

It's a little rainy, so I choose a longer dress to hide the goose bumps on my legs. The rust-colored Swiss Dot midi pairs nicely with ankle boots and a wide-brimmed fedora that I'm sure Charlie's hat-loving heart will appreciate.

The golf course where Kai works offers all kinds of ceremony sites, from the clubhouse to the greens to even a dock. Because it's October in Oregon, Meri wisely picked the marquee tent.

I'm a little sad the two of them didn't get married in the orchard last weekend. That sunshine and view were perfection, not to mention the Newberg family history there. In fact, it's so perfect I'm confused as to why Charlie hadn't suggested it for our wedding. Maybe he knew that without my parents paying for the ceremony, the two of us couldn't afford such a trendy location right out of college. We'd settled on a pretty little place in Aloha, Oregon. It's pronounced *uh-low-uh*, though maybe the Hawaiian meaning of the word should have been a sign as to how Charlie was going to say goodbye.

I arrive at the golf club early in hopes of spending more time with Charlie, but he's out on the miniature golf course with Kai. Even though I've got a hat to protect me from the drizzle, I decide to stay where it's dry and avoid the dreaded goose bumps. Instead, I help tie the white tablecloths to the legs of the round tables in case the wind whips up.

The sides of the tent are open to the greens, the trees, and mountains in the distance. The white awning is lit with chandeliers and strands of patio lights, which will be enchanting once it turns dark. A wooden arch covered in greenery sits at the far end with a hundred or so seats set up facing it in neat rows. And of course, there's the photo booth. Everything is what you'd expect for a tent wedding, except for the corner gas firepit surrounded by brocade sofas and wingback chairs. I appreciate the elegant touch and head to the firepit for warmth until everyone else arrives.

As usual, I hear Meri before I see her. She appears in a fluffy tea-length white tulle skirt with a sparkly gold sweater that matches her heels.

I'm a little underdressed, which is a first for me. "You look like an angel."

"Fear not. It is I, Meri Newberg."

As dramatic as ever. I hope this time the two of us can stay friends after Charlie leaves. I mean, I'm in her wedding, so that makes this a lifelong thing. Though it'll just be hard to hear about Charlie settling down with someone he meets in Manila or beyond. Not that he'll literally settle down.

I rise to give her a hug and hang on for a tad too long. The same way I did with her mom. Mrs. Newberg pronounced that they're both in good places, and I'm happy for them. As for me, I think being in either of their embraces is probably safer than Charlie's arms.

Meri's posse appears, sans the heart-shaped sunglasses, thus I'm forced to release my hold. They ooh and aah over her outfit, though Roxy does compare it to what her preschool daughter is going to wear as the flower girl.

I smile politely through it all, and I realize I'm just waiting for Charlie to show. This means I am definitely not in a good place. What's going to happen when he leaves?

I'll have the career of my dreams, that's what. He'll win another Emmy for the documentary I'm promoting. It'll go on my résumé, which could very well get me work with faith-based films. Then I'll be changing the world too.

Win-win-win. Me, Charlie, and the planet will all be better off. Even if I don't feel like it at first.

I rub a hand over my heart to soothe the muscular organ with a deep tissue massage. It thumps harder beneath my touch, alerting me to Charlie's presence.

I turn to find him striding underneath the awning with the groom. While Kai heads directly to Meri, Charlie's eyes are on me. This connection relieves my heartburn better than the strongest antacid. I smile for real this time, though my joy could be related to Charlie's getup.

He's wearing his standard flannel, but it's spiffed up with suspenders and a newsie cap.

"Were you playing mini golf or delivering newspapers?" I tease.

"Playing mini golf." He doesn't stop until he's directly in front of me. "Why would I be delivering newspapers? Most people read the news online these days."

A laugh shimmies through me. "I'm talking about your hat."

"Oh, right." He tips his hat. "Meri wanted me to dress up."

Only Charlie. "How do you know she didn't mean for you to wear your pirate costume?"

"She made it very clear." He adjusts his collar, then nods toward my fedora. "Though I'm sure she likes your hat. I certainly do."

I press my lips together to conceal my delight. "I thought you hated hats."

"Really? I wear them all the time."

Okay, I can't keep from grinning at how seriously he takes teasing. "I know, Charlie."

He tugs my brim lower, hiding my eyes so I can only see his smile above his beard when he asks, "You wore it for me?"

"Well, I wouldn't say that." But yeah.

Mrs. Newberg claps her hands. I fix my hat to give her my attention. She's upgraded her bright blazers to a blush-colored one with puffy sleeves, and her standard scarf has been replaced by something lacy. It's soft and feminine and similar in style to what my mom might have worn had she ever gotten to be a mother of the bride.

Charlie turns to stand by my side.

Mrs. Newberg starts strong. "Thank you all for coming and for taking part in this union. We're going to . . . we're going to . . ." Her voice fades, and she wipes a tear.

The Polynesian woman beside her takes her hand. "We're going to run through the ceremony quickly so we can get to the fun part of the evening where I tell embarrassing stories about Kai."

Oh, she's Kai's mom. She doesn't look much older than me, not to mention her body is more fit. She's wearing a coral dress that only covers one well-defined shoulder. It's something my mom wouldn't have even let me wear to prom. The one time I picked out a strapless dress, Mom bought me a shrug to wear over it.

She did her best, but I wish she'd put more energy into protecting herself than she spent on protecting me.

Kai groans at his mom's suggestion. I guess all kids wish their folks were a little different. "Nobody needs to hear those stories. Meri, walk as slowly as you can down the aisle."

"I'm going to put your fifty-yard-dash speed to shame." Meri kicks off her heels. "Come on, guys. Go, go, go."

We line up at the back of the tent in order of the processional. Pastor Greg stands up front with Kai.

When I met Kai, he was a skater with shaggy hair who dressed in a uniform of baggy T-shirts. After college, I didn't see him much because he got a night job editing clips for the morning news, meaning he slept during the day. He didn't date a lot, and I never expected him to beat me to the altar.

Yet tonight he awaits his bride-to-be in chinos, a button-up, and a grin that is both mischievous kindergartener and noble gentleman. He's changed.

A pang inside me wishes the same would happen for Charlie. Except Charlie doesn't need to grow up. Charlie was always the man of the house.

He steps beside me and holds out his arm. He's my escort in the same way he's dressed up for Meri. It's with as much enthusiasm as it is selfishness. Yeah, selfishness. He insists on doing things his way. Though who gets to draw the line between being oneself and being selfish?

I take a deep breath and hook my fingers around the crook of his elbow. Maybe I'm selfish too. Because I want him to do things my way. I want him to make me a higher priority than his dreams.

He reaches across his body to cover my hand with his other palm. This is how I'd imagined us walking down the aisle after becoming man and wife. I even imagined my goose bumps, because they are coming from his touch, not the chill.

"I like this," he says.

But like isn't enough, is it? It wasn't when he left for Peru.

Could I ask him to stay again? Would he even consider it? If I asked him now, I could ruin what we have in this moment. I'm just supposed to be enjoying this.

So I say, "I do too." Wondering how long I'll wait before requesting more.

Mrs. Kamaka motions us forward. "Your turn," she stage-whispers.

I take a step. Charlie surges ahead. I tighten my grip to slow him down as though he's a dog on a leash. The analogy fits in more ways than one. He's energetic, wants to get things done, and doesn't understand why others can't keep up. But this time he can't leave me behind.

He looks over his shoulder in question.

"It's not a race." Having to tell him this makes me want to google the awards show where Charlie accepted his Emmy. I can totally see him running up onstage. Maybe even stepping on chairs like that guy who won the Oscar for *Life Is Beautiful*.

"Meri told us to go fast." Charlie looks impatiently from me to the altar. "I've got some great stories to share about Kai, as well."

I continue my normal pace. "Meri was joking."

Energy radiates from his body like a jet engine, though he falls in step. He's choosing to slow down for me. Hope springs up and pools within. I could very well drown in it.

He turns his focus from the destination to our journey. His gorgeous eyes drink me in. "When I kiss you, whose hat do you think will fall off first?"

I hope nobody else heard that. Though it might not be a big deal to them. They see us as a couple.

We're a couple, whether I want to admit it or not. Whether we last or not. Whether we walk another processional or not.

"Is it a competition?" I ask about the hats. With Charlie, everything is a competition.

"I just want to knock your hat off."

I bite my lip to hold back a smile. No matter whose hat gets knocked off first, I'm going to win.

Chapter Twenty-Six

CHARLIE

Where there is love there is life.
—Mahatma Gandhi

I don't only want to knock Nicole's hat off. I want to have babies with her.

I'm thinking this because I'm reading all the stats on midwives in the Philippines. Less than half of births in their country have a trained birth attendant, and there's a high rate of mortality for both mother and child. Besides the economics, even if the lower-class women could afford care, they're often treated so unkindly by health-care professionals that they don't want to visit their physician.

I can't imagine letting a wife go through something like that. I can't imagine Nicole being pregnant with my child and not getting the care she needs. Falling for Nicole all over again makes this even more real to me. My heart aches for the families in crisis.

It has to change, and I can help change it. The only question is whether Nicole will go with me this time.

I haven't said anything to her yet because no contract has been signed. While I generally speak my mind, I'm a believer in things that are black and white. In this instance, ink on a dotted line.

Okay, I also want to make sure Nicole and I are on the same page before I propose again. With the way her eyes kept wandering to mine from her side of the wedding rehearsal, I believe we are. She's practically part of my family. She wore a hat for me. She likes me and might even love me. She's at least going to love what I offer.

Since I promised not to propose marriage, this time I'm proposing we partner for business. I'm going to offer her a job doing the same thing she does now, but globally. Starting with Manila.

If it was her job that kept her from coming with me last time, then it makes sense to start with the job. That way there's nothing separating us.

I click the touch pad on my laptop and listen for the whir of the printer. Warm paper slides into my hands. It's done. I've partnered with a ministry that trains midwives and provides free care to pregnant women. I'll be following around the founder, interviewing patients, and maybe even driving their ambulance through jungles.

My pulse surges with anticipation of this new endeavor. Promotion for *Sitting on a Gold Mine* has been excellent, and Nicole's got the premiere well in hand, so I'm going to sneak out to the Philippines next week to get things set up for the coming crew. Then I'll be back to attend the film festival, and we'll go from there. Now where did I put my passport?

"Bro." Kai appears in my doorway, fresh haircut slick from the shower. "Can you believe you're truly becoming my brother today?"

I grin at the guy. "It's going to be a day we never forget."

He nods, strangely somber. "I'm going to miss being your roommate, but having a ranch house in Happy Valley will be more ideal for raising a family. Meri and I hope to have lots of visits from Uncle Charlie."

I grin at the name Uncle Charlie. I know Meri is anxious to have kiddos, and I wonder if Nicole feels the same. We'd talked about having four kids, but that was when we were in our twenties. How has that changed for her over the years?

If we do get married and have lots of children, would I want her to go through labor and delivery in a country like the Philippines, or would I want her back here in the States? I'd need to be with her through it. Then there's the question of education. If we're on the road all the time, will we homeschool? That's not in Nicole's career plan, and I hadn't thought that far in mine. But I'm probably jumping ahead.

"I'll visit as much as I can, but right now I'm getting ready for Manila."

"Wait." Kai crosses his arms and leans against the doorframe. "You're still leaving?"

I wave the contract. "It's my job. I'm booking a red-eye for Monday night to scout it out."

Kai grimaces. "Déjà vu."

But he's thinking about the day of my wedding, not his. "This time it'll be different."

"You're not . . ." He rubs a hand down his face. "You're not going to tell Nicole at our ceremony, are you? Flowers are expensive, and I don't want her beating you with the bouquet as you walk down the aisle."

I chuckle. It's nice to know he thinks Nicole cares that much. "She doesn't need a weapon, she takes kickboxing."

Kai bugs his eyes, either in horror or warning. It's a rare moment when I make a joke, and he doesn't see the humor.

"Kidding." I hold up my hand to calm him. "I'm coming back for the premiere, so I'm not leaving for good. Though I'm going to offer Nicole a job, because I hope to take her with me."

Kai shakes his head. "And I thought I was bad at relationships."

First of all, the guy is wearing a tux for his wedding, so he can't be that bad. Second, my relationship is going well. We haven't referred to it as a relationship yet, but we hung out every evening this past week, so we probably spent more time together than most committed couples.

"Okay, Dr. Phil. What would you have me do?" I ask while entering my credit card info online to pay for my airline ticket.

"You made a local documentary on the police force. Why can't you do more of that?"

I stand straight to explain. If Kai hears the stats, he'll understand. "Think about Meri. If she gave birth in the Philippines, it's likely that either she or your baby would die. Or both. I'm going to bring awareness to the issue and inspire training and care to save lives like theirs. How can I not go?"

Kai takes a deep breath. "I'm not going. Does that make me a bad person?"

"Noo . . ." I wave my hand to let him off the hook. "You got a job as cameraman for that Bible story show. That's important too."

He shoves his hands in his pockets and rocks back on his heels. "I respect your passion. Just know you might have to choose between saving lives and a life with Nicole."

I refuse to accept his statement. There doesn't have to be a Y in the road. I know where I'm going, and I'm inviting Nicole along. We were created to work together. It's obvious. It's easy. I simply have to convince her.

As for Kai, he can think what he wants. Other people's opinions have never bothered me before. My purpose is not in doubt.

With conviction, I state, "I go where I'm called."

I'm called upon a lot that day. Because Meri is too happy to deal with any of the wedding worries—like wet leaves littering the dance floor or the flower girl getting stuck in a tree—I'm asked to step in and assist the event coordinator.

Maybe it's even my undercurrent of jitteriness about talking to Nicole that energizes me to get things done faster than everyone else. Delivery guy needs help carrying the expensive cake? I've got it set up on the table before he brings the last layer. Package of felt pens for the guest book out of ink? I rush to the store. DJ's sound system blows a fuse? I troubleshoot with the golf club's maintenance man.

Hence, I'm a little sweaty and out of breath when I hear music starting in the tent. Last night's rehearsal runs through my mind, and I scramble down the slippery embankment to take my place in time.

After wiping mud off my feet in the grass, I duck out of the rain and come face-to-face with the woman of my dreams. I pause to breathe her in. "Wow."

I see her dressed up all the time, so I'm not sure what it is that sends me reeling. The bridesmaid dress is a sage velvet with floaty short sleeves. Very soft and feminine. But the whole bridal party is wearing the same thing, and Nicole is the only one I can't take my eyes off.

She's made her usually sleek hair wavy somehow. It's pretty, but not anything that would normally stop me in my tracks.

Her bouquet includes more greenery than white flowers. It smells fresh, like roses, honey, and grass. I'll probably never come across a more intoxicating scent, but that's not it either.

It's not her shiny manicure. It's not her dewy lips. It's not her alluringly arched eyebrow. It's not the strand of Tahitian pearls.

It's nothing and it's everything. Though my eyes return to the black pearls as if I'm still in my Jack Sparrow costume. I'm overwhelmed with a memory I'd forgotten.

We picked out wedding rings at Alice's jewelry shop on Valentine's, and they had a kissing contest. There were five of us engaged couples, and whoever kissed the longest won the pearls. I'm personally not a fan of PDA, but I'm also not a fan of losing. So, I kissed Nicole three hours, two minutes, and fifty-six seconds straight to win her that necklace. I had to pee so bad it hurt, but valuable things are worth the sacrifice.

"Hey." I reach for the strand and roll one of the smooth beads between my fingers. "I remember these."

"Really?" She shrugs a shoulder. "I forget where they came from."

My mouth opens in protest, but then I see the corner of her lips curve up, and I know she's teasing me again. "Want me to kiss you for three hours, two minutes, and fifty-six seconds to remind you?"

"Not right now." She reaches for my face anyway, but only to wipe away the remainders of rain from my beard. Then she hooks a hand through the curve of my elbow, ready to take the next step.

My heart swells with pride that I get to walk her down the aisle. Yeah, she's stunning, but she's also smart, caring, and funny. We fit together in more ways than kissing contests.

Finally, we're heading the same direction, and I don't only mean the altar, a.k.a. wooden arch. I know I'm not supposed to propose marriage, but I want this for us. I want what Kai and Meri have. I want forever.

I will risk getting beaten with her expensive bouquet because I can't hold it in any longer. I whisper, "I love you."

Okay, I just figured that out, so I didn't hold it in at all, but it's Nicole's response that matters now.

She doesn't miss an excruciatingly slow step, but her perfectly sharpened nails dig into my forearm. "I've heard that before."

Ouch. Not the response I expected when I decided to declare my affection. In that fraction of a second, I'd thought she'd respond in kind. Especially since she's wearing our pearls. "I meant it before too."

She smiles straight ahead, and I don't think her lips even move when she responds, "Then I don't think you know what love means."

How are we back here? We were getting along so well.

While I'd been in a rush to get to the front of the ceremony last night, the aisle is way too short today. In a moment, we'll be parting ways to stare at each other during vows of devotion. I only have a moment to make this right. "It means I want you to go to Manila with me."

Her fingers slide from my arm, but she doesn't turn her back to take her place. Instead, she faces me, chest heaving. And though she's staring directly into my eyes, I can't read her expression. I just know it's not a good one.

Chapter Twenty-Seven

NICOLE

When you forgive, you love. And when you love,
God's light shines on you.
—HAL HOLBROOK AS RON, *INTO THE WILD*

I can't believe this is happening again. But instead of the wedding being canceled, I must face Charlie through an entire ceremony.

I feel the itch of his gaze, but I won't look at him. I can barely keep my composure as it is. My teeth are gritted to force this smile, and I have to blink a lot to prevent my vision from blurring. I really hope Kai's cameraman friend doesn't get a close-up of my face.

Charlie doesn't love me. His definition of love is wanting me to follow him around the world like an assistant. If I didn't do that before, there's no way I'm doing it now. How humiliating. And what a mockery of my emotions.

I put on these pearls for him, thinking we had another chance. But I was stupid to hope.

The ceremony drags on.

"Love is patient."

I almost snort.

"Love is kind."

Okay, Charlie tries. I'm the mean one who wants to bash him with my bouquet.

"It does not envy, it does not boast, it is not proud."

I blow out a breath, deflating a little with that one. Is my pride getting in the way? Or is it a boundary? I can't be a doormat. Again, where is that line?

"It does not dishonor others, it is not self-seeking."

Aha. Self-seeking. I want to point my finger at Charlie the way Esther pointed at Haman in my favorite Sunday school story from *The Picture Bible*.

"It is not easily angered, it keeps no record of wrongs."

And this would be the part where I'd have one finger pointed at Charlie and the others pointing back at me. But it's hard for a girl to forget when she's been abandoned the day before her wedding.

"It always protects, always trusts, always hopes, always perseveres."

My eyes leap to meet Charlie's. He looks as miserable as I feel. Nauseous. Like we booked a cruise during a hurricane.

"Love never fails."

There it is. This isn't love. He doesn't love me, and I don't love him. Neither of us are willing to lay down our lives for the other.

But we shouldn't have to. This isn't meant to be. We're simply too different.

Sure, we balance each other out in some ways. We have fun together. And we can kiss longer than the average couple. But there's no future here.

We both wanted so much more from this relationship, and we've both failed. My heart breaks all over again, but I'll own my part. I require more than Charlie can offer.

My rage settles into numbness. In the midst of this beautiful celebration, I've lost all hope. Was it only last night when Charlie held my hand under the dinner table, pulling it up to kiss my knuckles every time Kai and Meri kissed? That won't be happening today.

"You may now kiss the bride."

I lower my gaze to the cement, heart thundering in my ears.

Life isn't fair. I know this is true for families who lose their children to sinkholes in South America or poor health conditions in small island countries, so I should compare myself to them in order to make myself feel better. To help me let Charlie go. But those hurting families are not right in front of me. Kai and Meri are.

"Ladies and gentlemen, it is now my pleasure to present for the first time, Kai and Meredith Kamaka."

Kai swings his arms overhead in victory, taking Meri's hand with him. The crowd erupts. A Bruno Mars song plays over the loudspeakers. Not the "Marry You" song I'd expected, but "Count on Me."

My heart tears a little more. Because the sweet lyrics describe real love. It's not about what you can get from each other but what you have to offer.

Meri hops on Kai's back for a piggyback ride, and I realize in a moment I'm going to have to take Charlie's elbow again. The wedding party merges like a zipper, bringing us together way too quickly.

I'm a robot on the outside. I link arms mechanically. I take the preprogrammed steps. I smile an automated smile when the camera flashes.

On the inside, I've gone haywire. I can almost hear springs popping loose in my brain.

Charlie covers my hand with his palm like he did last night, only this time it feels like it's to lock me in place. To take me hostage.

"Can I talk to you?" He doesn't whisper because he's Charlie, but I doubt even he is willing to hash out our issues in public, and we're going to be in public for the foreseeable future.

"Sure. Whenever."

First, there are photos. Then there's dinner. And dancing. And cake. And toasts, which he handles with the experience of an Emmy winner. But there's no chance to speak privately.

We're together through it all, which is what I'd feared when I first learned he'd be my escort at Meri's wedding. While he hadn't planned it this way, if I'd known this was going to happen, I would have been even angrier at the time. Unfortunately, there's nothing I can do about it without making Kai and Meri's wedding all about me.

The DJ croons into the microphone. "And now is the moment all the unmarried folks have been waiting for."

Oh no it's not.

Gemma claps and rushes to the middle of the dance floor to the tune of "Single Ladies." I'll let her catch the bouquet.

Charlie beelines my direction. Is he going to try to give me advice to beat Gemma? He's competitive that way.

Even if I catch it, it doesn't mean I'm marrying him. I've already proven I can find another fiancé.

He grabs my hand and tugs me toward the photo booth.

I don't have enough energy to fight him. I slip through the curtain and plop down on the makeshift bench.

He lowers next to me, so close our thighs and arms press together. There's no room to scoot over. I try to and accidentally bump the button to start the timer.

"What is going on?" he demands.

The light flashes.

I close my eyes to avoid seeing our image reflected. I can still smell his mossy scent and feel the starch of his shirtsleeve. I don't want to admit it, but he cleans up nicely. "You're leaving."

His fingers thread through mine, and I pretend I don't know he's lifting my hand to press a warm kiss against my knuckles until it gives me shivers. "I want you to go with me."

The light flashes for a second shot.

I'd already determined I'm not going, but there's a soft part of my heart that didn't get properly guarded. "When?"

"Well, I fly out Monday night, but—"

My spine snaps straight. I snatch my hand away. "You're not even staying for the premiere? All that work I put into promoting—"

Flash.

"I'll be there. This is just a quick trip to set things up. Then you'll have until after the holidays . . ."

I clutch my pearls. He simply assumes I'm going with him? "I'm not going."

Flash.

His shoulders sag. His head tilts. "I thought this time was different."

"So did I."

Gemma squeals from outside the booth to cheers and applause. The old En Vogue song "Whatta Man" plays next, and I assume Karson is getting ready to draw his weapon on any other guy who tries to catch the garter. I wish Charlie and I had been in a place to challenge their succession to the altar.

Charlie's eyebrows draw together. His lips press into a straight line between his beard and mustache. He's not used to losing, but neither of us won this round. "I really am in love with you."

I'm sure he thinks he loves me. This is how my dad loved me.

"Charlie, if I went with you, I wouldn't let you crawl into mines that could cave in on you. I would stop you to keep you safe. Then you'd never get the footage that wins you awards and saves cities full of strangers." I let that sink in. "You don't want me there."

He shakes his head. "I'm done with mines. I'm not risking my life anymore."

We both know better. My own youth group pastor used to tell the story of hiding in the bed of a pickup to get past armed guards in the Philippines. The world needs people like that, but I don't.

"Charlie." I twist to better see him, but I can't stop there. Not if we're saying goodbye for real. I take his face in my hands, savoring the tickle of his facial hair against my palms.

His eyes plead with me, dark and sad, and I want to rescue him the way he thinks he has to rescue everyone else. Maybe I do love him. But then wouldn't I know how to get past this barrier between us?

"I'm glad you pursued working with me." I swallow the lump in my throat to finish what I have to say. "I'm glad we were both able to get closure."

The crowd outside cheers, making this moment even more surreal.

"No . . ." Charlie grips my forearms, and I prepare for a Rhett Butler–type kiss that's going to have me rethinking my whole speech.

The curtain swings wide. Karson and Gemma jostle the frame of the photo booth in a rush to have their pictures taken with the bouquet and garter before realizing it's already occupied.

"Oh." Gemma halts, her wide-eyed expression of shock making me wonder how she ever got work as an actress. "Sorry."

I drop my hands, which also releases me from Charlie's hold. "It's okay. We're done."

I return to being robot woman and rush from the booth toward the clubhouse, where nobody can look at me or ask me questions. And where I can safely mourn the loss of my goodbye kiss as well as that closure I so eloquently spoke of.

But first, I swiped the unwanted photo strip before anyone could see evidence of how unloved I am.

I stare at the photo strip. More accurately, I stare at the pearl necklace around my throat in the photos. Those poor college kids hadn't known what they were getting themselves into with that three-hour-two-minute-fifty-six-second kiss. Having my stomach growl for lack of food during the contest was nothing compared to its nausea now.

I stuff the strip in my purse so I don't have to look at myself anymore, but when I glance up, I'm staring at myself in the clubhouse's bathroom mirror. I raise my hand to the pearls around my throat, then reach behind my neck to unhook the lobster claw. What am I supposed to do with the necklace we won? I don't want to wear it, and I don't want to keep it as a memento. It's not like I'll have any kids to pass it down to.

Trembling, I pull out my phone and open my camera app. I select a filter that will blur the marble tiles and gold gilded mirror in the background and let the strand fall through my fingers in an alluring way. I snap a few shots and quickly post it to Craigslist before changing my mind. I'll donate the money it brings in to save the town in Ecuador. It's what Charlie would want.

I look back to the mirror. My collarbones feel exposed above the V-neck of my wrap dress. Sucking in a deep breath, I unzip my wristlet to retrieve the necklace Alice gave me. I'd taken it off this morning when daring to wear my pearls. Though the jewelry designer couldn't have known it at the time, she made the piece for this very moment.

"She flies with her own wings." I state the Oregon motto as my own.

Okay. I can do this. It's what I've been doing my whole life.

I stride out the door and through the lounge, posture tall. I'm going to go dance under the fading sky and wave the happy couple off with sparklers. Then I'll go home and kick the crud out of my punching bag.

"Nicole?" The voice is male, but there's a Southern drawl to it. "Nicole Lemaire?"

I frown and stop to study the guests seated in rolling brocade chairs around tiny square tables. Who would I know from the south that hangs out in a bar at a golf club?

A beefy guy with a round face removes his ball cap, revealing his bald head and his identity. Though he looks more gaunt than I remember. He's not your normal golfer, but people once loved him for it.

"Dante Sullivan?" Of all the times . . . I'm not sure how I'm supposed to feel about this. Under normal circumstances, it would be uncomfortable, but I was already uncomfortable, so seeing him here doesn't affect me much. "How are you doing?"

He slides his cap back on, shielding his bloodshot eyes. "I'm glad to run into you because I owe you an apology."

I blink. This is the last thing I expected from the man I'd once blamed for ruining my career. But I'm so past that now. Bigger issues. "Not necessary."

He motions to the chair next to him. "Nevertheless, if you have a moment, I'd like to ask your forgiveness."

If he'd kicked me in the gut, I wouldn't have been more shocked. Though I'd like to think I could have blocked that move.

"Oh. Okay." I look around to make sure there's nobody watching, but of course there is. I'm with Dante Sullivan. I sink next to him but point out, "You know I lost the Slice of Heaven deal because they were worried you might have been mixed up with me, as well. This probably isn't going to help those rumors."

He grunts. "I should have warned you."

I don't know what's happening right now. "Warned me of what?"

"Warned you I was going to confess my affair publicly."

I clutch my necklace, pulling it away from my throat as if that will resolve this choking feeling. "I . . . I figured you were caught."

He hangs his head. "My wife caught me, yes. And it turned out to be a relief not having to hide the truth from her anymore."

Once again, the best things for us are often those we fear the most.

He rubs his face. "She gave me another chance, and I didn't want her to have to bear the burden of lying about what a great guy I am to the media."

My heart squeezes tight. I didn't know confessing openly was an option anyone took.

Dante had been placed on a Christian pedestal. Doesn't the Bible say religious leaders are held to a higher standard? If his sin should cause another to stumble, he's accountable for them too. Or is that another verse Dad twisted to justify his cover-up?

"You . . ." I swallow over the lump, remembering the church service I recently attended with Charlie. "You abandoned your ministry platform for her? You left the flock that followed you in order to pursue one sheep?"

Dante swirls his drink thoughtfully. "King David also got caught in adultery. Nathan used a story about a rich guy stealing a sheep from a poor man as an example of what David had done. What I did." He blows out a breath. "We both went looking for greener pastures, but now I'm returning home. If that analogy makes my wife my sheep, then, yes. She should have always been my priority."

I'm overwhelmed with more emotions than I felt in the photo booth.

"My marriage is worth more than any success I can find outside my home. My wife is worth more."

Though this man sinned, he's trying to make it right. He's sacrificed his career, along with potentially sacrificing mine, yet I'm strangely jealous of his wife. She's loved the way I've always longed to be.

My dad, a pastor, didn't love me that much. My former fiancé, a good man who wants to save the world, doesn't love me that much. No, I've never been loved that much.

Though if Dante has that much love, he should be home with his wife, not drinking in a bar with me. "Then why are you here?"

He looks away. "It hurts to see the pain in her eyes and know I caused it."

The weight of my heart pulls me forward. I know Dante is talking, but I see my dad.

"I used to be so full of pride. I'd tell myself my wife was lucky to have me." He shifts his jaw side to side. "It made me feel good to think I was what every woman wanted. Ironically, what every woman truly wants is a man who will never tell himself things like that."

I've only considered this situation from a woman's perspective. From my mom's perspective. I never considered how the cheater feels. How my dad felt.

He shakes his head. "I don't deserve her."

"Dante." I grip his arm. I may not be able to save my relationship with my father or even my own romance, but I can help save Mrs. Sullivan's. "She wants *you* to be that man. That's why she's giving you another chance. Don't let the shame for what you've done hold you back from what you have the opportunity to do right now."

His gaze flicks up to meet mine, hesitant but hopeful. "I was ashamed to face you, but you're being much cooler about this than I expected."

"Oh, I'm so not cool." I roll my eyes at all the times I'd imagined his face on my punching bag, and I pull my hand away from his arm in case I could still be doing damage with this ridiculous manicure. "But I do forgive you as you requested. And as unexpected as it may sound, you've helped me understand God's love better than all the 'perfect' Christian leaders out there."

He leans back in his seat, studying me as if to see if I'm being honest. "Extremely unexpected."

God has used Dante in spite of himself, as He does for us all. The guy still has a way to go, but maybe now that I've offered mercy, he'll listen to me speak truth. "Go home, Dante. Your wife needs you more than you know."

He sets his glass down and stands. "You're right."

I watch him walk away, satisfied with the outcome of our conversation yet also more alone now than ever.

"You're feisty today." Workout Wendy holds the bag so I can bash it repeatedly.

"It's been a while." I alternately aim my sidekick lower and higher. Were I actually in the ring with Charlie, I'd be taking out his hip and chest. Hip and chest. Hip and chest. "I've got to make up for lost time." By lost time, I mean the Sundays when I canceled these sessions to go to church with Charlie.

"Right." Wendy nods for me to change legs. "I'm sure this has nothing to do with that guy you were supposed to guard your heart from."

Front kick. "I was in his sister's wedding yesterday." Roundhouse. "We walked down the aisle together as a bridesmaid and groomsman." Spinning back kick. "He said he loved me."

She lets me continue, understanding I need this. "You don't believe him?"

I jump kick to hit harder. It hurts to not be loved. I want to hurt back.

Finally, I stand down, gasping for breath. "I ran into another guy at the wedding." I wipe my forearm across my forehead. "Dante Sullivan. Remember him?"

"I can't keep up." Wendy hands me a water bottle. "Wait. Isn't that the golfer who got caught cheating on his wife?"

"Yeah." I guzzle the much-needed cool liquid. "Only he didn't get caught. Not by the public. He confessed."

"Really?" She hangs on the punching bag, swinging with it as she listens. I wonder if her other trainees regale her with such drama. My life has to be more entertaining than a soap opera.

"He . . ." I shake my head, still reeling from the news as if I took a hook to the jaw. "He's giving up his platform for her."

"Good." Wendy nods her approval.

A lump lodges in my throat, so I just nod along. Then I check my smartwatch to hide my emotion. I've burned over four hundred calories, and we still have fifteen minutes left. I lift my guard. "Shall we practice punches?"

"I think you should slow down."

My glare tells her I think otherwise. I need to power through.

She arches her eyebrows knowingly. "Have you been practicing your katas?"

I twist my lips in regret. Though if she wants me to slow down, I could really impress her with how much I'd slowed down this last month. "I've been sleeping in and using extra creamer in my coffee and taking bubble baths."

"I figured as much when you kept canceling our sessions," she states sagely.

Might as well confess. "I've been going to church."

She plants her hands on her hips and tilts her head. "Why aren't you at church today?"

My hands fall from guard position, and my head rolls back. "Because."

"Because why?"

She's going to make me say it. I just have to get it out. "Because Charlie isn't pursuing me like Dante wants to pursue his wife. He's letting me go in order to keep tending the rest of his flock."

"Darling . . ."

Her tender tone is my undoing. I haven't been anyone's darling in a long time. My pain pours out. "I know Dante Sullivan cheated on his wife and hurt her, but he's giving up everything else to be there for her now." I wipe at my nose to keep from blubbering too much. As if there's an acceptable amount of blubbering. "I've never been loved like that. I've always been the one sacrificed."

She wraps me in her sweaty arms. The same arms that attack when sparring now shield me from the world.

"Just once . . . just once I want someone to come after me like a lost sheep." I curl into her embrace and let myself sob. I hate feeling this weak, but at the same time, I can rest in Wendy's strength. "I'm supposed to believe God loves me, but He's left me on my own."

She rubs her fat gloves down my spine. They're designed to protect her hands, but they've become my safe place. "Are you alone right now?" she challenges.

I squeeze her back, thanking her for being here for me. Even as I pout. "No, but I pay you to come over."

She places her gloves on my shoulders and pulls away to look me in the eye. "I've never worked on Sundays before."

Unsure of what she's trying to say, I swipe tears away to better read her expression. It's patient. And kind. And all the things that describe love.

"You're my lost lamb."

My heartbeat hitches. Wendy's always been a mentor figure. A physical trainer. But if she's left her flock to come after me, that makes her family.

"I'm your lost lamb?" I squeak. Nobody wants to be considered a lost lamb, but everyone wants to be found. Pursued. Worthy even when we've wandered off.

It hurts in the best ways. In healing ways.

"I'm here for you," she vows.

God did send someone to love me. It's just not who I'd expected.

Chapter Twenty-Eight

CHARLIE

Love is not only something you feel,
it is something you do.
—David Wilkerson

This is not how I wanted to leave for the Philippines. I'd wanted to head out overflowing with love. Instead, my heart is empty. I'm distracted. I'm sick to my stomach because I know how this ends. I've lived it once before.

Nicole doesn't seem as affected as she did last time. She was actually going to kiss me goodbye before we got interrupted. She called it closure.

Afterward, I followed her up to the clubhouse and saw her talking to some guy. He looked vaguely familiar, and I assume he's her other former fiancé. She then returned to the wedding all pleasant and polite, as though we were nothing but acquaintances.

I would've asked if she was driving home in a new Porsche if Kai hadn't cornered me and scolded me for doing exactly what he'd asked me not to do. But it's not as if I'd anticipated things going this way. I'd mistakenly assumed telling a woman I loved her during a wedding ceremony would add to the romance of the moment.

I bet it would make Kai feel better if he knew I don't have any more excitement for this upcoming documentary. Part of my excitement had been the opportunity to share it with Nicole. Now that I've worked with her, I'm ruined for all other marketers.

I punch her number into my cell phone. Though I detest acting like a lovesick ex, I've got things to say and nobody else to say them to.

Her phone doesn't even ring but sends me directly to voicemail. She didn't come to church yesterday. She's avoiding me again.

If she doesn't want to talk to me as a boyfriend, that's fine. I'm still her client. She can't avoid that.

Grabbing my keys, I head out the door. I drive through the maze of skyrises I've memorized to get to her office and ride the elevator to her floor. Then I barge silently right past Morgan.

She doesn't even try to stop me this time. Good woman.

But Nicole's chair is empty. Did someone alert her to the fact I was coming? I trudge to the doorway and glare at Morgan as though she's an accomplice to this crime.

"Hello, Mr. Newberg," she greets cheerfully. She's only cheerful when bearing bad news. "Miss Lemaire is out sick today."

Now what? I sigh and surprise myself by strolling over to sink into a seat across from Nicole's assistant.

She arches dramatically dark eyebrows above her glasses. "Would you like some coffee? With arsenic?"

"If that's what you're offering."

She rises and bustles to a built-in shelving unit by the door with a Keurig and, presumably, arsenic.

"Did Nicole tell you I'm going to Manila?"

Morgan retrieves a mug from the cabinet and pops a pod into the machine. "She might have mentioned it."

That's a yes. "Did she mention I invited her to join me?"

"Hmm?" She watches coffee trickle into the mug as if it's more interesting than talking to me. Then she stirs in what appears to be powdered creamer but could very well be rat poison. "You didn't seriously expect her to take you up on your offer, did you?"

I stare at her as she carries the full cup my way. "Why not? I'm in love with her."

"Are you, though?" She hands me the warm mug.

I study the milky brown beverage suspiciously and sniff. "Arsenic smells like caramel."

"What a way to go, right?" She returns to her seat.

I sip slowly, concerned more for burning my taste buds than the threat of death. "You think if I was really in love with Nicole that I'd stay here?"

Morgan turns her chair to face her computer in the corner of her desk and starts typing. "Not necessarily."

She's just being difficult. I don't know why I'm still sitting across from her. I should be in Zoom meetings with investors and packing my suitcase. But I don't have the energy for it. "Then why don't you believe I'm in love?"

"What is love?" she challenges.

"I'm . . ." I shrug and resort to quoting the movie *Bambi*. "Twitterpated."

Her gaze slides my way for a moment. "We know."

We being the world? Thanks, lady. I cross an ankle over one knee. "Fine. Tell me what you think love is."

She continues to type without answering. I study the photos on her desk. Her family. I bet she'd rather be home with her baby and toddler, but she's working here to provide. Maybe she does know something about love.

Could I trade traveling to stay here for Nicole? I could, but I might make her as miserable here as she thinks she'd make me there.

Morgan interrupts my thoughts. "I recently had this discussion with Nicole, and I told her I believe love is the perfect blend of truth and mercy."

Startled, I turn back toward the admin assistant. It takes me a minute to soak in her words.

First of all, Nicole had been pondering love, as well. That's a good sign.

Secondly, Morgan's answer is deeper and more profound than expected.

"I'm all about truth." I nod in agreement. "Mercy too. I'm offering mercy to those I help with my documentaries."

Morgan grunts.

"What?" I demand. "My job is all about love."

She lowers her glasses on her nose like a disapproving schoolmarm. "I thought we were talking about Nicole, not your career."

I reel back, sloshing coffee on my jeans. I ignore the spill to focus on the reason I scalded myself in the first place. How could I claim to love Nicole when I was offering truth and mercy more to people I've never met than to her?

My whole career is based on feeling called to make a difference in the world. To touch lives. To inspire change. I felt called to Peru and Ecuador. I felt called to reveal how defunding the police affected law enforcement officers, their families, and the community at large. And then I felt called to love Nicole.

Marrying and loving are two very different things, but I'd confused them. The idea of marriage benefited me. While loving means giving when there's no guarantee of getting anything in return.

If I'm called to love her, I have to make the sacrifice. I must risk my heart the way I'd rather risk my life. But how do I do that?

I know one way . . .

"I'm going to make a documentary about her."

Morgan's hands drop to her lap. Her mouth falls open. "You're what?"

"Don't tell her. I want it to be a surprise. I can show it to her at the theater after the premiere." The ideas are coming faster and faster now. I stand and set the mug on Morgan's desk, energy renewed. Caffeine beats arsenic. "This is what I do to show my love. Thanks for the idea."

She reaches out like she can stop me. "I didn't mean . . ."

I turn at the door and shoot her a confident grin. "But God did."

I don't know how I'm going to do this. My best cameraman is on his honeymoon. I guess I could film with my phone. Some Academy Award winners have been filmed with phones. Not that I expect to win an Oscar for a story about a pastor's daughter from Kansas.

Of all the places I've been, I've never been to Kansas. I've never cared to see Nicole's hometown. I've never asked to meet any of her family. No wonder she doesn't believe I love her.

The more I think about it, the sadder this makes me. Nicole had no siblings and her mom died shortly before she moved to Oregon for college.

As for her dad, he seems to have disappeared from her life right after he got caught cheating on her mom. I know she wishes they were closer. Her heart softened toward being paired with me in Meri's wedding when she realized it meant Meri was going to have a father figure walk her down the aisle. If I want the best for Nicole, then I am going to try to give her what she really wants. What she's wanted longer than she's wanted to be with me.

There's no guarantee Nicole's dad longs for the same reconnection, but I won't know if I don't ask. All I have to do is find the man.

I remember the name of Nicole's old church because whenever she talked about her dad's affair, she'd refer to it as his fall from Grace Chapel. It's been over a decade since she attended the church, and the congregation could be completely different by now, but it's a place to start. And I know just the person to help. Someone well-versed in matters of the heart and sweet enough to coax little old ladies into sharing their potluck recipes.

Before even leaving the parking garage, I cancel my flight to Manila and book two tickets to Wichita. Then I pull in front of my townhome and sprint through the front door. "Gemma?" It's close to five. She's usually off work by now.

My roommate emerges from her room at the top of the stairs, eyes wide behind some kind of dried green face mask. "Are you okay?" she asks. "Do you need a ride to the airport? Because I'm supposed to leave this on for half an hour."

"I do need a ride, but I also need you to get a sub to teach your high school classes and join me."

"It's homecoming week." She cringes, and the mask cracks across her forehead. "Also, I'm scared of giant spiders."

Giant spiders? I'm going to Kansas, not Middle-earth. Oh wait. She thinks I'm still going to Manila. "I need your help as a romance writer.

I'm making a documentary about my love for Nicole, and I have to track down her father, friends, and childhood home. We're going to Kansas."

She cheers from the top step, à la Rocky Balboa meets The Hulk. "Well, why didn't you say so? Let me make a phone call."

Chapter Twenty-Nine

CHARLIE

The love we give away is the only love we keep.
—ELBERT HUBBARD

As much as Dorothy claimed, "There's no place like home," Nicole didn't seem to share the sentiment. She'd left Kansas at the age of eighteen and didn't return. How have I never wanted to know more about this story before?

My flight lands in Wichita at twilight, and I film the purple sky through the window to use for documentary footage. There are no mountains, which I would miss if I lived here, but the flat land sets a grander stage for sunsets.

Water towers are also displayed like I've never noticed before. In Portland, the area is so hilly, and there are so many trees, that the tall structures are often hidden. Here they truly seem like attacking spaceships, the way radio listeners once assumed after mistaking the adaptation of *The War of the Worlds* for an actual news broadcast.

I wish it was still summer so I could experience the lightning bugs and lightning storms Nicole once mentioned. The temperature gauge in the car says it's fifty-eight degrees, which is the same as the weather we left in Oregon, but the air feels chillier here. That could be due to the humidity. Or the wind. Probably a combination.

Gemma and I retrieve our luggage and rental car, then check into the hotel rooms I booked downtown along the river. It's too late to visit Grace Chapel this evening, but we can get some footage of the city at night, not to mention this giant Native American statue on a little island.

With purpose, I stride down the street toward the park where a white footbridge leads to said island. Its modern suspension style looks new with the way it's lit up. I wonder if Nicole has seen it or if it was built after she left.

Gemma halts directly in front of me. I do a funky hop on one foot to avoid running her over.

She doesn't even notice my funky hop because she's entranced with the storefront of a pizza place. "Sunflower seed pizza? Does that mean seeds on top, or is the crust made of seeds?"

Being from Oregon, Gemma and I are the tree huggers here, but sunflower seed pizza sounds a little nutty to me. "Sunflower seeds are nothing more than an excuse for spitting in a Coke bottle on car trips."

"They reduce inflammation." She points through the window. "Hey, look. Sunflowers are the state flower. I have to try some now."

With her allergies, she doesn't get to eat pizza very often, so I wave her inside. I'd rather try an Indian taco with fry bread. Nicole told me she ate them while watching a native dance demonstration at some kind of river festival. Was that here? In this same area?

"I'm going to walk out to the island. Can you pick me up something with meat on it?"

She pauses to look at me. "You okay?" She's not asking about my growling stomach . . . She's asking about my heavy heart.

I try to shrug off the not-okay feeling, but it sticks to me like the humidity. "If we find Nicole's dad, should I ask his permission to marry her?"

Now that I've said it out loud, I have to face it. I'm hunting down the man years after I abandoned his daughter in order to pursue my own career ambitions. I never considered asking for his blessing before, because I saw him as a man who deserted his wife and daughter. But am I any better? Even if he reconnects with Nicole, why would he walk her down the aisle to me?

Gemma studies me. "Knowing Nicole, you never would need her

dad's permission. She's a pretty independent woman." Gemma places a hand on my arm. "But if you believe God sent you here, then Nicole's heavenly Father has already given you His blessing. Isn't that what really matters?"

I'm sure Gemma meant her words to soothe, but they are more like water poured on the hot rocks of a sauna. All the while I'd thought God was telling me to marry Nicole, He'd needed to protect her from my selfishness.

"Thanks, Gemma." I'm thankful she's here. I'm thankful for her reminder that I should be going to God with this.

So I do. I cross the bridge over one of the lazy rivers that converge here out to the statue named the Keeper of the Plains. It's sculpted from metal and stands about forty-five feet high. Details include fringe along his pants and sleeves, and feathers from his headdress. A ring of fire like torches illuminates the steel to appear gold against the dark of night.

I pause to read the lighted plaque about the statue's symbolism and its dedication during the bicentennial.

With his face raised to the sky, he extends his arms in supplication of the Great Spirit.

Another reminder.

I'm alone, but I'm not alone.

At one time, there was nobody on this land other than tribes like the Cheyenne and Comanche. But even before that, God knew I would end up here right now. So how can I go around acting like He needs me?

"I'm sorry, Lord." I take a deep breath of honeysuckle-scented air. "I'm here now. I'm here for Nicole. I'm here for her dad. Use me how You want to."

My throat tightens at the idea that God might not use me. He might have brought me here only to get my attention, like when the fish swallowed Jonah. He doesn't care so much if I win an Emmy as if I grow. Which is the hardest thing to accept.

I want to be the one who saves others. I don't want to need saving. Even though that's how I became a Christian in the first place.

If the Keeper of the Plains knows to lift his hands to heaven, so should I.

I flip my hands over, palms open. "Work in me however You want."

If I don't go to the Philippines, there will be someone else God can use to save mothers and babies. At the same time, if I don't stay here with Nicole, God can provide someone else for her too. Both of those things are good things to do. The problem is that I've been doing good things for the wrong reasons.

I want to feel important, the way I felt when I was a kid who was also the man of the house. But the truth is, if I don't obey God's will, I'm the one missing out.

My imagination pictured a church in Kansas as looking like a one-room schoolhouse. Maybe my mom made me watch too much *Little House on the Prairie* as a child. Maybe I just figured that since Nicole's dad had been having an affair while pastoring, his church couldn't possibly have been thriving. I should have known better than to stereotype, as I'm reminded the next morning.

"This place is massive." Gemma is supposed to be filming as I drive into the Disneyland-sized parking lot, but she's leaning forward to see the top of the cross that rises above the center of the modern brick-and-stone structure. The camera on her phone is pointed toward her feet.

"Camera," I remind her.

She jolts back against her seat to refocus.

I'm certainly not winning another Emmy.

"Did you know it was this big?" she asks.

"No." I park as close as we can get to one of the multiple sets of glass double doors at the front of the place. I wonder if they have parking attendants on Sunday mornings. "I expected a few large families who dressed like they were on *The Sound of Music* and homeschooled together."

Gemma pops her door open. "Was Nicole homeschooled?"

I pull out the keys and click the lock to follow. "Private school."

"There's a difference."

We pass a trickling fountain. "Apparently."

Gemma twists her lips in thought. "I don't know any homeschool families who dress like they're from *The Sound of Music*. Are you talking about the scene where they're wearing clothes made out of curtains?"

I shake my head because that's not the point. "I'd hoped to get names of a few families whose kids grew up with Nicole, but from the size of this place, her dad's affair must have caused a huge scandal. I hope people aren't too angry to help us."

"Nicole was a kid. They can't be mad at her."

We finally reach the front door, and I hold it open. The foyer is massive with shiny cement floors, exposed pipes along the high ceiling, and barstools lined up along the walls of windows as if it's an airport or something. An information booth sits in the center of the space, and an open staircase leads up the left wall to what I must assume is the balcony of the sanctuary.

I look for a hallway with the hopes of offices, but Gemma heads toward a reclaimed wood wall displaying the cutout of another cross. It's surrounded with black-and-white headshots that I assume must be the current staff. "Let's find a friendly face. Then maybe we can send a message through Facebook for help."

Not a bad idea. I probably would have done so already if this was a normal documentary.

I take a quick glance at the staff photos. They're all pretty clean-cut, and I appreciate the ethnic diversity. I point to the guy with a trimmed beard and flannel shirt, then look for his info on a little white plaque next to his photo. "I pick Sean Brumley."

Gemma gasps, hand over her mouth.

"Do you have something against beards and flannel shirts that I should know about?"

Gemma's big blue eyes meet mine, and for some reason the concern I see sends a chill down my spine. She slowly points to the picture at the top.

The man in question is middle-aged, with a full head of gray hair and dark eyebrows. He wears a confident smile and stylish glasses. His nose is also a little wide at the base, reminding me of the Iranian documentary and . . . Nicole.

My gaze zips to the plaque of Head Pastor David Lemaire. Nicole's dad never left? Did he confess his affair? Or was it a secret she was forced to keep? No wonder she stayed away.

Gemma lowers her hand to speak. "Am I reading that correctly?"

If she is, it makes me like the guy even less. And it's going to make this documentary more challenging than it already is.

"We shouldn't jump to conclusions," I say. Because I don't want to believe it. But I'm looking for that hallway of offices with more determination than before.

"It's been over a decade. Maybe he went through church discipline and had his position restored?" Gemma is always hopeful.

"Maybe." I beeline to the information desk and riffle through pamphlets and newsletters to find a map.

Gemma trails behind. "Or maybe it's her uncle? Ministry could be the family trade."

Aha. Offices are upstairs.

"Can I help you?" The voice comes from behind us, and I turn to find a man with a beard exiting the bathroom. He's not wearing his flannel today, but even in his boring navy polo, he looks like the guy from the photo.

I stride his way, hand extended to shake. "Sean Brumley?"

He squints at my face as if trying to recall how we know each other. His grip is solid, but not too solid. "Yes. Were you looking for me?"

"Actually." Gemma rushes to join us. Probably knowing I'll blurt out things that shouldn't be blurted. She may not be good with a camera, but she's good with people. "We're friends of Nicole Lemaire. Do you know her?"

He blinks and steps back. "Is she . . . is she okay?"

So he does know her.

Gemma waves her hands to wipe away any of his concern. "Oh,

yes. Charlie here wants to marry her, but he's never met her family or seen her hometown."

Sean's head tilts my way. He studies me with new awareness. He looks back to Gemma. "And you are here because . . . ?"

By *you*, he means Gemma. I can see how it might be weird that I'm visiting the hometown of the woman I want to marry with another woman. But I *am* a weirdo.

So I explain. "I'm a film director. I make documentaries. *Dirty Gold* won an Emmy a few years ago, if you've heard of it."

He shakes his head, even more confused than before.

"Well." I didn't really expect him to recognize the title. "My name is Charlie Newberg, and—"

"Oh." He snaps his fingers. "You did that earthworm documentary."

Behind him, Gemma opens her arms wide and looks at me with even more shock than when we first saw the photo of the man we suspect to be Nicole's dad.

I ignore her.

Sean gushes, "I watched it in an airport on my way home from a pastor's conference. I've never seen a more beautiful leaf with dew on it."

I cross my arms and lean forward. I knew I liked this guy. "Thank you." It's good to meet a fan.

"Yeah, my flight out of Portland got delayed, and I was exhausted but too stressed to sleep. That film helped me relax for a much-needed nap."

I press my lips together before responding. "The Lord works in mysterious ways."

Gemma bursts out laughing.

His mouth rounds and his cheeks ripen. He holds up a hand in apology. "I didn't mean . . ."

I want to put on my tricorn hat and quote Jack Sparrow. *"But you have heard of me."*

Instead, I focus on business at hand.

"It's okay." I stroke what's left of my beard. "I'm here now because

I make documentaries about what I love, and I'm in love with Nicole. Did you know her well enough to answer some questions on film?"

His hand drops. He glances toward the balcony upstairs, then back toward me warily. "Where will it be shown?"

I steady my gaze. "It's for her alone."

His face softens. "Like a proposal video?"

"Something like that."

"Aww . . . I'm happy for her." He stands taller. "Nicole and I attended youth group together, though she turned me down for prom."

This is a man after my own heart. We both have good taste in facial hair and women. Plus, it's nice to not be the only one she's rejected. "Do tell."

His smile fades. "I didn't know it at the time, but I think things were tough for her at home."

So maybe he does know about her dad.

Sean sighs. "Nicole told me she didn't want to go to the dance, but later, after Mrs. Lemaire overdosed, I think she knew her mom was struggling and tried to stay close by."

My gut clenches. Nicole never mentioned drugs. And overdose? She must have felt like she was abandoned by both parents.

Gemma steps closer to put a hand on my tricep. I barely feel it through the buzzing of my brain.

My roommate speaks for me. "I didn't know she overdosed."

Sean nods sadly. "We think it was accidental. She'd been prescribed both antidepressants and sleeping pills, and got the two confused."

Pills for depression. Nicole's mom was probably in pain from her husband's affair.

Sean winces. "Nicole left right after that, and I've thought about her a lot since then. Wondered what more I could have done for her."

Gemma shakes her head. "You didn't know," she reminds him.

He shoots her a grateful smile. "I'll be happy to tell some funny stories for your film. But I'm not sure how many other people will have nice things to say." He sighs. "Some people feel as though she kicked her dad when he was down. The prodigal daughter and all that."

"Huh." I slide my eyes toward Gemma to see if she's thinking what

I'm thinking. I'm not normally the one to read between the lines, so I need to be sure.

Gemma gives me the slightest chin lift, which really isn't helpful for someone who also struggles with body language. But then she says, "And her dad is . . . ?"

Sean motions toward the wall of picture frames. "Pastor David Lemaire. He started this church in the '90s, and he's been leading it ever since."

Nicole's dad chose his church over his daughter. No wonder she thought I was choosing my documentary over her. It's time that girl finds out how much she's loved.

Chapter Thirty

NICOLE

There is no surprise more magical than the surprise
of being loved: it is God's finger on man's shoulder.
—Charles Morgan

After Wendy's hug, I don't feel as nauseous as I did at the wedding, but I still called out sick this week because I've got some healing to do. Today's treatment involves selling my Tahitian pearls.

I received a few offers on the strand right away, but one prospective buyer sent me a link about how much the necklace is worth and offered five times as much as I'd been asking. It's enough to donate to Charlie's fundraiser *and* take me to Peru, which I think might be the next step on my healing journey.

Because the necklace is so valuable and I don't want to get scammed, I suggested we meet at Sunstone Jewelers. It's a public place, and there are sure to be appraisers available.

It would also be nice to see Alice again. I could tell her how well the Gold Standard campaign is going and thank her again for the necklace she gave me. I hope she's not hurt that I'm selling the pearls, though she seems to be the kind of person who cares more about the meaning of a piece than its price tag. She'll understand that I can't keep the strand for the same reason I couldn't keep the engagement ring.

My phone vibrates, and my heart jolts like it does every time Charlie calls. I want to talk to him. I may even want to give up my every desire in order to be with him. But that's exactly why I can't. It's what killed my mom.

I dig my pointy fingernails into my palm until the call goes to voicemail. Then I resume my stride from the parking lot toward the jewelry shop. With a deep breath, I enter the place that's now decorated with all that glitters, but somehow remains as simple and pure as its founder.

"Nicole." Alice glides toward me in her bright caftan, greeting me with yet another motherly hug. "It's good to see you again."

"Thanks. It's good to see you too." I hug her back. "This necklace you gave has meant more than you can imagine. It's given me strength."

"Aww . . ." She nods with perception and takes my hands. "Where is Charlie boy today?"

I take a deep breath, though it doesn't sting as much as I expected it to. "Manila."

"I see," she says, and I wonder if she can see more than I do. "How is his fundraiser going? I plan to attend the premiere and help out with the auction."

"Oh, I'm so glad." I squeeze her hands. "The fundraiser is going better than I expected. That's partly why I'm here. I wanted to let you know that since you've collaborated with us, we've gotten most of the big jewelry chains on board. They're starting to refer to the Gold Standard in all their advertising now."

"As they should." She nods approvingly. "What is the other reason you're here?"

I twist my lips, not sure I want to tell her now. But she's so understanding. "I hope you aren't offended, but do you remember the pearls Charlie and I won the day we bought my engagement ring?"

"Yes." Her eyes have this way of caressing. Of soothing my fears.

"They're beautiful, but with Charlie leaving again, it's too hard to keep them."

Her smile is sad for me, not for herself. "Yes."

I look away from her compassion, then exhale out as much emotion as possible to face her again without breaking. "I posted them on Craigslist, and I'm meeting the buyer here. I hope you don't mind."

"I don't mind." She gives a cute little old lady wink. "It's rather convenient actually, since I am the buyer."

I reel back in shock, and it's a good thing she's holding my hands to keep me upright.

"What? No. You can't buy back the necklace. If you want it, I'll give it to you." My brain scrambles to connect the pieces. "You're the one who offered five times the amount I asked for? Alice . . ."

She chuckles. "I don't want it for myself. I want to donate it to be auctioned off at the premiere."

I can't even. "I'll donate it. You don't have to spend anything. I was going to give the amount I asked for to Charlie's cause anyway." This is crazy. "How did you even know I posted it for sale?"

"I've been watching for you to sell it ever since I saw you last."

Did she view me as a taker? As if I take necklaces she gives me, then I take money from her to buy them back? "Why?"

"It's what people do to heal from heartbreak. They sell the piece that reminds them of the one who broke their heart."

I study her, wondering how she could possibly know this would happen.

"Come back to my office. We'll negotiate our transaction."

I laugh dryly, but she lets go of one hand to tug me after her with the other. "Alice . . ."

After we cross into the more private area, she lets me go to sit, primly facing me from the other side of her mahogany desk.

I shake my head but sink down across from her.

"Do you have the pearls?"

I stare at her, considering my options. I can't sell her the pearls, but I could give them to her and then refuse to take her money. With a deep breath, I pull the black velvet pouch from my purse and slide it across the table.

She removes the strand. "Oh, yes. These are as fine as I remember." She flips on an LED lamp to look more closely. "Black pearls used to be so rare they were only worn by royalty. The shinier and more round they are, the more expensive."

They are shiny. "That explains the price you gave me."

"Mm-hmm." She lifts her gaze from the jewelry, but her expression doesn't change. As though she thinks I'm rare and royal too. "There's a lot of mythology around them. The Polynesian belief is that it represents eternal love."

"No wonder you knew I'd be getting rid of them." I roll my eyes.

"Others say they symbolize hope for wounded hearts."

I guffaw. "Are you just making this stuff up?"

"Oh no. That's real." Her wrinkles deepen, and I wonder if she knows from experience. "Do you want to tell me about your heart wound?"

I drop my gaze to the pearls, wishing they had the magical powers she speaks of. But it's more likely they were cursed like the Black Pearl in *Pirates of the Caribbean*.

Of course, I've been taught that healing power only comes from God. With the way Workout Wendy has come after me like a lost sheep, I'm starting to believe it. "I caught my dad having an affair on my mom."

"Oh, child." Alice leans back in her chair. "Is that what you expect from a marriage? Is that why you keep breaking off engagements?"

I look up to meet her eyes. Such a wound is probably sadly common. Though I think mine goes deeper. "My dad was a pastor. And he warned me that if I told anyone, it would affect the whole congregation. There would be a church split, and church members would fall away from faith."

She clutches her own necklace but remains quiet, inviting me to tell the whole story for the very first time.

"I told my mom anyway." My heart clogs my throat. "She confronted Dad, but then she agreed to keep it a secret to protect the church."

Alice shakes her head, confirming what I always suspected. God is never in favor of the cover-up. I'm released to continue.

"It messed her up. She ended up with a prescription for antidepressants and sleeping pills."

Alice's chin puckers. I see horror in her eyes as if she fears what's coming.

"She overdosed. I believe it was an accident, but that only made the loss more tragic."

Alice's eyes close. She leans forward, as if somehow praying right now will be retroactive and make a difference in the devastation that was my childhood. When I was supposed to be going to prom and planning for grad parties, I was attending my mother's funeral with the weight of her death on my shoulders.

"I am so sorry." She opens watery eyes. "You know it wasn't your fault, right?"

She's the first person who has had the knowledge to tell me this. She's the first person to know I need to hear it.

"It hurt too much to think if I hadn't told her about Dad's affair, she would still be alive. So I blamed my dad and left."

Her wrinkly lips press together. She's poised and controlled in sharing my grief. If I'd told this part of my story to Workout Wendy, she probably would have tracked down my dad to punch him. My desire to defend him is new.

"Until this weekend, I never considered that he might have blamed himself as well. I just figured he didn't come after me because he was relieved when I left. I took his secret with me, thus removing the threat of losing his position." I shrug away the assumption, remembering Dante's shame. "But part of me is starting to wonder if rather than being glad I'm not in his life, maybe he thinks I'm better off without him in mine."

"That is a heavy burden to bear. Especially as you were a child." She taps her chest. "Does Charlie know this?"

Charlie didn't break my heart. He just shattered one of the remaining pieces. "He doesn't know the specifics."

"That might change things."

"I don't see how." Charlie shouldn't have to give up his dreams to hold mine together.

She lifts her chin to study me down her nose. "Who have you shared this story with?"

I hold up a finger as if I'm going to count on my hand the number of people I've told, but I stop at one finger and point toward her.

She shakes her head in confusion. "Why me?"

"You asked," I say simply, though that's not entirely true. I scratch my cheek, recalling another deep conversation. "Up until Sunday I thought I had to do this by myself. I thought the necklace you gave me meant I fly alone. But for the first time, I'm starting to realize it wasn't God's will for my dad to choose his flock over me."

Alice leans forward. "Did God send someone to rescue you like a lost sheep?"

"Yes. My friend Workout Wendy." And maybe He loved me so much He sent more than one shepherd. I mean, I'm not alone right now either. "But also, I think, you."

She blinks back tears. "What a blessing to be used by God."

As if she doesn't make a difference in lives around her all day every day. "You are a blessing," I affirm, then I ponder the irony of my situation. "All this time, I've been afraid to share my secret, as if whoever knew wouldn't be able to love me anymore. But I think it's the other way around. Nobody can truly love me unless they truly know me."

"You are truly loved."

I let her words wash over me, expecting the drowning sensation that normally accompanies such a statement. But for the first time, I don't fight the current. I float on top.

Alice lifts an eyebrow. "You feel free like a bird?"

Her question reminds me of a video about ducks that went viral a while back. The birds swam in a river, their backs obliviously toward the waterfall that threatened to suck them over the edge. A group of onlookers chattered with growing concern about what appeared to be the birds' inevitable doom. Panic rose to a crescendo as the first duck reached the precipice. But instead of tipping over the falls and plummeting into the whitewater below, it simply soared away.

The viewers laughed with relief as much as with embarrassment because they'd had no reason to fear. The ducks had certainly never been afraid.

This is what it means to fly with my own wings. "Yes."

"May I ask you a question?"

"Absolutely." At this point, if she asked me, I would pay the woman for the pearls I brought in to sell.

I'd trade the world to continue feeling this loved. And maybe that's what Jesus was talking about when He told the parable of the pearl of great price. It's referring to the value of the kingdom of heaven, but this is heaven on earth. Is there anything better than being known and being loved?

Alice reaches across the table to grab my hand. The light in her gaze turning sober. "Child, is there anyone in the world who knows your dad enough to truly love him besides you?"

Chapter Thirty-One

CHARLIE

One does not fall in love; one grows into love, and love grows in him.
—KARL A. MENNINGER

Friday morning, Reverend Lemaire rises from his desk, looking the part of the dad who cleans his gun when a boy asks to date his daughter. He doesn't realize I'm armed with the truth.

"Sean told me you're working on a proposal video for my daughter." He lifts his chin to look down his Persian nose at me when we shake hands. "If you're planning to marry Nicole, it's about time we met."

I realize he's sizing me up, and I'm probably coming up lacking. While he's dressed in a plaid sport coat over his denim shirt, I'm wearing a hoodie. Though I picture myself in a hooded robe and boxing gloves as I enter the ring for round one.

Somehow, I play it cool the way Meri taught me. "I'm sorry I haven't gotten a chance to meet you before now." Because I am sorry. I'm sorry it took me flying halfway across the country to discover why his daughter's terrified of reaching out.

He returns to his spot behind the desk and motions for me to take one of the two cranberry leather chairs that look big enough to be recliners. If he's nervous that Nicole told me about his affair, then he's not showing it. Or I'm just that bad at reading body language.

"Charlie Newberg, is it?"

"Yes, sir." I settle in, placing my laptop bag on the desk between us and resting my forearms on my thighs. I believe this is the brace position demonstrated on our flight here, so apparently I'm prepared for things to get turbulent.

I didn't bring Gemma into the office, and I'm not filming our conversation. Though I have lots of footage to show Reverend Lemaire.

He motions to my laptop. "Sean told me you're the earthworm guy."

I wonder if Sean also told him about my Emmy, but he's trying to put me in my place. Good thing I've never really cared what others think. "I'm the earthworm guy."

He motions for me to proceed. "You're here to ask me for Nicole's hand in marriage?"

Loving Nicole means confronting her father with his extreme arrogance that he would expect anyone to ask his permission to marry a daughter he hasn't spoken to in over a decade.

I take a deep breath and meet his gaze. "The truth is, if I were going to ask your permission, it would have been five years ago when I first proposed to her. We planned a wedding that you weren't invited to, but she never walked down the aisle because I left to film a documentary in Peru."

He blinks, and I could be wrong, but his eyes harden as if he's angry at me. "You left my daughter, and now you're trying to win her back? You think getting me on your side will help your case?"

Oh boy. His hypocrisy is mind-blowing.

"This isn't a proposal video. It's a documentary about her life. I make documentaries when I love something, and I should have done so sooner. If I had, then I would've realized why she thought I was abandoning her when I was offered the opportunity in Peru."

His jaw clenches. His eyes narrow. Though he remains silent.

"I wanted her to go with me, but she must have felt I was choosing my ministry over her. The way her father did."

He bolts to his feet. "Is this some exposé on the church? Because if so, 'get behind me, Satan.'"

Whoa. I reel back at his response. Gemma tried to warn me he'd see himself as the good guy, which makes me the bad guy. But Satan?

"It's not an exposé." I rise to face him head-on. "I'm not here for me. I'm here for you. This project is for your daughter's eyes only. It's a chance for the two of you to reconnect."

He crosses his arms, but his chin drops. Does that mean he's considering?

I slide my laptop from its bag and open to clips I edited together just for him from the week's filming.

I started with his secretary. "Nicole was always a good girl. I don't understand how she could desert her father the way she did. I saw her in a television interview recently but was afraid to tell Pastor Lemaire in case it would cause him more pain."

Her old youth group leader. "I think there was a lot of pressure for Nicole to be perfect. When her mom died, she couldn't pretend anymore."

The neighbor lady. "I heard her yelling at her dad one night. He'd just lost his wife, and she blamed him. I'm amazed the poor man was able to keep it together and keep preaching. It's nothing short of a miracle."

Her best friend. "I still pray for her to come home."

I snap the laptop closed on the most powerful piece of film I've ever put together. This is not an exposé, but it's also not what Jesus ever intended for His followers. There's a pastor's daughter who has been very hurt by the church, and her dad would rather the congregation think she's in the wrong.

Reverend Lemaire rubs a hand over his face. It's shaking. "Why are you doing this?"

This is what I do. I believe it's why God brought me here. "Because I'm the only one who can."

He averts his eyes. "You know why she left?"

Is he still hoping I haven't put the pieces together? "She told me you cheated on her mom."

He gives a shaky breath. "Oh, God."

As backward as it seems, I do believe he's praying. "She couldn't keep your secret, and you let her go."

His eyes jolt up, frantic yet with a touch of remorse. "She told her mom about . . . about me, and it hurt my wife so much that she over-dosed. Can you imagine the pain if she'd told the church? I'd have all their lost souls on my hands."

He sounds as if he really believes it. "Keeping the secret is what killed your wife. Are you willing to sacrifice your daughter in the same way?"

"What? No." He pounds a fist into his opposite palm. "I'm sacri-ficing myself for God's work."

I frown at the mixed-up theology, but my narrowed gaze reveals a little of myself in him. I've been just as selfish.

Maybe I need to share what God's been teaching me through this. "Jesus left the flock to save one lost sheep."

Reverend Lemaire staggers toward his chair. He rolls it away from his desk far enough to drop in. What sounds like a sob escapes, though there are no tears.

I can't help wondering if it's theatrics. I wait.

He sits tall. Takes a deep breath. "God didn't remove King David from his position."

I hate it when sinners compare themselves to King David without having the same heart of repentance. David Lemaire is no David. He's a Saul, asking for undeserved honor. "God also didn't keep David's sin a secret."

This David turns his head toward me, dark gaze almost daring me to destroy God's reputation by telling the truth. Once again, I'm reminded of the Persian documentary I watched.

"Sir, I don't know your heritage because I don't know much about you at all, but you do share a wider nasal dorsal projection with your daughter."

He looks at me as though I'm a weirdo, which also reminds me of his daughter. I consider this a good sign.

"I watched a documentary recently on the Persian obsession with nose jobs."

His mouth opens as if to defend himself or maybe attack me. But I'm on his side, so I don't let him cut me off.

"The documentary explained the record-setting rate of surgeries as part of the Islamic culture that pursues perfection. In this same way, Muslims don't understand the Bible because it includes all kinds of scandalous stories about the heroes of faith."

He closes his mouth.

"But actually it's the Bible's honesty about those scandals that makes God's love even more amazing. He can handle our messes."

Reverend Lemaire looks away again.

"I personally relate to Jonah. God called me to love Nicole, and I ran the other way."

The man reaches for his throat in a gesture that is, once again, reminiscent of Nicole. "I can't . . ."

"I'm sure this is all a shock."

His hand slides up over his face and through his thick gray hair, making it stick up as if he has devil horns.

Who's Satan now?

"You're honestly not going public with this?" he asks in the voice of a scared child, and I'm reminded that our battle is not against flesh and blood. This guy is loved by God as much as I am. As much as his daughter is.

I take a deep breath. It's tempting to play the role of prophet here, but I want more for Nicole. More for him. "I'm a truth teller, but this isn't my story to tell."

He nods and stares off into space.

"Would you like to say anything on camera for Nicole?"

He shudders. "I can't . . . I can't take the chance that she'd use it against me."

"Okay." I stand. But I have one more thought. "Do you know how I ended up here?" Of course, he doesn't. Rhetorical question. "She's a marketing director for Slice of Heaven Pizza. She signed a deal with PGA golfer Dante Sullivan to represent the pizza company."

He comes out of his fog. "Dante Sullivan just confessed to cheating on his wife."

"Exactly." I slide my laptop into the case and grab the handle. "Nicole lost the deal after that. Which freed her up to sign me as a client."

His dark brows draw together, obviously not connecting the dots.

"I've discovered what love really is because a Christian celebrity confessed his sins. What the enemy planned for evil, God is using for good. And He can do that in your life too."

Reverend Lemaire's shoulders sag. His countenance droops along with it. "Tell Nicole I love her."

I stride to the door. "When you learn what real love is, you'll be able to do that yourself."

Chapter Thirty-Two

NICOLE

Oh, how a quiet love can drown out every fear.
—JESSICA KATOFF

My nausea is back. I hold a hand to my stomach and stare at Alice in shock. "My dad cheated on my mom, lied to the whole church about it, and expected us to do the same. She died trying to keep that secret. I told him I wouldn't lie for him, and he let me go at the age of eighteen. He's the one who should be making amends. He's the parent."

She nods along, not arguing with one word.

"When I spoke with Dante, I told him he needed to pursue his wife, not the other way around."

Alice nods again.

I throw my arms in the air. "If you agree with me, why are you telling me to rescue my dad? He's not a lost sheep. He's a wolf in sheep's clothing."

Alice tilts her head in compassion. "I don't want you to get bitten again."

"Thank you."

"But you can keep your distance while extending your crook."

I had a pink plastic crook when I was little. It went with the Bo Peep costume I wore for our church harvest party in second grade. Dad had been Buzz Lightyear.

My chin quivers at the happy memory. It's been a long time since I've had any happy memories of him. But that doesn't help me understand where she's coming from. I cry aloud, "What does that even mean?"

She leans forward. "It means you don't go into the dark with him. You invite him into the light."

She makes it sound so easy. But it's not. "I still don't understand what you want me to do."

"Jesus is the light. Stay with Him, and He'll give you direction." She opens a desk drawer and pulls out one of those huge checkbooks that holds three checks per page. I suppose she's still going to try to pay me for the pearls I once won from her store.

I push to my feet. I have to move. Yes, I've found freedom in being loved, but the idea that I'm expected to know how to love others makes me feel trapped back in my birdcage.

"Alice, don't write a check. I'll just put the pearls in the silent auction, and all the money can go to Ecuador. You've already given me too much."

She glances up, then points at the bottom of her lip. "You okay? You look like you have a red bump forming. Is it hives?"

Oh, great. I rub my lips together, causing pressure to reveal the tender spot. My cold sore is back. And with the red-carpet premiere coming up. As if I'm not under enough stress. "I get these sores when I'm tense. I'd better go put some ointment on it."

She rises and walks me to the door. "If you change your mind about the necklace and decide to keep it or want a check from me, those are both acceptable decisions. I support you."

I sigh because I don't know what to do with all her analogies and advice, but I appreciate her support. "There you go again. Being amazing."

She smiles and pauses at the corkboard by her door. It's littered with all kinds of thank-you cards from people like me. There are also a few articles about her shop. My gaze snags on one that looks familiar. It's the one that includes the photo of Charlie proposing to me on the aerial tram.

I grimace, pointing to the photo. "You printed it out?"

"Of course. It's the moment that brought you to me."

I stare at the happy couple. Their happiness didn't last ever after, but it did bring Alice and me together. Her love is helping me heal. "Of that, I'm grateful."

I don't believe God sent Charlie to marry me, but I do believe God allowed Charlie to believe it for many reasons. One being our partnership for the Gold Standard. Besides saving a city in Ecuador, it saved my career. It helped me reconnect with Alice. It got me back in church. It showed me what love really is.

I'm not ready to rebuild any bridges with my dad, but maybe I do want to reconnect with my heavenly Father. And what better way to do so than on a hike to the highest point of the city?

The trail part of the 4T Trail is harder than I remember. Perhaps because I haven't hiked for years. Perhaps because there are gray clouds forming in the distance, and I'm a little concerned about not bringing a jacket with a hood. Perhaps because when Charlie was with me, I was too happy to feel the pain of exertion.

I cross the bridge over the loud highway and almost get lost when the path runs into the side of a road. But I follow the signs and breathe in the evergreen and damp-earth scent that remind me so much of my ex.

On the day Charlie proposed—the first time—we were also trying to beat a storm to the top of the peak. Of course, I didn't know he was planning to ask me to marry him, and I'd rushed him from the peak into the aerial tram, where we ended up getting engaged.

If I could go back, I'm not sure I would do anything different. Getting engaged had made it a beautiful day. It didn't turn out the way I'd hoped it would, but other beautiful things came from it.

I emerge into Council Crest Park with its breathtaking views. The peaks of all three mountains are hidden by clouds, but I can still see the city and colorful trees in the valley below. Because it's a workday, and probably because it's chilly out, I have the area to myself. But I can't explain why there's a white piano in the center of the round cement viewpoint. If Charlie were here, I'd play him a song, but since he's not, I walk to the stone wall surrounding the area and take a seat.

This peacefulness is a far cry from the city below, and I'm reminded that I enjoyed hiking for reasons other than time with Charlie. I enjoyed it for all the things that drew me to Oregon in the first place. The mountains. The pine trees. The waterfalls. Clear lakes.

Of course, there are things I miss about Kansas too. Unlike Portland, our summer showers were warm. I'd ride my bikes through the puddles afterward and never get a goose bump. Our nights stayed warm too.

Yeah, tornadoes were scary, and our church would band together to help clean up homes that had been destroyed, but I have many fond memories of playing Uno in the musty basement as the driving rain pelted the roof and the lights flickered. We always prayed for those in the path of danger.

I found comfort in my dad's prayers as a girl. He wasn't only my father, he was the pastor. He could do no wrong. Or so I'd thought.

I still believe what my dad taught from the Bible, but only because I've read enough Scripture to understand it on my own. I've come to rely on my personal study now because I don't trust pastors. Or men.

The thought strikes me from out of the blue. I don't trust men?

Alice was right about my hang-up with marriage. It's the same hang-up I have with church. I've been flying alone because I feel safer flying alone.

An eagle soars overhead, catching my attention. Its huge wings flap high and low as it swoops straight past, white head leading the way. I sit back in awe, feeling this moment was crafted just for me in the same way my necklace was.

My eagle circles and darts. No destination, simply enjoying his journey. I enjoy it too. The majesty. The splendor.

Sadly, for both of us, that storm is still coming. Billowing gray clouds slink over the trees, threatening to block my view. I expect the eagle to take off to find shelter. Instead, he turns toward the weather and rides the wind higher. He's above the clouds.

My heart thumps with new meaning. If I'm going to fly with my own wings, I must take that which comes against me and use it to lift me higher.

My dad failed me. Charlie failed me too. But that doesn't have to be the end. I can accept the truth and offer mercy. I can love them anyway.

A light raindrop grazes my cheek. It's no Kansas shower, but it's the mist and trickle that bring constant growth. I feel it in my heart. In my toes. In my fingertips.

I rise, but instead of running toward the aerial tram to escape the storm this time, I turn toward the piano. Mom and I used to play together. She taught me the basics for church and Christmas. She also taught me "Tears in Heaven" by Eric Clapton to play at funerals.

I run my fingers over the keys, and the melody unlocks so many childhood memories that I don't know what to do with them all. I watch my former life like an old-fashioned slideshow. It looked so perfect before it fell apart.

I'll never be that little girl again. I'll never have my mom back. But maybe I could have my dad back.

If I reach out, what's the worst that could happen? He could reject me. He could lie and/or blame me for his mistakes. But I wouldn't be any worse off than I am right now. In fact, I'd be better, because I'd know I'm capable of loving people who don't deserve it. Which is the only kind of love that lasts.

My fingers slip against the wet ivories, ruining the song but not ruining the moment. "Tears in Heaven" should always be played on the top of a mountain in the rain. Then when the sun comes out, it would be a reminder that Jesus said He'll wipe away our every tear.

If my mom is watching me from heaven right now, I hope she knows I miss her, but I don't blame her. In fact, I wonder if part of her reason for keeping Dad's secret was to protect me. That doesn't make it right, but it makes it relatable.

In what might have been Mom's best effort at keeping our family together, I ended up losing both parents. It was a tragedy for us all, and I've spent a long time mourning the life I should have had. But now it's time to use that which comes against me to lift me higher.

It's time to fly home.

Chapter Thirty-Three

CHARLIE

You don't love someone because they're perfect. You love them in spite of the fact that they're not.
—JODI PICOULT, MY SISTER'S KEEPER

Gemma watches the mini documentary with arms crossed. "You did fine, but I was hoping for more."

"Same." I sigh and close the laptop. We've been here almost a week, and our flight home leaves in three hours. "There are some cute things, like the photo of Nicole playing piano with her mom and the video footage of her knocking her dad into the dunk tank at a church picnic. I'm just afraid that without Reverend Lemaire participating in the documentary, the memories won't be happy ones."

"It makes me sad." Gemma sniffs, though she's been known to sob in the shower over the imaginary characters she makes up for her screenplays.

I shrug, helpless. "I don't know what else to do."

My phone buzzes in my back pocket. Probably Meri from Maui. She knows what we're up to and is dying to see the final result, even though she's on her honeymoon. I guess people in love just want everyone to be in love.

Grace Chapel.

"What's wrong?" Gemma asks before I even realize I've stiffened.

I hold the phone up for her to see.

"Answer it."

I swipe and try to come up with some scenario where it's not Nicole's dad on the phone calling to say he's changed his mind. I don't want to be disappointed when it's simply Sean asking what beard oil I use. Yeah, it's probably Sean.

I announce myself. "Charlie Newberg."

Someone clears his throat.

My pulse quickens. Sean wouldn't need to clear his throat before asking about beard oil.

"Charlie, this is David Lemaire."

I hold a finger to my lips to hush Gemma, even though she's not making a sound. I just need total silence, and she tends to squeal about exciting things.

"What can I do for you, Reverend?"

Gemma squeals.

I plug my ear that's not pressed to the earpiece.

"I've decided I have something to say for your documentary."

I cannot wait to hug Nicole. I don't know what her dad is going to say, but it has to be something good. Right?

I glance at my watch. We'll make this work. "That's great, sir. Our flight leaves in a few hours, but we can stop by the church on our way."

Quiet. Then . . . "I was hoping you would stay for the whole service."

My heartbeat drums in my ears even louder than Gemma's squeals. I cannot wait to get off the phone and ask her if this means what I think it means. So I ask Nicole's dad. "Does this mean what I think it means?"

"I don't know yet."

But he's asked us to be there with the understanding that we know his secrets and could at any time spill them to someone in the congregation. If he's at least considering a public confession, our presence might encourage him that direction.

I hadn't intended for a public confession. I thought maybe he'd want to talk to his elders first. Or even simply tell his daughter he misses her.

This news will devastate many. Hearts will bleed. Faith will be shaken. And he's going to lose his job.

"I'm praying for you." I hang up and hit my knees.

What did I do?

Gemma and I sweat through worship, and it looks like Reverend Lemaire is sweating in the front row too. His glasses keep slipping down his nose anyway. I feel bad that Nicole can't be here, though I'm filming from the front row of the balcony for her.

The building is too modern to have traditional pews. In fact, it's more like half a stadium with normal chairs on the floor level while the risers around have the kind of seats that have to be folded down. We face the stage with five screens that show enlarged versions of what's going on from different angles. I wonder if this building was even here when Nicole attended Grace Chapel.

I scan the crowd. Though I interviewed quite a few people this week, I don't recognize a familiar face. I wonder if that's better or worse than if someone were to wave at me now, then get angry later when they realize my presence played a part in what happened.

Though what if it doesn't happen? What if Reverend Lemaire doesn't go through with it? That doesn't mean he never will. He might even be better off getting some counsel from leadership, or at least giving them a heads-up.

All too soon he rises to take the stage. He wipes his forehead and asks an usher to bring him a glass of water.

Please, Lord. Be with David Lemaire. Be with everyone here listening. May hearts be healed. Give them all faith in Your relentless love.

"I want to thank everyone for coming today." Reverend Lemaire's head moves to look across the rows and stops when he's facing me.

I nod from behind my camera phone.

His chest rises and falls in a close-up on all five screens, and I wonder if the sermon is being shown live over social media or even on television. If it's being recorded by cameras other than mine, video clips could make the evening news. He's not only talking to the couple thousand or so in this sanctuary. He's talking to the world.

He pauses and looks down at his notes. "As some of you know, there's a man here who is making a documentary about my daughter, Nicole."

My stomach knots.

"A lot of you haven't met her because she hasn't been home since she left for college twelve years ago. Until I watched recorded footage, I didn't realize that those of you who do remember her have negative opinions of her for leaving." He looks up. Looks toward me. "So I need to set the record straight."

A murmur sweeps through the crowd.

Gemma grabs my arm, bumping the camera.

I jab her away with my elbow.

"Oh sorry," she whispers when she realizes what she did.

I'll have to edit that out.

"Nicole is a better person than I am." Reverend Lemaire nods as he says this, as if confirming it to himself.

Nervous chuckles.

"She left because I asked her to keep a secret, but no more. I'm here to confess that . . . I've broken every single one of the Ten Commandments."

The murmur rises to a dull roar.

I am so proud of this man I could cry. He's got some ugly truths to confess, but the truth is about to set him free.

"Commandment number one." He holds up a finger, reclaiming the congregation's attention. "We are to have no other gods before Him. I've put your opinion of me above God's opinion of me."

The crowd simmers with almost a collective sigh of relief. They're okay with being his god. That's probably what many churchgoers look for without realizing it. They want a pastor who gives them what they want.

"Number two. We aren't to have idols." Reverend Lemaire shakes his head. "I've been arrogant, and an arrogant man is a god unto himself. I've become my own idol."

A few people even chuckle at this. Apparently, arrogance is acceptable, as well.

"Number three. We aren't to use the Lord's name in vain." He sighs. "I've done this in my self-centered prayers. I've done it every time I preached a sermon that I myself don't follow. I've used God's name for my own glory and have become a hypocrite."

Heads turn toward each other, likely sharing concern once again.

"Number four." Now that he's got the ball rolling, he's powering through to the biggie. "The Sabbath is for intentional time with God. I've been intentionally avoiding Him."

Whoa.

"Number five. I have dishonored the heritage of faith my parents passed down. They'd be ashamed of what I'm about to tell you. They trained me better. Number six—"

Murder. I glance at Gemma.

"I killed my wife."

No . . . My mouth parts.

All around me people gasp and shout and get halfway up out of their seats. One woman breaks out in hysterical sobs. I briefly wonder if she's the other woman. Or a new wife. Could Reverend Lemaire have remarried?

"I didn't give Melanie the pills, but I'm the reason she was taking them. Because number seven—"

The room collectively freezes.

"I cheated on her."

More gasping and crying. Gemma's even crying, and she knew about this. I guess she's crying because her heart breaks for things that break the heart of God.

"My daughter, Nicole, caught me with another woman and told her mom. I apologized to them both as well as to the other woman. I promised never to cheat again. But I also asked them not to tell anyone. I claimed it was to protect the church, when really it was to hide my own guilt." Reverend Lemaire continues on as though he doesn't know most public confessions tend to be vague and presented in a way that displays the pastor in the best light possible. "My wife respected my request to her own detriment. My daughter could not, so she left."

Heads shake. Noses sniff. A couple in the front stands and walks out as if in support of Nicole. Except I know she wouldn't want this for anyone.

"This is how I broke commandment number eight. I stole Nicole's good reputation."

How will Nicole feel when she sees this video? Will she rejoice to discover that her dad does love her, or hurt all over again for the pain this community is now experiencing?

I give a sad smile. This is the saddest moment of my life. Thousands of people are having their hearts shattered.

"Number nine includes over a decade of lies. This brings me to number ten." He looks to heaven as if praying for help. "After destroying my family with my sin, I have coveted every one of your happy families." His face crumples and his body racks with sobs. He wipes his tears and fights for composure. "I am so sorry. So, so sorry."

The crowd stares in shock. The man they revered as the Great and Powerful Oz has pulled his own curtain back to reveal himself as a mere human. Broken. A sinner.

A couple of men in ties climb the stairs to wrap an arm around Pastor Lemaire in a hug. One on either side of him. They seem as stunned as everyone else, but they are offering mercy.

One of them steps in to pray, while Nicole's dad sobs in the other man's arms. It's a rare sight. So rare that Alice once told me there is folklore about pearls being the tears of Adam and Eve, with the rare black pearls as Adam's tears since men cry less. My throat constricts as if choked by black pearls.

The prayer ends too soon because, in this room where confession pours forth and mercy mops it up, there's a sense of holiness. A sense of rightness. A sense that Nicole's dad has led by example, and everyone else is going to have their eyes opened to sins in their own lives.

I know I have.

"Thank you." The reverend blows out a loud breath in the microphone, then laughs at the unexpected sound. It echoes throughout the room, as well. "I didn't even know if I had the guts to confess this morning. I've been so afraid, and now I don't have to be afraid anymore."

Sean stands and yells out, "We love you, Pastor Lemaire."

Someone else starts a slow clap. Around us, a few people join in. It turns into applause.

"No. Stop." The reverend weeps once more as the cheers slow to a trickle. "I appreciate your support, but I don't deserve any praise. That would mock the lives I've destroyed."

Whoa. This is for real.

"All this time I've pretended to be an example of God's love, but I'm nothing but an example of why we need God's love."

I pray David Lemaire remains this sincere. And I pray this congregation supports his healing process. When he gets attacked on social media or ripped apart by the press, which he will, he's going to need a core group to help him stay focused on God's truths.

He wipes his face, and someone in the front row tosses up a tissue box. He blows a little too loud, but it's not any worse than the other things he's already asked forgiveness for.

Nicole's dad clears his throat in the same way he did over the phone this morning. "I'll be stepping down and letting the elders take over with what happens next. They're finding out about this along with you, so please give them mercy as well. I don't know what I'm going to be doing other than tracking down my daughter to seek her forgiveness. Please keep us both in your prayers."

Oh, I will.

The band steps back onstage to lead us in subdued worship, creating an environment for continued prayer. As the assistant pastor encourages us to examine our own hearts, I ask God to prepare Nicole's heart for an upcoming reunion.

Chapter Thirty-Four

NICOLE

I saw that you were perfect, and so I loved you.
Then I saw that you were not perfect, and I loved
you even more.
—ANGELITA LIM

I stand in front of William's desk with my hands clasped. I'm not even taking the time to sit down. I've been running around like crazy this week, trying to plan my trip home while finishing up Charlie's premiere planning, and there's still too much to do.

William motions to his lip, obviously referencing the spot on mine where the old cold sore is back in full force. Crazy how I've forgotten about it, but then again, I accidentally put mascara on only one eye this morning too.

"You need some more of my ointment?" he offers.

"If you have any handy. Otherwise, don't worry about it. I'm headed out of town."

He leans back in his chair. "Really? Don't you have a movie premiere this evening?"

Charlie. I hate to miss his moment, but if I want a solid foundation for spending the rest of our lives together, I have to confront my daddy issues first. "I'm sending Morgan in my place and taking two weeks of vacation, effective immediately. I put in for the days off with HR, and they've been approved."

His eyebrows arch. "Where are you spending your vacation?" This isn't business anymore. I love that he cares enough to ask.

"Wichita, Kansas."

"Naturally." He scratches his head. "This doesn't have anything to do with avoiding your client, does it?"

"It has everything to do with Charlie. But not in the way you would think."

"I have no idea what to think." He holds out a hand. "I've never had a publicist so inspired by a client that she takes off the most important day of their campaign to head to the heartland of America."

I smile. I've never thought of Kansas as heartland before, but I like it. "I'm in love with Charlie, so I'm going to attempt to make things right with my dad in order to love from a healthier place."

"Love is a beautiful thing." William chuckles, but not in a mocking way. He's happy for me. "I hope that works out for you." He removes his glasses and uses them to motion toward me. "I mean the dad thing. I know the Charlie thing will work out."

I sigh in contentment. Charlie has no idea I won't be at the premiere. He has no idea I'm going home. He has no idea I want to spend the rest of my life with him. But I'm pretty sure we'd both agree it's God's will now.

William folds his hands together. "After these two weeks, should I expect you to return to work for me?"

I've been debating that one. I want to work with Charlie, and only with Charlie, but there's no rush for me to take off to foreign countries yet. We can date long distance and figure this out as we go. We could have figured it out five years ago if we'd each been a little more willing to put the other before self. We obviously had some growing to do first.

"Would you be willing to let me work with Charlie exclusively? I can continue running the Gold Standard campaign until his next documentary is ready to be promoted."

William slides his glasses back on. "I'll consider it. But let's see how well the premiere goes first. You sure you don't want to attend?"

I motion to the open lesion. "You want me to go like this?"

"I guess you have a point. We have a reputation to uphold." He huffs. "By the way, what is going on with your eye makeup?"

"I was in a rush this morning."

One corner of his lips curves up. "Did you ever think love would do this to you?"

"I didn't know what love was before now."

Chapter Thirty-Five

CHARLIE

*In the absence of love . . . there is nothing, nothing
in this world worth fighting for.*
—KEVIN COSTNER AS STEPHEN, *THE WAR*

I know Nicole wants to avoid me, but I never imagined she'd no-show my premiere. I thought she'd be right here by my side as I step out of the limo onto the red carpet. She seemed to like my beanie with the sport coat idea, and I wanted to see her reaction.

Cameras flash. Paparazzi shout my name. Where were they when I released my earthworm film?

I make my way up the carpet, scanning for her dark brown bob and some stylish dress in the color of a Kansas sky. But she's not here. I'd feel her presence.

I stop to answer a few questions from reporters. They only want to know about the gold and jewels being auctioned off. It's not so much me the media is interested in as it is the glitz and glam. We'll see what they think after I'm almost buried alive in an attempt to save a South American village. There's no glam in that.

I make my way into the lobby. Armed guards monitor the tables set up with jewelry that's been donated for the auction. Alice stands at the end.

I stride over and give her a kiss on the cheek. "Have you seen Nicole?"

"Not since she tried to sell me this." She nods down to a black pearl necklace. It looks like the one Nicole wore to Meri's wedding. The prize for winning our kissing contest.

"Why?"

Alice presses her lips together, her eyes missing their twinkle. "I think she was trying to get rid of the reminder of you."

Dagger to my heart. Will anything change after she reconnects with her dad? That's not why I went in search of him, but it's my deepest desire.

I glance at the prices listed as bids for the pearls, then add a grand to the highest number. "Will you keep an eye on this for me?" I request. "I want to be the highest bidder."

She nods approvingly. "I'd love to."

Morgan heads my way with her clipboard. She's frowning, so she's probably coming to tell me some good news. Hopefully it's that Nicole is on her way and will be taking over the event momentarily.

I sigh with relief. This is the night I've been planning for, and not because I'm premiering my latest film.

"Mr. Newberg?" The assistant leans forward to speak into my ear and above the noise. "I have bad news."

"Great."

She pulls back far enough to shoot me a puzzled expression. "What's great about Nicole not coming?"

I run a hand through my hair, knocking my beanie to the floor, and ruining my artsy appearance. "I thought you were going to tell me she's almost here. You're only cheerful when you have bad news, and you're glum when things go my way."

Morgan pauses to consider. "I guess I have been that way." She squats and retrieves my beanie.

I accept it cautiously. Who is this woman?

"After you told me you were making a documentary on my boss, I stopped hating you so much."

"Fabulous." But not what matters in this moment. "Why isn't Nicole coming?"

Morgan taps a pen against her dimpled chin. "She's taking a vacation. To Kansas."

Nicole is planning to reconnect with her dad? How did that happen? I hope I didn't ruin everything when she gets there and finds out her dad confessed to the congregation and resigned.

Gemma bounces over, looking as angelic as ever and with her soldier of a boyfriend in tow. "I'm so excited. Where's Nicole?"

"She's not coming."

Meri picks that moment to pop her nose into our conversation. It's extra freckled from her time in Hawaii. "Nicole has to come."

Kai strolls up, munching popcorn. "I thought you were going to give her a private showing of the documentary you made afterward."

The crowd streams past us to find their seats. We're going to have to start the film while Nicole is heading to the airport to fly away.

Morgan looks between us, then arches a sculpted eyebrow my direction. "So you did make the documentary?"

"I did." The assistant doesn't know the half of it. This is crazy. With all the money Nicole helped me raise, Ecuador is saved, but I can't tell her that she's the real treasure in my life.

Morgan pulls out her phone. "I'm going to text her that the old equipment here corrupted the film roll. Then she'll have to bring down a digital file."

I want to jump on board with the plan, but all of Nicole's relationships have been corroded by the lie her dad had wanted her to tell. "You're going to lie?"

Morgan taps on her phone and sends the text. "It's not a lie. It's a surprise. Like a party or a gift."

"I don't know. What if she brings the digital file up to the projector room and sees the reels still intact? She'll feel manipulated, like the last time we were here." I can't hurt her more.

Morgan's phone chimes. She glances at the incoming text, then looks up with a shrug. "Too late. She's heading to the airport, but she's got the film on her computer drive, and she'll drop it off on her way. I'll tell her to let the valets park her car. She's only five minutes out."

My heart hammers. Nicole's coming. This is happening. If I don't mess it up. "I've got to destroy the reels."

"What?" Kai demands around a mouthful of popcorn.

I dart up the stairway and into the projector room.

He follows.

Ace looks up from where he's adjusting dials. "Everything's set."

"We have to mess it up."

"Nerves?" He nods with empathy. "It's going to be all right. This flick is even better than your earthworm film."

"No. Remember the short that I asked you to play later tonight? The girl I want to play it for wasn't going to come, but her assistant talked her into it. Only she said the film reel was corrupted. So we have to corrupt it to keep her from thinking I'm trying to manipulate her."

"That sounds kind of manipulative to me."

I reach around him, trying to pull the spool from the frame. "It's sacrificial. I'm willing to ruin my film debut for her benefit."

He karate chops my arm away. "Don't touch my equipment."

For the first time ever I wish I'd taken more kickboxing classes with Nicole. I might need backup. "Kai, go get Karson."

Kai slides me the side-eye. "What for, dude? You want to arrest the theater manager for protecting his equipment?"

"Yes. You get it."

"Charlie." The deep voice comes from the man watching our scuffle from the corner. He was supposed to stay hidden until after Nicole sees his confession on tape. "Why isn't my daughter coming?"

I drop my arms. How do I tell Nicole's dad that she's on her way to Wichita after he came all the way here for her? Maybe he'll be touched. Though it doesn't help our goal. "She's heading to the airport to fly to Kansas."

His eyebrows quirk in and out a couple times. "She is? She's going to see me?"

I lift a shoulder. "It looks that way."

My watch vibrates. I glance down at the message on my wrist. "It's Morgan. She says Nicole found her in the theater below and handed over her laptop. Now she's trying to leave."

Kai takes off for the door. "I'll stop her."

He has a better chance of catching up with her than I do. "He ran track in college," I explain to her dad.

Reverend Lemaire—or should I say Mr. Lemaire?—is quiet as he leans to peer through the window at the crowded, dimly lit theater below. He points to the woman in pigtails by the right exit. "Is that her?"

I do a double take. She's not wearing one of her fancy dresses. She's in sweats, and yes, pigtails. Certainly not how I imagined tonight going. "That's her."

We watch her head toward the swinging door. I hold my breath, waiting for Kai to intercept her.

The swinging doors on the left fly open. He's at the wrong set of theater doors.

I tap on the glass to try to get his attention. "Kai. Other door."

He looks around, but there's still a bunch of people at the back of the theater. He can't see her.

She turns to exit.

Mr. Lemaire blows out a deep breath. "Play Nicole's story."

Ace rolls his lips together and bugs his eyes my way.

I'm the one who rented the theater. I have the final say.

Mr. Lemaire looks down toward his daughter. "If you really are willing to sabotage your premiere out of love for my daughter, the least I can do is sacrifice myself as well."

I want to savor the beauty in this moment, but we don't have time. "Hit it, Ace."

Chapter Thirty-Six

NICOLE

Love is a game that two can play and both win.
—Eva Gabor

I look at my watch and smile at the memory of Charlie talk-texting me over his watch the last time I was here. I'm excited to be reconnecting with him, but I don't want him to see me now. I don't want anybody to see me right now in sweats, pigtails, and this huge sore on my lip. But Charlie in particular, because if I see him, it will be so hard to leave him that I'll be in danger of missing my flight.

Going to find my dad has to be my first priority. He's my lost sheep.

The event seems to be a smashing success. Morgan handled it well. Except for the destroyed film reel, though I can't blame her for that.

There was even a huge bidding war on the black pearl necklace. My heart mourns the loss, though I know the money is going to a good cause. And hopefully the strand becomes a symbol of unending love for another woman who needs it.

I turn and jog toward the back door of the theater. This is when wearing my cross trainers to a red-carpet movie premiere comes in handy.

"Nicole Lemaire." I hear my name but not from anybody around. It's coming through the sound system. Everyone in the theater heard my name.

The lights dim and color reflects off the screen behind me. I turn to see what's playing. I watched all of Charlie's documentary, and my name wasn't mentioned once. I would have remembered that.

"Nicole Lemaire." A woman's voice.

"Nicole Lemaire." Is that my old youth group leader? He's lost some hair.

"I called her Nikki." Sean Brumley. My high school crush apparently turned out more handsome than expected. Or maybe I just find beards attractive now.

But what is he doing talking about me on-screen at Charlie's premiere? I've got to be dreaming.

I look up toward the projection room.

Charlie waves. I recognize his silhouette. With the facial hair and beanie, it's hard to miss.

This isn't a dream. It's Charlie's premiere. But this isn't the film Charlie made.

Is it?

There is no way he went to Kansas instead of the Philippines. No. Way.

If Charlie went to my old church and met my dad, he would have found out my dad's still preaching. He would have confronted him. That couldn't have turned out well.

Even if my dad is as sorry as Dante Sullivan, he doesn't know Charlie. He doesn't know I've been engaged twice without inviting him to either wedding.

I was supposed to tell Dad all of that. I was on my way to do so.

Charlie appears on-screen in front of the giant Native American statue in Wichita. He's at the Keeper of the Plains.

As a teen, the island had become my sanctuary, and the sculpture a reminder that there was Someone greater than my dad in charge. He was the one I looked up to when my dad let me down.

I cover my mouth and press backward against the wall.

"My name is Charlie Newberg, and I'm in love with Nicole Lemaire."

The crowd in front of me turns their heads to look at each other. This isn't what they expected either.

Who does this?

"We were engaged once, but I messed it up. Now that she's back in my life, I realize I need to show her I understand love this time around."

"Charlie . . ." He's dumbfounded me yet again.

He continues in his authentic way, reminding me that other people's opinions shouldn't matter so much. "Thus, I did what I always do when I'm passionate about something. I filmed a documentary about her."

I'm the subject and the audience. He did this for me.

A laugh bursts out. Okay, I'm both dumbfounded and happy.

A video of my kindergarten Christmas program plays on-screen. A photo of middle school camp in our matching T-shirts. My volleyball team at the state playoffs.

Back to Charlie. "This was my first trip to Kansas. I never even met Nicole's family before this week. And I realized, rather than her choosing to spend the rest of her life with me, the more important option is the possibility of reuniting her with her dad."

My heart throbs bigger and bigger as if it might explode.

Dad appears on-screen. "Hey, sweetheart."

He's talking to me. I don't remember the last time my dad called me sweetheart. Yes, I do. It was when he took me out for a root beer float the night before I found him with Ms. Shannon.

Charlie again. "I noticed something strange when I talked to people who knew Nicole as a child. They all seemed to think she'd deserted her dad, though I knew that's not how things went down."

I ball my fingernails into my palms. Dad was already in the film, so it couldn't have gone too horribly.

Dad. "I failed you, Nicole. And I need to ask your forgiveness."

I gasp for air.

Because there's also footage of him asking the whole church for forgiveness.

He confessed to breaking every one of the ten commandments.

He sobbed in another pastor's arms.

He silenced applause.

He's not the father I left.

"You deserve better than me."

Tears rain down, and I smear them out of the way so as not to miss a frame. I don't care so much that my dad messed up as I do that he wants to be my dad again.

I'm not lost anymore though. I can't wait to run to him. But I'm going to miss my flight now. I'll have to settle for running to Charlie. I can hardly wait until this story of my life ends, so I can move forward into our future.

The film is well done. Silly when I knock my dad into the dunk tank. Poignant when my mom and I play "Tears in Heaven."

The lights flip on overhead. Everyone is wiping tears, and I feel bad for the women who wore lots of makeup for this event. At least I only had mascara on one eye.

The theater crowd stands and cheers. Their ovation thrums through my soul. This isn't a religious crowd, but we all want redemption, don't we? We all want to be loved.

What my dad thought would turn people away from the church could very well do the opposite. Because that's what truth and mercy do.

The audience kind of looks around as if trying to figure out what happens next. I'm right there with them. I may have planned this event, but it was never in my hands.

Another round of applause, and I check to see what the crowd is cheering about now. They're looking past me.

I bite my lip above the sore that must be bleeding because it tastes like copper, and I turn to greet the man who loves me despite my imperfections. Charlie has outdone himself.

Except it's not Charlie.

It's my dad. With gray hair.

I gasp. And I run. I wrap my arms around the guy who taught me how to drive and always beat me at Uno. The guy whose leather scent brings back even more memories. I want that for us again. And he must have wanted it enough to let go of the rest of his life for this.

"You're here," I cry, and lean back to look at his face.

"I'm sorry it took me so long."

I hold his cheeks between my palms. He wears glasses now. His skin droops around his jaw. He's got hair coming out of his ears. And I've never seen anything so wonderful in all the world.

I'd thought I wanted a quiet life by myself. I thought I wanted to avoid church and relationships. But what I really wanted was to believe in love again.

"You look so much like your mother," he whispers. And we both cry.

Then we have to go out to the lobby, because the real film premiere is starting and they don't want us talking in the back row as we catch up on things from the heartland.

Alice is there, and I introduce her to my dad. Though I'm a little sad to see the pearls are gone.

"Nicole Lemaire?" This time the voice isn't booming through the loudspeaker. It's right behind me, and it's achingly familiar.

I turn to face the other man who loves me enough to pursue me. "I can't believe you did this."

He shrugs. "It was Morgan's idea."

"How is that possible?"

He steps forward. "I'm not sure. I thought she was trying to poison me with arsenic."

"That sounds more like her." I grin and shake my head. "Yet she colluded with you to get me here tonight, huh?"

"It was fun while it lasted." He grimaces. "Unfortunately, Morgan also heard me tell Alice to bid on the pearls for me. She drove the price higher and higher."

I gasp. I'd seen the bids. "She didn't."

"She did. But you're worth it." He lifts the strand. "They can be yours again if you make out with me for three hours, two minutes, and fifty-seven seconds."

He added a second, and I adore him for it. "Is that all?"

He steps behind me to clasp the necklace around my neck. His roommates watch from the stairway, while Dad and Alice are lost in conversation. Something about starting a retreat center for fallen pastors the way my mom had once suggested.

And I can't help thinking I'm glad Charlie and I didn't get married back when we were first engaged.

We would have missed this moment of redemption.

Charlie spins me to face him and adjusts my two necklaces so they don't tangle on each other. He lifts the one with the inscription. "Is it cliché if I tell you I want to be the wind beneath your wings?"

As cliché as it is, his words give me warm fuzzies. "Just don't say it too loudly or Gemma will come try to rewrite this scene. She's very anti-cliché."

He glances over my shoulder to make sure he's in the clear, then whispers, "Well, it's true. I want to help you soar."

He already has. In his own unique way.

"Weirdo," I whisper back.

"Hey," he murmurs. And because we're speaking so quietly, we have to get closer and closer to each other in order to hear. Our noses almost touch. "If you call me weirdo again, I'm going to propose marriage."

They say third time's a charm, so I whisper, "Okay, weirdo," and wrap my arms around his neck.

Chapter Thirty-Seven

NICOLE

Above all, love each other deeply, because love
covers over a multitude of sins.
—1 Peter 4:8

It wasn't too long ago that I mourned not having a father to give me away at my wedding, yet here I stand while he officiates. In fact, he's choking up as he reads the love chapter.

His eyes jump to mine, and he clears his throat. "Love never fails."

He failed, and he knows it. But love is an invitation to try again. To learn from mistakes. To let your own life be a warning so others don't have to go through the pain you've endured . . . or even caused.

Which is why after a year of counseling and reconnection, Dad purchased a retreat center on the Oregon Coast for pastors brave enough to confess they've fallen. Falling had once been his greatest nightmare. Yet, like those ducks who floated toward the edge of a waterfall, God had already given him the wings he needed to fly away from what some considered certain doom. That's what God's love wants to do for us all.

Dad will never pastor a church again, but his heart has embraced ministry more than it ever did before. Watching the way it affects him to perform a wedding ceremony makes me think it's not only redeeming his future but healing pain from his past.

"I now pronounce you man and wife."

My heart swells, and I turn my gaze toward Charlie in the golden glow of sunset. He's not the guy I once fell in love with, but he's become the man of my dreams, Oregon State Fair–winning beard and all.

That scraggly looking thing has to make him extra sweaty when living part-time in Manila to film his latest documentary, but the man is nothing if not determined. It's how I know he'll make a good husband and father. I mean, he's already saving babies around the world.

I've gotten to volunteer in the Philippines this year too, when I'm not doing marketing for our new nonprofit. Our lives have become a great big adventure, and I'm just thankful Charlie made it home for this wedding.

"You may now kiss the bride."

I bite my lip in expectation.

Charlie waggles his eyebrows.

Then Gemma and Karson kiss, becoming man and wife.

It's one of those kisses where the guy dips the girl, everyone cheers, and doves fly overhead in slow motion.

Well, not really. There are no doves. But it's still pretty magical here in an enchanted forest that used to be the gun range behind Karson's house. I guess this is where the bride and groom also shared their first kiss.

"It is my great honor to present . . ." Dad pauses dramatically. "Mr. and Mrs. Karson Zellner!"

Karson rights Gemma with a twirl as a Mexican guitar strums the introduction to a Latin song. We're all supposed to salsa dance up the aisle, but even after hours of rehearsal last night, Charlie is a lost cause.

The wedding guests stand, whooping and hollering at the skill with which Karson cha-chas and Gemma shimmies. She's always been beautiful, but today she's a woodland fairy with flowers appliquéd over the sheer, floaty layers of her dress. Karson's attractive too, but usually in a gruff sort of way. Today he can't stop smiling, which makes him appear years younger.

The wild applause fades until clapping matches the beat. I can't clap because I have a bouquet in my hand, so I drop my arms to my sides and sway to the tunes. I'll simply enjoy the show that will eventually bring Charlie and me together.

Gemma's and Karson's niece and nephews served as flower girl and ring bearers, and they follow first after the bride and groom. The little girl pirouettes and sashays while the boys partake of a playful shoving match.

Gemma's sister and maid of honor covers her face in mock embarrassment at her son's antics, though her escort, Karson's old partner, performs some antics of his own. Drew dances around Jewel, pretending to reel her in like a fish and all that. The big guy seems pretty light on his feet, and I've heard rumors he's sweeping Jewel off of hers. They're as unlikely a pair as they are perfect together.

Next in line, Meri reaches the aisle before Kai, as if she's been waiting her whole life to dance the Charleston to salsa music. Step kick, step tap, repeat. It's a great reminder that I'm not dating the only weirdo in the family. Meanwhile, Kai does some kind of manly hula.

Maybe Charlie and I won't be so out of place after all. There's one more couple before our turn.

Gemma's high school friend from Salt Lake City, Lacey, came out for the wedding. Gemma played a part in getting Lacey together with a real-life wise man at Christmas, so she was part of their bridal party, and now they're repaying the favor. Of course, with the way Mr. Wise is also funding Gemma's next film, there was probably no repayment necessary.

The two link arms for some kind of country two-step, leaving me and Charlie as the grand finale. Last time Charlie escorted me out of a wedding, I'd been ready to kiss him goodbye. A few things have changed since then.

I bend my elbows to roll my arms along with my hips in the beginning of a merengue and dance Charlie's way.

He stands at attention. Oh no. He wouldn't.

He salutes.

I can't help laughing when we meet in the middle. "Again?" I ask, as dumbfounded and happy as ever.

He marches beside me toward the dance floor. By dance floor, I mean Karson's back patio. Though with all the greenery and flowers surrounding the place, it's no normal back yard. Garden lights shine above the stone pavers in the growing dusk, and Karson leads Gemma to the center as if it's a spotlight for their first dance. The music slows.

I wish love were always this beautiful. But then it wouldn't be real, would it?

Real is a man with a ridiculous beard who can't dance but will change the world, starting with mine.

"Marching like this got you to kiss me once," he claims.

"I'll kiss you if you stop." I might as well have ordered, *At ease, soldier.*

He drops his posture just as fast as he turns to face me, arms wrapping behind my back. He's warm and woodsy, but rather than kiss me as I'd expected, he walks me through a curtain into Kai and Meri's photo booth.

My pulse picks up speed. Not because we're alone, but because we're surrounded with memories.

Memories of the photo strip from when we were first dating.

Memories of the photo strip I tried to hide from Charlie after we reconnected.

Memories of the photo strip that accidentally documented yet another breakup.

"We need to redeem this photo booth," I declare. It's a good day for redemption.

Charlie holds my hand like a gentleman as I sit. He takes his spot beside me and grins at the camera. My, how I love his smile. I love it almost as much as serious Charlie who gets things done.

"So here's the plan . . ." Using the camera image as a mirror, he straightens his bow tie even though it's hidden by his beard. "We'll turn back-to-back for the first photo. Second, we'll smile at each other. For the third, I'll kiss you. The fourth is to be determined."

"Way to be spontaneous," I tease.

He's not laughing. In fact, he looks stern as he reaches for the button to start the process. "Turn around."

I consider messing with him, but I'd rather just get to frame three. The kiss. "Back-to-back," I repeat, turning to face the side of the booth. I make a finger gun as if I'm on *Charlie's Angels*.

The camera flashes.

"Hey, Charlie. I'm your angel." I turn to point out my pose captured on the screen, but it's not my pose that matters. Because the image reflects Charlie holding an open ring box.

"What?" I spin to face the real man.

The real ring.

And by real, I mean not a lab-created diamond. Not a diamond at all. This ring has a golden pearl at the center. The kind that comes from the South Sea. He must have found it in the Philippines.

The camera flashes.

"I'm sorry it's taken me so long to propose. I was waiting for Alice to finish designing your engagement ring."

Tears spring into my eyes, and I swipe quickly to keep them from ruining my makeup. Unlike the last time I cried at a big event, I have mascara on both eyes, so it's probably a lost cause. But the thing about happy tears is you're still happy even if they make you look like a monster in photos.

My chest swells. I love the ring, but it's only a symbol of what I really love. I love this second chance at forever. I love that I'm going to appreciate being together more than I did when Charlie first proposed.

"Yes." I reach for the sides of his face in the same way I did the last time we were in here, only everything is completely different.

His lips meet mine.

The camera flashes again.

"I didn't ask you to marry me yet," he murmurs against my lips.

I laugh, realizing he hasn't actually said the words. Not today anyway. "Yes, you did," I counter. Though when he showed up to propose in my office last year, I never would have imagined this moment. "Twice."

He pulls back far enough to slide the ring on my finger. An exact fit.

The camera flashes one final time.

He really did plan out the perfect photo strip, didn't he?

Holding my left hand between us, he looks into my eyes. "I'm never going to stop asking you to be my wife."

My heart skips a beat. This is what it means to be loved. "And I'll never stop saying yes."

The curtain flies open. Karson and Gemma stand there just like before but, again, everything is completely different.

Gemma squeals. "She said yes?"

How long had they been standing there? This is their wedding day. Had they known Charlie was going to propose? Probably, if they knew the ring was finished. Charlie doesn't keep secrets well.

"Yes! Get in here." Charlie motions them to join us.

They squeeze inside, Gemma's skirt taking up all the floor space.

Then the back of the curtain rises so Kai and Meri can pop their heads in too.

Charlie holds up my left hand and shows them my new bling. It shines with classic elegance, like a candle or chandelier, and my heart feels just as warm.

Meri squishes us together in a hug from behind.

"Congrats, dude," says Kai.

Charlie pats his sister's arm while at the same time attempting to squirm from her embrace. "I didn't mean to steal the show, but I love that you all want to share our celebration."

Meri releases her hold, then winks the way only she can. "I've been waiting a long time for this."

"*You've* been waiting?" I tease.

Laughter echoes all around.

Then Gemma points at the image of all six of us on the screen. "We must commemorate this moment."

Almost a decade ago, Charlie and I posed for our first photo booth strip. I'd been happy with him then, but it didn't compare to this lasting joy that has come through self-sacrifice and healing. Through mentors and friends. Through growth and God's love.

We are all so loved.

Charlie hangs on to my hand with one of his and reaches for the button to start the camera with the other. "Ready?"

My picture-perfect family surrounds me. This is everything I ever wanted. In fact, it's more than I'd dared imagine.

I take a deep breath. "Yes, finally, I'm ready."

Acknowledgments

While I had the idea to write a trilogy when I first pitched *Husband Auditions*, Kregel only contracted the first book. I didn't think to pitch a series after that one released, so I'm grateful my editor Janyre Tromp suggested it. She also helped me soften the hard parts of *Fiancé Finale* . . . so you wouldn't throw it against the wall and quit reading before you reached the characters' redemption.

After Janyre shaped the story, Christina Tarabochia cleaned it up. I met Christina at my very first writer's conference in 2006, and she's the first critique partner I ever worked with. We've been through a lot together, so I totally lucked out when she became this award-winning editor. She makes me do hard things, but she also makes it fun. I can't help feeling sorry for all the other writers out there who don't have a brilliant bestie getting paid to fix their mistakes. It's really the way to go.

My new critique partners are also two of my favorite authors. Sarah Monzon and Heather Woodhaven cheered me along with this story, which I absolutely needed. See, I'd made the mistake of double-booking my deadline month with a heavy workload in my job as a flight attendant.

Finishing *Fiancé Finale* was a blur as I flew across the country during the day and wrote in hotels at night, but the most memorable moment came when author Pepper Basham met me for dinner in Asheville. Her ideas were exactly what I needed to create the redemptive moment that would make you glad you didn't throw this book across the room (hopefully).

Of course, I also must thank my agent, Cynthia Ruchti, who

receives my writing before editors have fixed it. She gets to see the messiest side of me, yet she loves me anyway. Which, as Charlie and Nicole find out, is a requirement for lasting love.

This whole publishing experience has been amazing—from my family traveling to Nashville with me to attend the Christy Awards along with my publisher, Catherine DeVries, to the cover of *Hero Debut* winning a Top Shelf Award. I wish the series didn't have to ever end, but as Nicole's assistant says to Charlie, "What a way to go, right?"

Charlie and Nicole's story is very dear to my heart. Not only do I adore Charlie for his literal take on life and enthusiasm about changing the world, but as a pastor's daughter, my heart goes out to Nicole. I've seen families sacrificed for the "good" of a congregation, and sometimes the ministers themselves are the lost sheep. I don't believe any of us get everything right, and there are no easy answers. There's only belief in the God of all hope who gives us personal direction when we seek it.

So I also want to acknowledge you. Wherever you're at and wherever you've come from, it's likely you've been hurt by the church before. It's likely you've been lost before too. And I'm absolutely positive there is hope. God is coming for you. May you seek His direction and be surprised by His love.

I'll finish by acknowledging Him, the Author of Life. I've lived through plot twists that have been doozies. Some things happened even though I didn't want them to. Other things I expected to happen, but then my plans fell apart. In the end (middle?), God brought me to a spacious place. It all worked out for good. And that, my friend, is a finale worth waiting for.

About the Author

Angela Ruth Strong survived breast cancer, works as a flight attendant, and uses her own crazy life experiences as inspiration for the stories she writes. She has been a TOP PICK author in *Romantic Times*, a finalist for the Christy Awards, winner of the Cascade Award, and an Amazon best-selling author. She and her husband also got to play extras when her novel *Finding Love in Big Sky, Montana* was adapted for film. To help  aspiring authors, Angela started IdaHope Writers in Idaho, where she lives. Find out more or write her at www.angelaruthstrong.com.

Join Cara Putman alongside authors Angela Ruth Strong and Crystal Caudill in *We Three Kings: A Romance Christmas Collection*, as they craft tales that will warm your heart and kindle the festive spirit.

KREGEL
PUBLICATIONS